PRAISE FOR TERRI THAYER'

"Superb, the perfect cozy to ... y afternoon."

—*Mystery Scene Magazine*

"Extremely well written, the book not only kept me turning pages, but had me nodding delightedly at the dead-aim Terri takes on the contemporary quilting world."

—*A Charmed Life*, the blog of *Quilting Arts*
Features editor, Cate Prato

"As much as this is a murder mystery, [*Old Maid's Puzzle*] is also a story of women, their crafts, and their lives and loves."

—*Gumshoe Review*

"Enjoyable."   —*Kirkus Reviews*

"A fun mystery with as many pieces as a complex quilt, *Old Maid's Puzzle* has much to offer readers."   —*Mystery Reader*

"Readers will eagerly await the next book in the series to see how things go after the surprising conclusion of this book."

—*Fresh Fiction*

"Terri Thayer has once again created a true cozy mystery. The twists and turns are really well done and you truly don't know who did it until the end."   —*OnceUponARomance.net*

"A very refreshing approach ... one doesn't have to be a quilting aficionado or even know the first thing about quilt patterns to appreciate the mystery crafted in Old Maid's Puzzle."

—*Mysterious Reviews*

"A near perfect cozy mystery with a great intergenerational cast."

—*Cozy Library*

Monkey
Wrench

OTHER BOOKS BY TERRI THAYER

Wild Goose Chase

Old Maid's Puzzle

Ocean Waves

A QUILTING MYSTERY

Monkey Wrench

TERRI THAYER

MIDNIGHT INK
WOODBURY, MINNESOTA

Monkey Wrench: A Quilting Mystery © 2012 by Terri Thayer. All rights reserved. No part of this book may be used or reproduced in any manner whatsoever, including Internet usage, without written permission from Midnight Ink, except in the case of brief quotations embodied in critical articles and reviews.

FIRST EDITION
First Printing, 2012

Book design and format by Donna Burch
Cover design by Lisa Novak
Cover illustration © Cheryl Chalmers—The July Group
Editing by Connie Hill

Midnight Ink, an imprint of Llewellyn Worldwide Ltd.

This is a work of fiction. Names, characters, places, and incidents are either the product of the author's imagination or are used fictitiously, and any resemblance to actual persons, living or dead, business establishments, events, or locales is entirely coincidental.

Library of Congress Cataloging-in-Publication Data
Thayer, Terri.
    Monkey wrench : a quilting mystery / Terri Thayer. — 1st ed.
        p.   cm.
    ISBN 978-0-7387-3126-1
    1. Quilting—Fiction. I. Title.
    PS3620.H393M66   2012
    813'.6—dc23   2011049216

Midnight Ink
Llewellyn Worldwide Ltd.
2143 Wooddale Drive
Woodbury, MN 55125-2989
www.midnightinkbooks.com

Printed in the United States of America

ACKNOWLEDGMENTS

Thank you to my lovely critique goup—Becky Levine, Beth Proudfoot, Cyndy Furze, and Jane McBurney-Lin. Your encouragement and great ideas make all the difference.

Thank you to my steadfast pharmacist, Gene Togioka, for answering my silly questions with wonderful seriousness.

MONKEY WRENCH

Monkey Wrench is only one name for this traditional block. Other variations include Churn Dash and Shoo Fly.

ONE

"Kevin, you're killing me."

My brother grunted. That was no answer.

"I need that bathroom finished. We're less than two weeks away from the Quilters Crawl. Do you know what that means?"

I felt free to yell at my contractor. Pellicano Construction was my dad's company.

I didn't wait for him to answer. "Those are the four days each year where hundreds of women visit multiple quilt shops to win prizes. Including my shop. Driving, Kevin. Long distances. That means potty breaks. Plenty of them." My voice ticked up. I yelled. "I need a working toilet!"

I was standing in what was supposed to be QP's new bathroom. As we were on our cell phones, I had no idea where my brother was standing. But he wasn't where he should have been—in the bathroom of my quilt shop.

Here, there was no sink, no toilet, no tile floor. My voice echoed in the emptiness. There were only open walls and pipes. This remodel was taking too long.

"Not to mention the fact that Mom's dresser is in the hall, taking up too much room. Someone trips over it once a day."

"Mom's dresser with the hole in it?" Kevin sneered.

"Get my bathroom finished already!" I hollered. He didn't like the idea of changing the antique dresser piece into a vanity, but I didn't care.

"This is on you, Dewey," his deep voice booming. "We can't go further without the city inspector signing off. You knew that. And yet, no one was at the store yesterday when he came." My younger brother's tone was way too smug for me.

I stopped in front of the empty hole where the commode would be placed. "What do you mean? Vangie was here. I left around five. She promised to stay and let the inspector in."

"Well, she didn't. He got there around five-thirty. Said he banged on the door for at least five minutes. Back and front," he said, preempting my last argument.

My heart sank.

Kevin continued, "No rough-in inspection means I can't finish putting in the fixtures—"

Which means I wouldn't have a bathroom. A vision of dozens of quilters with their legs crossed flitted across my mind. "When can you get another inspector out here? Tomorrow?"

I walked into my office to check my calendar. I'd have to make sure *I'd* be here when the inspector came.

Kevin said, "I highly doubt that. I'd scheduled that one a week ago."

A red circle reminded me. My throat tensed. Yikes. Never mind the actual Crawl. I had bigger troubles. I had twelve quilt shop owners gathering here on Friday for a Crawl powwow.

"No, Kev, no. I don't have another week. I have a very important meeting in four days."

The final Quilters Crawl planning meeting was being held here. I tried to picture the chairwoman, Barb V, peeing at the burrito place next door. She'd probably turn yellow first—and blame me when she got a bladder infection.

"I don't know what to tell you," Kevin said. "Welcome to my world."

Out of the corner of my eye, I saw Vangie heading in from the parking lot. Her steps were heavy as if she was carrying not just a lot of books but also the fate of the entire world on her hunched shoulders. I waved at her.

She started to say something as she entered the office we shared but I held up my hand, showing her the phone. She nodded. Her backpack thudded as it hit her desk.

"Call Uncle Joe," I suggested to my brother. Our father's best friend had risen through the ranks and was the city's chief inspector now. I hadn't seen him in years, not since Mom's funeral, but certainly he'd be willing to help.

Kevin's voice rose in a squeak. "No way. I can't call in a favor like that. I might need him on a big job later."

My job didn't count. I got mad, just like when we were kids and Kevin would quit playing tag with me and run after our two older brothers. "Never mind, I'll do it myself. Be sure your guys are ready to work Wednesday."

I hung up the phone. Vangie looked up from booting up the store computer. Vangie had thick brown eyelashes framing her pretty eyes. Today though, the lashes only accented the brown circles under her eyes.

"My brother," I explained. "This bathroom is going to be the death of me."

Her hand went up to her mouth. I waited for her explanation but she shook her head.

I said, "What happened last night? The inspector came but you were gone."

Vangie's face turned red. "I'm sorry, Dewey. He was late. I couldn't hang around. I had study group. I tried to call you, but you didn't answer."

It was my turn to flush. Buster had had a rare night off work and we'd gone device-free. Anything with a plug or an on/off switch was strictly forbidden. Well, most devices anyway.

Vangie slumped in her chair, feet splayed beneath her. She was wearing black denim shorts and an SJSU hoodie. I could see her legs hadn't been shaved in weeks. "It's so much harder being at State full-time than I thought it would be. There's so much reading, I'm barely keeping up," she said.

My anger faded. Vangie was the assistant manager at my quilt shop, QP, and I needed her here, but she was also a twenty-three-year-old who was trying to secure her future by getting a degree. Neither of us had anticipated what the switch from community college to San Jose State would mean. It was only six weeks into the semester and already Vangie was struggling.

"It's okay," I said. "I know you're trying. Don't worry about it. I'm going to call a family friend. We'll have a new bathroom before Friday."

Vangie smiled. Her usually wide grin was somewhat stunted by worry.

"Was this the *Wyatt* study group?" I asked, teasing, trying to break up the gloom. She'd mentioned a guy named Wyatt more than a few times.

I regretted my words almost immediately. Vangie didn't answer, stared at the computer screen instead. At thirty, I was much too young to be turning into my father. Next, I'd be asking. "So what does this Wyatt character *do* for a living?"

We worked in silence for a few minutes. This time together was rare. I missed Vangie when she wasn't in the office.

An item on my to-do list caught my attention. "I hate to ask," I said. "What about the presentation for Friday's Crawl meeting? You know, the one about the special Twitter prizes?"

Vangie gathered her thick brown hair up in a ponytail and rubbed the back of her neck. She had blemishes on her cheeks. Stress-related I knew. Her eyebrows furrowed.

"I'll finish it, I promise."

She sounded so unsure I couldn't resist emphasizing its importance. "Because this is my last chance to convince the committee to go along with our idea."

Vangie nodded. She knew how much I wanted to put my stamp on QP's first foray into this annual event. "I'll email it to you in plenty of time. All you'll have to do is open up your laptop. The slides will be up and ready to go."

"I wish you could be at the meeting."

She turned back to her screen and pulled the keyboard toward her. "I'll try. Now let me just get these online orders filled. I only have about an hour before class."

I left her to it and went next door to Mrs. Unites's burrito shop to use her restroom. I tried to only take advantage of her generosity once a day. This time, the price I paid was listening to her theory that a toxic cloud that came from the dry cleaners across the street added to the demise of the long-time pet store next door. At least she'd waited until after I used the facilities.

When I came back, Vangie had her head on the desk. I could see the tension in her shoulders.

"What's up?" I asked, laying my hand on her back. She dragged her head up and looked at me. More pimples had appeared on her forehead.

"Pearl," she said, her phone in hand. "I was supposed to take her to the doctor but I wanted to come here and work so I asked a friend to take her. He did, but now she refuses to ride home with him. She wants me to come get her."

"So go," I said.

"He's got my car." Vangie's eyes filled with tears. "I can't handle her right now."

I patted her between the shoulder blades. Pearl Nakamura was a Quilter Paradiso regular. Along with her friend, Ina, she'd been an original member of the Stitch 'n' Bitch group that met here every week for years. I'd often done my homework between their sewing machines. Vangie and I both viewed Pearl as a grandmother, although Pearl preferred to be seen as an older sister.

Even when she was well past her seventieth birthday, Pearl would race through the classroom, ear buds dangling, wheels on her sneakers out, her short black hair highlighted with red or pink or blue, depending on her mood. Her hands glittered with six gold rings and her eyes sparkled with a joy that age couldn't diminish.

She was Pearl, one of a kind. Or she had been.

That Pearl disappeared when her husband of fifty years died eight months ago. She and Hiro had met as kids in the Manzanar Internment camp. Their bond was so strong that without him, the unthinkable had happened. Our Pearl faded away.

Vangie had spent a lot of her summer running Pearl's errands and playing endless rounds of Blackjack with her. But now with school back in session, Vangie's time was limited. Pearl's needs were unlimited.

Vangie was caving under the pressure.

I glanced at the clock. It was a few minutes after eleven. Uncle Joe, the city inspector, said he'd be here at noon.

"Tell me where she is," I said. "Maybe I can go get her."

Vangie's face shifted as relief flooded over her. I saw a ray of hope in her eyes. "Would you? The doctor's right in Japantown. Practically around the corner from her house."

Japantown was a neighborhood in San Jose, close to downtown and not far from QP. It was the place to find homemade tofu, study Ikebana, or worship at the Buddhist temple. The surrounding streets were filled with neat bungalows and a lot of second-generation Japanese-Americans like Pearl.

"I don't have much time," I said.

Vangie broke in quickly. "All you'll have to do is get her and drop her off. She'll be okay at home. These doctor visits wear her out. She'll probably want to nap."

Vangie threw her arms around me. "Thanks, Dewey. I'll get my life under control soon, I swear."

I drove right past Pearl the first time through the medical complex. I was searching out the right building, and barely registered the old woman seated at the bus stop whose feet didn't reach the pavement. Instead, I recognized Vangie's car. A tall young man was leaning on the trunk.

Then I saw Pearl, wearing her favorite plaid capris. She didn't usually pair them with a striped shirt. The orange Crocs dangling from her toes clashed with both and looked to be about two sizes too big.

I slammed on the brakes and stopped my car in a red zone. "Pearl?" I called.

She looked up slowly. I opened the car door and waved her in.

"Ready to go home?" I asked.

"Where have you been?" she said petulantly. Her face looked nearly as gray as the streaks in her hair. I hated seeing her like this.

Vangie's friend came over, trying to help Pearl into my car. She shook him off and climbed into the back seat on her own. He shut the door after she was in.

I got out and approached him. "Thanks for bringing her. I'm sorry she's being such a pill."

He laughed. "Oh, I've got a grandmother. I know how they can be."

"I'm Dewey Pellicano," I said, offering my hand. "Vangie's boss."

"Wyatt Pederson," he said. He shook my hand with a light touch.

Wyatt was pale. And skinny. His blond hair fell in shoulder-length dreadlocks. Not what I'd have called Vangie's type at all. Her frequent lament was that Buster didn't have a younger brother or even better, a clone. There weren't many six-foot-three, black haired, blue-eyed boys out there.

Wyatt was the anti-Buster. At least in looks. Maybe he had Buster's good heart.

Pearl rapped on the window. "Let's go," she barked.

I saluted her and smiled at Wyatt. "See ya," I said.

"How was the doctor?" I asked Pearl as I settled behind the wheel.

I got no answer. In the old days, Pearl would have been the first one to yell, "Shotgun!" She always sat up front, usually with her head stuck out the window like a dog. She'd never wanted to miss a thing.

It was only a few blocks to her house.

I chattered to quell a tightness growing in my chest. "We're so busy at the store, you know. QP is doing the Quilters Crawl next week. We haven't participated in years."

No response. I looked over my shoulder. Pearl's eyes were closed.

"You used to work that with my mom, right?" I knew that she did.

Nothing. I kept up the small talk until I pulled up in front of her house.

Pearl's cottage on Fourth Street was painted pale yellow. Ordinarily, only the purple trim and fuchsia door set it apart from the other bungalows on the street.

Today Pearl's house stood out for the wrong reasons. Her lawn had gotten spotty, with patches of brown larger than actual grass.

Landscaping had been Hiro's domain. The evergreens in front of the bedroom windows were so overgrown, an intruder could get in without ever being seen from the street. Someone had mowed the remaining grass, but not for a few weeks.

A black cat sat on the edge of the koi pond, staring through a layer of dead leaves. She must know something I didn't. I'd have bet the beautiful speckled fish that had once flashed through the depths were long gone.

"Did the doctor give you a prescription to fill?" I asked after throwing my car in park. I checked the time on the dash. I had ten minutes to get back to QP. I would need every minute of it, but if Pearl needed me, I wanted to help. I could come back later.

She shook her head and pulled open the door and scooted out of her seat. I got out on my side, but she was already halfway up the walk.

"I don't need anything, Dewey," she said over her shoulder. "Go on back to work."

I wanted to at least see that she was settled inside. I caught up to her on the porch. She went through the unlocked front door without a word.

"Pearl?" I said. I'd always been welcome in her house.

She closed the door firmly. Wow, that was abrupt. I felt like a fool.

I dialed Vangie as I pulled away. "Vangie, what's the deal? Pearl looks awful. And she wouldn't let me in the house."

Vangie's voice sounded muffled. I could picture the pose. I'd seen her stuff her phone under her chin many times in order to multitask. "Can hardly hear you," she said. "I'm in the parking garage."

Wyatt must have gone straight to QP and picked up Vangie if she was at school already.

"Fine? She's not talking, she looks like she's wearing Hiro's clothes and she's moving like a hundred-year-old. Talk to me."

Vangie came through clearer. "Sorry, you know how she is about her privacy. She'll be okay. I'll go there after school and check on her."

If Pearl didn't want my help, I had to respect that. Vangie would look after her.

"All right, keep me updated."

"Will do." Her voice faded.

———

When I got back to QP, Ursula greeted me with the news that there was a man in the bathroom asking for me.

Ursula had come to work for me after our Asilomar adventure last fall. Her mature calmness centered me.

Now she looked a little frazzled and cut her eyes to a customer whose quilt top was laid out over the cutting table. I didn't recognize the frowning woman. Six or seven spools of thread were laid out. The woman had pulled a long strand from each. She sighed, and tried another color.

Ursula had outlived an abusive husband, but a demanding perfectionist could bring her to her knees.

"I've got to check on the bathroom," I said, dropping my keys in my purse.

She nodded but her eyes begged me to stay. I gave her a half-smile of encouragement and kept going.

The bathroom door was open and a light was on. I didn't hear any banging so it wasn't one of Kevin's workers. It had to be my inspector.

It was.

"Uncle Joe!" I threw my arms around the tall guy on his knees near the stack pipe. "You came!"

I nearly knocked him over but he had good balance for an old guy.

"Anything for my almost-goddaughter," Joe said, standing and kissing my hair. Our private joke. It had always been his contention that my parents should have named him my godfather instead of my real Uncle Joe, who'd moved to Europe soon after my baptism.

Joe McCarty, despite humble beginnings in East San Jose, had a patrician air. His hair, now white, was combed as always, straight back from his face, giving his wide brow plenty of play. He was dressed in a pinstriped suit and red tie. His shiny shoes were a far cry from the work boots he'd worn as a plumber. As a kid, I used to love to visit my father's job sites. Uncle Joe was always there with a stick of Juicy Fruit.

I squeezed his upper arm. "Oh man, you can't believe how good it is to see you. Kevin started remodeling my bathroom and it's been nothing but excuses. I need a working toilet, Uncle Joe."

"Don't we all, sweetheart. Don't we all."

"Do you see any problems?" I asked. I crossed my fingers. No more delays.

"Looks like typical Pellicano Construction work. Very well done," he said, consulting a pad on his clipboard and making notes.

"I'm glad to hear that. Kevin's in charge now and I was afraid he would cut corners."

"So your dad's completely retired now?" Joe asked, his eyes casting over the installation. He squatted and ran his hand down a stack pipe.

"Yup," I said. "He's fishing full-time."

"That's great. No one deserves a break more than Nick Pellicano."

"Dewey, peaches," Ursula called from the store. "Pee-aches."

Uncle Joe cocked a trimmed eyebrow at me inquisitively.

"It's code, Uncle Joe," I whispered. "Means a customer is giving my staff a hard time. We don't like to use negative descriptors around here, so we call the tough ones 'Peaches.'"

Joe laughed. "Well, I've had my share of those."

"Let me know when you're done," I said.

"You bet."

———

I was about to convince Ursula's Peach that she was getting the best possible quilting thread for her son's-girlfriend's-baby-who-was-not-her-granddaughter-and-he-better-be-happy-she's-getting-a-quilt-at-all quilt when Uncle Joe came to the front of the store. I smiled and let Ursula ring her up.

He said, "You're all set. Tell Kevin he can have men on the job here tomorrow. In fact, tell him I said he'd better have men here tomorrow."

I laughed and kissed his cheek. He smelled the same, as if the Brut he'd worn all those years ago had seeped into his bloodstream.

"Don't be a stranger," I said. "Dad has Sunday supper most weeks. Stop by."

As Uncle Joe left, he held the door open for Peach to leave, and a pudgy woman bounced into the store. She saw Ursula and me standing by the register and loped over.

"Hi, I'm Lois Lane," she said, smiling as if she knew her name would produce a giggle. Physically, she was the opposite of Superman's girlfriend. Short, round, and blonde. No reporter would be caught dead in her outfit: an electric blue tracksuit with pink sneakers and pink sweatbands. Not exactly dress code for the *Daily Planet*.

"I was born right after the first Superman comic. My dad was a fan," she said quickly. "If I had a nickel for every time I said that," she laughed.

I looked to Ursula to see if she recognized this ball of energy. She answered me with a nod of her head and a laugh. This woman was the perfect antidote to a Peach. Ursula's shoulders came down a notch.

Ursula said, "Lois was in here last week getting fabric for a ..." she paused, trying to recall.

"A purse," Lois filled in. She produced a handbag made of quilted patchwork. I recognized the pattern and the latest Joel Dewberry line as ones I carried.

"It's beautiful," I said.

"Matches my outfit," Lois said, holding it against her chest. Indeed, the rose-colored top under her tracksuit matched the floral print. "And it has plenty of pockets inside so I don't lose things. I love that. Screwy thing is that I had enough fabric to make two."

Ursula said, her voice filled with concern, "Oh, no. I'm sorry. We followed the directions on the pattern, right? Did you buy extra?"

"A little," Lois admitted. "It's really okay. I made two! But I wanted you to know so you can tell your customers that those requirements are a little off."

"Thanks," I said. "I do appreciate the feedback."

"Well, my neighbor will *love* having the same purse as me. She's always copying me anyhow." Lois smiled as she bounced from foot to foot. Maybe that was the secret to staying youthful. Perpetual motion. "While I'm here, I want one of those Quilters Crawl thingamajigs."

I looked on the counter where we kept the colorful Quilters Crawl maps. The space was empty.

"Ursula? Are we out?"

Ursula had returned to the cutting table and was winding a bolt of fabric. She looked up. "I must have given away the last one."

"I'm sorry," I said to Lois. "Can you go online? There's a great interactive map on the website."

Lois frowned. "I guess I could ask my grandson. He knows all that Internet stuff."

Her eyes strayed past me. I was used to being ignored in my store. In fact I relished it. If my customers were distracted by the quilt displays, the fabric, the class samples, I was doing my job.

"This place looks so different. You know when I came in last week, I wasn't sure I was in the right place."

"Oh, you've been in before?"

"Not in forever, honey. Maybe ten years ago. There was a different owner."

I felt the tiny pang I always felt when my mother's presence was invoked. It happened less and less as time went on and I wasn't sure if I was happy or sad about that.

"That was my mother," I said.

"Why, bless your heart. You do look like her. I have time to quilt now that I finally quit working. At seventy-five," she crowed. "Can you believe that? I've worked for sixty years."

I laughed. "I can't believe that you're seventy five," I said.

"Going on seventy-six. Will you get more brochures? I like to hold a map in my hand," Lois said. Her round face wrinkled up in worry.

"Of course," I said. "Leave me your phone number and I'll call you when they're here."

Lois beamed. "I sure don't want to miss the Crawl. I think it's going to be the best one yet!"

TWO

"I WOULDN'T MAKE TOO much coffee," Freddy Roman said, settling into a chair in the store kitchen as I filled the old twenty-cup urn. "You don't want folks getting themselves killed in your very rustic *salon de bain.*"

"Make yourself useful." I tossed a bread knife and a bag of bagels his way. "Cut those into quarters."

It was Friday morning, the day of the Quilters Crawl meeting. Freddy had just returned from washing his hands in my still work-in-progress bathroom. Kevin had not been able to finish. The toilet and sink were in, but the tile guys had not been here yet so the concrete board subfloor was showing. The mirror over the sink wasn't installed and the entire room needed to be painted. The bathroom functioned fine but it looked butt ugly.

Freddy hung his aviator sunglasses off the neck of his T-shirt and pushed up the sleeves of his cardigan. Freddy dressed differently now that he'd moved his sewing machine store to the Bay Area. Gone were the Hawaiian-style shirts made of prints that featured voluptuous, half-dressed women. No more dashikis or gauzy wedding tunics. He'd adopted an urban, hip vibe that suited him much better. Today he was wearing a gray cardigan and black T-shirt with expensive jeans. He'd cut his hair too, and he looked far more handsome without the scraggly ponytail. His sharp features looked less feral.

He still haunted the tanning booths though.

"I'm serious," he said. "You'll get sued if someone trips over that uneven floor in there."

I waved away his concern. "The bathroom will have to do. I couldn't very well change the meeting. If Barb V had her way, we'd meet at her place every time. I wanted the committee to come here."

The Quilters Crawl was made up of twelve shops, and the owners got together once a month to go over plans. As the newest member of the Crawl, I had been assigned the last meeting. Freddy got a bye as we only met eleven times, taking off the month of December.

"I thought you and Mr. Wonderful were going to paint the walls last night."

A stab of loneliness developed in my chest. "Buster had to work."

"Oh, is he out there making the streets safe for us mere mortals?" Freddy asked.

Freddy's jabs at my lonely nights stung.

"Buster's on the Joint Task Force for Drug Elimination," I defended, wishing I could take back the words as soon as they came out. Buster's work was confidential. He'd told me little else than what I'd blurted to Freddy. "You can't tell anyone," I said hurriedly.

"Who am I going to tell? I don't know any drug dealers. I do know a few drug takers, however," he said with a lupine grin. "Ecstasy, a little Oxy for the pain, some Prozac to smooth out the rough spots. I could use a little something right about now. Did you bake any funny brownies?"

"Freddy..." I warned. He was so full of baloney. I was sure the only pill he took was a little blue one when he was with one of his ladies. "I need you on your best behavior today."

He held a bagel aloft and took a deep bow, one that ended with a face plant into the table. "At your service," he intoned into the wood. I giggled at his welcome silliness.

We carried refreshments into the classroom. I set out cups, milk, and sweeteners. Freddy put his basket of bagels on the center of the table.

"Yoo Hoo!"

Freddy caught my eye. "Vampira in the house," he whispered.

Barb V's last name was a constant source of amusement for Freddy. She wasn't forthcoming about her surname. No one seemed to know what it was. She owned a quilt shop called Barb V's Quilting Emporium. No one cared as much as Freddy. He liked to fill in the blanks.

He was sure she was a Voldemort.

Barb V entered the room, pulling behind her a file box on wheels. Inside I knew were color-coordinated folders on each of the participating Crawl shops. QP's was a bright magenta. Not my color at all.

Also on file were summaries of the past fifteen Crawls, names and addresses of every winner from each year and other viscera that Barb V felt necessary to haul out at every meeting.

She was as coordinated as her filing system. Her tight curls were growing in gray. The top was cropped close to her head, but the back was long. She was tall and thin, never touching the goodies, often homemade and decadent, that were served at these meetings. Today she was in layers of navy blue and white. Supportive shoes squeaked across the linoleum.

She stopped and surveyed the tables Freddy and I had pushed together. "Is there enough room for everyone?" she asked.

"I think..." I stopped to count the number of chairs I'd put out.

Freddy spoke up. "Of course there is, Barb. Twelve of us, twelve spots at the table. Just like the Apostles." He folded his hands and bowed his head. I hid my giggle.

She pursed her unadorned lips. "You know sometimes Cookie likes to bring her assistant. She has to drive all the way from Aptos, and she doesn't like to do it alone."

"If her assistant comes, I've got plenty of extra chairs," I said.

Barb V set her file box at the end of the table, where I'd been planning to sit, and began unpacking. She looked up, surprised to see Freddy and I watching her.

"I smell coffee. Is it ready?"

Freddy and I scurried to the kitchen. "How does she do that?" I asked. "I go from quilt shop owner extraordinaire to blithering idiot in sixty seconds."

"Don't let her," Freddy said. "Do what I do."

I remembered the advice of my college speech teacher. "Picture her in her underwear?"

"Oh god, no. Yuk, what a thought."

Freddy banged on his temple with an open palm. He crossed his eyes and shook his head, as if trying to rid himself of the image. I laughed, forgetting Barb V's officiousness. I was so glad Freddy had moved up here. He always made me laugh.

"So what do you do?" I asked.

"Turn off my hearing aid."

Freddy had perfect hearing. I shoved him toward the refrigerator. "Get out the creamer."

Twenty-five minutes later, all the participants were present and ready to go. Two of the storeowners had used the bathroom without incident and without comment.

We all knew that the meeting would start exactly on time. Barb V didn't believe in tardiness.

She enjoyed her space at the head of the table. She sat up straight enough to make the fussiest mom happy and projected so that her voice was easily heard by everyone in the room. At times, her tone was her best weapon, quelling unasked questions and squashing objections before they were aired.

"I want to thank our hostess for this meeting, Dewey Pellicano."

There was a smattering of polite applause. We'd taken turns hosting the Crawl meetings. It was no big deal.

Barb V wasn't finished. "It's lovely to be back at Quilter Paradiso."

No one called it that anymore. I'd changed its identity to QP two years ago.

"Back at the very place where Audra Pellicano and I conceived of the very first Quilters Crawl, fifteen years ago," she continued.

I looked up, surprised. My mother? I didn't remember that she'd started the Crawl. I knew she'd taken part in them, but had it been her idea? Fifteen years ago, I'd been sixteen. My mother's doings at her quilt shop had not been my priority.

I looked over at the picture of my mother that hung on the classroom wall. It had been taken during her tenth anniversary sale and she looked exhausted, but happy. I gave her a mental thumbs up.

"Of course," Barb V said, casting a critical eye around the room. "So much has changed since then."

My face flushed hot. QP was my store now, and it was very different.

Freddy pushed a scribbled note in front of me. "Hey, Barb Vicious. The eighties called. They want their mullet back."

I covered the note with my hand and hid a smile.

"We have many items on our agenda to cover, so let's get started."

I raised my hand, feeling silly but knowing there was no other way to get her attention.

"Before we begin, I'm out of Quilters Crawl maps," I said.

"We have no more," she said, her eyes never leaving the page in front of her. I could see highlighted lines of text, some bright yellow, others green.

"Let's get some then," Freddy said.

"I don't see why," Barb V said. "Just because you've given all of yours away ..."

She made it sound like handing out promotional material was a bad idea.

22

"I'm almost out, too," said Cookie. Several other shop owners nodded.

Barbara D'Angelo, Barb V's co-chair frowned. "Those maps are quite expensive to print."

Freddy had nicknamed her Barbara the Damp because she sweated profusely no matter the outer temperature. A rivulet of sweat was tunneling through her makeup now.

"I thought that the San Jose State art department designed them for free and gave us a break on the printing," I said.

"I keep those maps on my front counter year-round," said Cookie. "They're a wonderful reference, with all of our shop information right there. My customers hang on to theirs."

"We need more," Freddy said.

Barb V's eyes narrowed at her mutineers. "Fine. But I'm much too busy to contact our person at the college."

"I'll do it," I said. Maybe Vangie could stop by on her way to class. "Give me the number."

Barb V reached into her file box and drew out a folder. "Her name is Sonya Salazar. Return that to me as soon as you write down what you need to know."

"Let's move on to our agenda items, please," she said, pulling down eyeglasses that were perched on her forehead.

"Varmint," Freddy whispered. He was doodling V words. He'd written Vixen, then circled it in red and drew a line through it.

Barb V slapped down a baggie with fabric in it. "The Monkey Wrench blocks, people. I want to show you the proper way to distribute the free block.

"All of you have received the block pattern and printed it out. Include one of these." Barb V waved the instructions. She folded it crisply, into thirds, and then in half.

I rolled my eyes at Freddy.

Barb V said, "Everything will fit nicely if you do it my way." She could scold without even looking up. She must have been a grade school teacher in another life.

"Each shop has chosen their fabrics, staying within our theme of blue and orange. Mostly. Cut one strip of each of three fabrics, five inches by twenty-two. That will give your customer enough to make the block. If the customer goes to all the shops, she'll have twelve blocks."

Barbara the Damp put in, "The customer will need to purchase several yards of fabric for sashings and border fabric so that could be a good sale for you."

"I have one finished," I said.

I held up the quilt that Ursula had made for our display. She used all the blocks and set them on point. A large floral served as setting triangles and unified the disparate fabrics of the blocks. I loved the look and was satisfied by the murmurs of pleasure that came from most of the group.

Barb V was eager to move on. She slapped a shrink-wrapped bundle in front of her. "Next, the Crawl passports, people. This year they are numbered. I have assigned your store one hundred passports. Mark your store's initials in the top right-hand corner. That way when the customer turns in her completed one, we will know where she began her quest. Also, we will be able to tell which shop had the most customers finish the race."

In order to be eligible for the prizes, including a new top-of-the-line sewing machine and a weeklong quilting seminar, quilters had to go to all the shops within the allotted time frame, and get their passport stamped. Most made a game of it, rushing from shop to shop. Many traveled in packs. Quilters came from out of town.

For some, it would be the first time they'd visited QP.

QP hadn't participated since my mother died, four years ago. I wanted back in so I could reintroduce the new and improved shop to customers.

Barbara the Damp distributed the bundles to each of us. I resisted the urge to wipe her wet fingerprints from the plastic. Freddy was not as restrained. He used his napkin to swipe at it. Crumbs from his earlier bagel went everywhere.

I tuned out Barb V and thought about my own presentation. Vangie had worked my idea of a special Twitter promotion into a lovely series of slides with illustrations and graphs explaining everything. I only wished I'd had this idea two months ago. We didn't have much time to implement it.

A discussion about the amount of money allotted for food dragged on. I kept watching the clock. Barb V not only started meetings on time, she ended them as well, sometimes in mid-sentence.

At least no one had complained about the bathroom or stubbed their toe on the dresser in the hall. Yet.

Finally, Barb V pointed at me.

"Dewey, you have something to discuss?" Barb V put a tick mark next to my name on her agenda. "You'll have to be quick. We only have six minutes left."

I stood and pushed in my chair. Freddy flashed me two fingers in a victory sign. I smiled at him and the group, hoping the act of smiling would quash the butterflies in my stomach.

"I have an idea I'd like to run by you. How many of you know what Twitter is?"

Most heads nodded. The shop owners varied in age, although I was by far the youngest. If I had to guess, I'd say Freddy was the next in line and he was in his late forties. These women represented long-established quilt shops that had withstood the battering of the last couple of years. Several shops had closed their doors and nothing new had opened in the valley, except for Freddy, in at least three years. Only the strongest shops survived the economic downturn, and these were the last standing. Collectively, they represented hundreds of years of experience.

"I'm on Twitter," Summer said, waving her arm burdened with dozens of silver bracelets. Her shop was in Santa Cruz. "I mean, the shop is. I have no clue. My granddaughter does all that stuff for me."

"Me, too," said Roberta of Quilting Pals. "Except it's my husband who does it all."

"Well," I said. "It's not as difficult as it might sound. I'll explain it the best I can. Feel free to interrupt me with questions."

I opened my laptop. It was already connected to the screen. I clicked the mouse, but nothing happened. I checked the connections and clicked again.

Still nothing. Several committee members looked at the blank screen, then back at me. Barb V cleared her throat significantly. I glanced at the wall clock. Five minutes.

I had to wing it. I closed the laptop and tried to remember Vangie's highlights. "Twitter is a free service. A tweet is a short message that goes out to all your followers. We can get a lot of free advertising, tweeting ahead of time about the Crawl."

Summer said, "We've been doing that already."

I nodded. "Me, too. But—I'd like to do something very special the days of the Crawl."

I stopped, trying to gauge how much of this was getting across. Summer and Roberta were nodding, but the two Barbaras had their mouths in a straight line. Barb V had crossed her arms across her chest for good measure.

The rest of the owners looked confused.

"I'd like to target four shops each day during a special Twitter promotion. We would do one in the north and south, morning and afternoon. I would tweet the location of the shop and encourage the Crawlers to get over there within the hour."

Gwen, the quilt shop owner from Half Moon Bay, was a weathered woman in a red vest and orange T-shirt. The dirt under her fingernails never seemed to go away. At least I hoped it was dirt. Freddy said she had a sheep farm.

She asked, "Why would we promote one particular shop? What would happen to the others?"

Barbara the Damp chimed in, "I don't want all my customers leaving and going somewhere else. That's not the point of the Crawl. The object here is to give everyone an equal chance."

I nodded, feeling my mouth go dry. This had made sense when Vangie and I had hashed it out. Vangie's presentation would explain all this. If only I could get it to work.

I pulled my eyes off the laptop, dragging myself away from the technology that wasn't helping. "Umm … shop hops like this one have become pretty common. We need to give the quilters an extra reason to come out to ours."

Roberta said, "My granddaughter uses Twitter all the time to plan events. One moment she's sitting at the kitchen table looking at her phone, the next minute, she's off to a party."

Barbara V frowned. "Maybe you should keep better track of her."

Roberta flushed, her chubby cheeks turning bright red. She added, "Another time a bunch of her friends got together and cleaned out a neighbor's basement and painted her kitchen. Planned it on the spot," she said proudly. Her pigeon chest expanded.

Cookie put in, "The Twitter alerts *could* add some excitement. Lots of people have smart phones these days. If the customers get online and tell their friends, we'll attract even more participants. Isn't that what we want to do?"

Cookie ran a very popular quilt shop in Aptos. She was a businesswoman first, and quilter second. I had been hoping she would understand.

Barbara the Damp wiped her hands on a crochet-trimmed handkerchief she pulled out of her sleeve. "We *have* been losing participants …" she began. Her voice faded out as she caught a glare from Barb V.

I broke in. "You've been telling us that there are two kinds of Crawlers. Ones who shop and the others who rush in only to get their stamp. This would be a chance to get those customers to stay a bit longer. And spend money."

"What would happen at the tweeter shop?" Barb V asked.

I ignored her mangling of the word. "We would award a special prize basket to one of the customers who got there during the allotted hour," I said. "You'd have to be present to win, so—"

Half Moon Bay threw up her hands. "Where am I supposed to get the money for more prizes?"

Others joined in. Barb V held up her pen for silence, and they ceased their chatter.

She said, "Dewey, you know that we have strict budgets for giveaways. You remember how difficult it was to negotiate a figure that everyone could afford."

I looked behind me. I thought I'd heard the back door open. I was so hoping Vangie would appear and get me out of this mess. But it was only a customer who moved on through to the front. My heart sank. I had two minutes to convince this group that my Twitter idea would work.

"It won't cost you anything. I'll get the prizes donated and put together a special basket for each shop. The days of the Crawl, I'll handle the tweeting. All you will have to do is greet the extra customers who come to your shop."

"And take their money," Freddy said.

"Time is up," Barb V said. "This meeting is over."

"I'll take that as a yes," I whispered to Freddy.

"*Vamonos*," he replied.

———

Freddy stayed behind to help me clean up. We cleared the table of used cups and plates. Most of the bagels were gone.

"I guess that was a success, even though now I have two major new tasks. I have to set up a Twitter account for the Quilters Crawl *and* track down free stuff to give away, I said."

I cracked my neck to the right and then to the left, in an effort to relieve some of the tension I was feeling. "Can you help?"

"I'll call Lark and get her to give us some of her books," Freddy said.

"That's big of you," I said, hitting the sarcasm hard. Freddy could take it. "That's a no-brainer and will take you all of about three minutes." We both talked regularly to Lark Gordon, star of a hit quilting cable show. She was an easy touch for door prizes.

I continued, "I'm going to talk to my scissors guy in Brooklyn. He'll be good for a dozen mini-snips. If he hasn't already sent my order out, we'll get them in time."

Freddy rubbed his neck. I could see a new tattoo peeking out of his collar. It looked like the head of a tiger. He refused to act his age. "I can get a hold of embroidery designs."

"Not everyone has a machine that can handle those," I pointed out. I couldn't let Freddy off the hook. He had to chip in with some help. I already had too much on my plate.

He stacked the coffee mugs precariously in the cabinet over the sink. I took two off the top and set them on a different shelf. "Okay, some high-quality thread, then. The big spools. And some stabilizer. Even the regular sewers can use stabilizer. Can you get Vangie to set up the Twitter account?"

I shook my head and filled the sink with soapy water. "I'll do it. She's got a full load at school. I want her available to work on the Crawl weekend."

"I haven't seen her in weeks."

Since opening a shop nearby, Freddy had become a bit of a fixture around my place. He sold sewing machines, so we weren't in direct competition. I sent my customers who needed a machine to him, and he sent me those looking for fabric and quilt classes. It was a good business relationship.

"Is she okay?" Freddy asked me.

I stuck my hands in the water. It was too hot but I didn't want to back away. I didn't want Freddy to see my face. He could tell when I was lying.

"She's fine. Can you buy baskets for the prizes?" He nodded

Buster came in the QP kitchen as Freddy was drying the knives. He was wearing his tightest SJPD black T-shirt and black jeans. I could tell he hadn't stopped at home yet because he was still wearing his gun. It was as if he knew Freddy was going to be here. Intimidation was the name of the game.

He said hello, and went straight to the refrigerator. His six-foot-three frame filled the open space. He peered into the interior like he was sixteen and in his mother's kitchen. I didn't mind the rear view but couldn't help but fret about the electricity being wasted.

"Hi, babe," I said. "Sorry, we're out of Vitamin Water."

Buster grunted and took out a quart of milk. I have three brothers, I knew what came next. I held out a glass. Buster ignored it and twisted off the top.

Freddy said, "Late night again?"

Buster turned to me. "So what, now. You talking about me?" he asked. He had a dangerous glint in his eye. He took a long drink from the container.

I shook my head. My guilt about slipping about Buster being on the drug task force found its way into my voice. "Of course not."

Buster caught my hesitation. He tilted the milk and looked at Freddy. "She been complaining about my rotten moods? How I never have time to take her out anymore?"

"It's pretty evident that you're busy. The bathroom ..." Freddy said. He was trying to be diplomatic. I had to give him that. That was not Freddy's usual modus operandi.

Buster was relentless. "Since you're over here all the time already, maybe you'd like to paint the bathroom."

Enough. I took the milk from Buster and poured the remainder into the glass. I rinsed the container. "Buster, Freddy and I have work to do. We're working on the Quilters Crawl together, you know that. Knock it off. You're out of line."

Freddy dried his hand on a paper towel. He gathered up his Quilters Crawl notebook. "We're done for today," he said.

He walked to the doorway and turned back, stroking his beard. His eyes sought Buster's and held them. "Your girl has not spilled your deep dark secrets, I guarantee that."

He managed to make it sound like just the opposite. I blushed. Buster glowered. Freddy disappeared.

I turned on Buster, with the milk container in my hand. Buster took it from me and tossed it into the recycling bin.

"Geez, Buster, that was unnecessary," I said. "I know you're tired and cranky, but come on."

"You do understand he moved up here to be near you, don't you?" Buster said, washing his dirty glass. He could only push the caveman act so far before his natural need for order took over.

"Not at all. He wanted to be closer to his brother."

"That's what he tells you, maybe, but I know the real reason. He fell for you when you two were at Asilomar last year."

I wiped down the countertop with vigor. Buster was pissing me off. "When do you get off that task force? You're getting paranoid."

"Think what you want. I know a smitten man when I see one." Buster helped himself to a stale bagel from the morning Crawl meeting.

I rinsed off my sponge and took a breath, letting the running water soothe me. Buster was miserable at his job right now. He'd asked to get off Homicide because he was dissatisfied only doing computer work on cold cases, but working the drug scene was souring him. I had to cut him some slack.

I faced him. "Freddy is not the problem. You need sleep, and lots of it."

He nodded reluctantly. "I'm sorry. I'm just upset at how long this is taking. If it was up to my superiors at SJPD, we'd have made arrests already. But they have to answer to the FBI and the DEA. Those guys are dragging their feet. Meanwhile, there are so many kids on campus becoming addicted to pills, it makes me sick."

"But it's out of your hands."

"That doesn't make it any easier when I know the amount of painkillers and Prozac that's being ingested. Those kids need help. And those dealers need to be locked up."

I dried my hands on the towel he was holding and reached for Buster. He came into my arms and let me stroke his lush hair. He'd been out all night again. I felt how weary he was as he sagged against me.

"When are we going to get our life back?" I asked.

Buster shook his head. He pulled away, brushing his hair back from his forehead. He looked so tired and vulnerable, I forgave him everything, even drinking from the milk carton.

"HQ's not telling me anything," he said. He fought off a yawn. "I'm going to go home and sleep."

"You're working again tonight?" I asked. Ugh. More hours in front of HGTV. I was even tiring of Josh Temple.

He grabbed his leather jacket. "Yup. Going in at seven."

"I'll come home early and make dinner," I said. That would be our only time together.

"Thanks," he said. His eyes were getting heavy. He started down the hall to QP's back door.

"Okay if I invite Freddy?" I called after him.

He didn't turn around, just flipped me off without looking back.

THREE

I LOGGED ONTO TWITTER and started an account in the Quilters
Crawl name. I tried to import the Quilters Crawl logo, a sea otter
draped incongruously in a patchwork quilt. The file was the wrong
size. I could not get the picture to appear next to the Quilters
Crawl name.

Frustrated, I gave up. I could be here for hours trying to figure
out what I was doing wrong. This was exactly the kind of thing
Vangie could do in three minutes. I gave up and wrote a note to
ask her to fix my mistake. I hadn't seen her since the day I picked
up Pearl, but she often came in late at night after I was gone.

For now, I would concentrate on finding followers. I tweeted
from QP's account about the promotion and urged my followers
to join the Quilters Crawl feed. I sent an email to the quilt guild
and our mailing list. I put a note on QP's Facebook wall. I wasn't
sure we'd get enough people online by the beginning of the Crawl,
but I was going to give it a try.

I had a bright idea. I could slip a note onto the new maps when we got them. Vangie had brightly colored stickers somewhere. I found them in her bottom drawer under her extra set of car keys and an expired coupon for Hot Diggety Dog.

I wrote *Follow the Quilters Crawl on Twitter for special prizes.* I printed this out and left a note for Ursula to attach them to the brochures before she handed them out. That might attract a few more people.

Flipping over to Twitter, I saw we'd gained a dozen people. Not so bad for an afternoon's work.

That was all I could do for now. The growth now would come from within the social media community. Word of mouth, so to speak.

I turned my attention to prizes. I'd gotten an email from Felix in Brooklyn saying he would send a dozen extra scissors in my regular order, early next week. One prize down. Only a dozen more to go.

————

The store was empty. Ursula was thumbing through a magazine. It was the latest edition of the *Ten Best Quilt Shops*. Every owner wanted their place featured in the magazine's biannual issue. I was no different. I let myself imagine QP on the cover. Some people wanted to be on the cover of the *Rolling Stone*, I'd rather be on this one.

"Hey, boss," she said. "Been kind of quiet around here."

"No worries. Any display ideas we can steal?"

Ursula shook her head. "Not unless you want to feature deer antlers?" She held up the page for me to see. A shop in Montana seemed to be using Bambi as design inspiration.

"Whatever works. Of course, our idea of a wild animal around here is a geek separated from his iPhone."

Ursula laughed. "Horrors. I hear they can get might testy."

Ursula had a great booming laugh. I hadn't heard it until she'd been working for QP for about four months, but now she let loose all the time. Each guffaw reminded me how lucky we'd been to find each other.

Ursula looked prettier than she had a year ago. The death of her abusive husband had released her and freedom was better than a hundred Botox treatments. Her forehead was unlined now and her eyes were clear and bright. Watching her blossom had been like watching someone get off drugs. She'd had to detox from the stress of her old life, but once she did, she radiated good health, except for some lingering injuries courtesy of her ex-husband.

"How's your shoulder today?" I asked.

Ursula had been absent-mindedly rubbing her upper arm. Legacy of having her shoulder disconnected too many times.

With her working at QP, my business had grown. She was great with customers, a natural salesperson who could suggest tools and extra rotary blades without being pushy. She always remembered to ask the customer if she needed thread before completing the sale. And my customers left feeling happy, secure that they had everything they needed to make their new project.

Sales were up twenty percent in the year she'd been here.

"Any sign of Vangie?" I asked.

Ursula shook her head.

"I guess I had my days mixed up. I thought she was coming to the Quilters Crawl meeting."

"How'd that go? By the way, someone else came in asking for the map."

I snapped my fingers. "Thanks for the reminder. I'm going to call right now and get us some more."

I turned back to Ursula. "Let's get out of here right at five. You can close out the drawer a little early if we don't get any more customers."

"Date night?" Ursula asked, with a twinkle in her eye.

"Buster promises to be home for dinner," I said. "I plan to make the most of it."

My step lightened as I walked away. The idea of spending even just a couple of hours with Buster made me happy. Most of the time, he came in well after midnight and crashed. Sometimes he went to his own place and skipped my house all together. I hated those days.

Why did it seem like I couldn't have everything I wanted? Successful quilt shop, loving boyfriend, good gal pals. QP was booming but both my best friend and my best guy were missing in action.

At 4:45, Ursula stuck her head in my door. "Pearl's in the classroom."

My heart thunked. I hadn't seen Pearl since she'd slammed her door in my face.

"Is she okay?"

Ursula's lips thinned and she looked over her shoulder at the open door to the classroom. "She's pretty testy. She said she wanted to work on her quilt. I told her we'd only be open for another few minutes and she told me to get lost."

Testy. Not what I wanted to hear. "Thanks, I'll deal with her."

I took a deep breath and braced myself for what I'd find. She hadn't been in the store for several months. Would her hair be combed? Would she be wearing a plaids and stripes combo again?

I thought about calling Vangie, but decided I could handle this. All I had to do was move Pearl on her way home so I could go cook dinner. I pushed open the door to the classroom. The curtains on the window wall were closed up and the room was dark.

I flipped on two sets of fluorescent lights.

Pearl was seated at a table, her back to me. She put a hand over her eyes and turned to me.

"You trying to blind me?" she said.

Testy, just like Ursula said. Or maybe a return to feisty.

She looked pretty good. She was neatly dressed in a white T-shirt and black long shorts. Her feet were in sandals and her toenails were painted bright blue. The back of her hair was smooth. All good signs. Perhaps the doctor had give her some medication.

"Whatcha up to, Pearl? I didn't hear you come in."

"Ursula said you were busy with the Quilters Crawl stuff," she said, returning her attention to the task at hand. I walked over to see what she was doing.

She was beading by the light of a small daylight lamp that was plugged into the strip on the table. Her feet dangled in the office chair. She opened a prescription bottle with her teeth and spilled out the needles inside. I used a similar container to store broken sharps or bent pins. The little bottles with the tight lids were just the right size to dispose of pointy objects.

She sorted through the contents of a zipper bag. She grunted, not finding what she was looking for. Frustrated, she dumped the bag.

Hundreds of seed beads bounced off the table and hit the floor. I gasped. She didn't seem to notice, picking up the bead she wanted and poking at the needle with clear beading thread.

I got down on my hands and knees and began picking up the tiny glass balls. I emptied the pile in my hand into her bag and went back on the floor. "Have you seen Vangie?" I asked.

"She stayed with me last night," Pearl said. "We watched movies all night. She knows how to get that 'flix thing going. We watched all of the Toy Story movies. I cried."

Vangie had told me about their *Toy Story* marathon. It had taken place over a week ago. Pearl was clearly confused about time.

"I loved *Toy Story 3*," I said. "Especially—" I stopped when I realized the losses in *Toy Story* might hit too close to home for Pearl, whose own loss was not fictional, nor did it involve inanimate objects.

"Vangie been staying with you a lot?" I asked. Maybe I'd been looking for Vangie in all the wrong places.

Pearl still hadn't managed to thread the needle. I wanted to take it from her and do it but she would hate that.

"We can't sleep," Pearl said. "She comes over when we're both awake. Which is like every night."

I doubted Vangie was there nightly but she might be sleeping there once in awhile. Vangie had had to move back home in order to afford school, so maybe she was staying more often at Pearl's. Her parents' house was full of younger siblings and grandparents.

Pearl pulled out a quilt. I glanced at the large clock. We had to be out of here in ten minutes.

"Pearl, I've got to close up in a few minutes."

She held up the quilt. The design was pictures of her late husband that had been transferred to fabric. Pearl had colored four of them into an Andy Warhol-type arrangement. Hiro's big smile and crinkly eyes were surprisingly lifelike.

Pearl stroked the quilt. "Do you like it? I'm going to bead it. Diamonds in his dimples."

"Great, Pearl, it's great."

She stood and stepped over me as I crawled under the table to get the last of the beads. "But first, I have to make sure these transfers are stuck really good. I hope you don't mind me turning on your iron. I needed really high heat. You've got the best iron around."

"Really, we've got to get a move on."

"It won't take long," she said.

I poured more beads back into her zipper bag. Giving in to Pearl was easier than arguing with her. I could only hurry her along. "Okay," I said. "But I will turn it off in five minutes, so hurry."

She pounded the iron down in emphasis. Her little triceps bulged from moving the heavy iron up and down. Her face was twisted in concentration.

When she set the iron back down on the board, the soleplate facing me, I gasped. The iron was black.

"Pearl, have you been using fusible web?" My throat was dry.

She looked at me and back to her piece laying on the ironing board. She nodded.

She'd been pressing on the wrong side of the fusing, transferring the sticky gluey stuff to the surface of the iron instead of her quilt.

I grabbed her quilt. Just as I feared, she'd used the iron on the front of the piece. Two of Hiro's faces were covered in the burnt glue.

"Okay, Pearl, you're done for today."

She looked at me blankly, all the early animation gone from her expression. Did she comprehend what had happened?

The soleplate of my hundred-dollar iron was ruined, covered in burnt fusible web. I wasn't sure there was enough elbow grease in the world that would get it looking like new again. Worse yet, there would be no way to salvage the top of her quilt. I couldn't send it home with her.

"Arrgh," Pearl said. She had picked up a needle in one hand and was poking the thread in the direction of the hole without success.

Ursula appeared in the doorway. She had her sweater on, her purse in hand. She was carrying her VTA pass, ready for the trip home.

"Okay, Pearl, shop's closed," I used my chirpiest voice. I held the quilt behind my back, hoping out of sight meant out of mind. I tucked it onto one of the high shelves and put the iron on a lower one. "I've got to meet Buster. Want me to drop you off at home?"

I gathered up her beads and needles.

Pearl said. "I have my car."

I wasn't sure she was okay to drive. I looked over to Ursula for her opinion.

Ursula caught on quickly. "How about you give me a lift as far as your place, Pearl? I'll catch the bus on Fourth Street."

"Sure, whatever," Pearl said.

I caught Ursula's eye and smiled. Going to Pearl's neighborhood first would be taking her in the opposite direction of her apartment in South San Jose, but that would ensure Pearl got home safe. That was a weight off me. I grabbed Ursula's upper arm and mouthed "thank you."

Pearl and Ursula went out the back. I heard Pearl's black and white Mini start up and saw it go past the window.

———

I felt the emptiness the minute I unlocked my back door. No gurgling from the shower, no gentle snoring coming from the bedroom, no cup of tea poured for me. No Buster.

The note was on the kitchen table. "Sorry, duty calls."

No details. I crumpled up the paper and tossed it toward the trash. I hated this job as much as Buster did. While a homicide meant late nights and intense days of non-stop investigations, they didn't happen that often. Drugs were another story.

The Task Force Buster was on was a joint federal and state and local force coming together to crack down on prescription drugs getting into downtown San Jose. Students at the college were selling their medications. Some got the pills legally from their doctors and sold them for a huge markup. Others visited pill mills—pain clinics—where unscrupulous doctors would give painkillers and stimulants to healthy kids.

I checked my phone for messages. Nothing more from Buster, but Sonya Salazar, Barb V's contact at State had called. Her message said she had more Quilters Crawl maps in her office at San Jose State and that she would be in before her evening class started at six.

Vangie had sent a text saying she was in the library, studying.

I saw a tweet from a Vietnamese food truck that I followed. The truck had no permanent home. Each week, they sent out tweets giving out their not-so-secret location for that night. According to this, PhoHo would be in front of the San Jose Museum of Quilts and Textiles tonight at six.

I glanced at the date. Today was the first Friday in October. Perfect. First Fridays were a big deal at the museum and all around the arty SoFA district with exhibits in odd venues. The vibe was hip, and I'd find plenty to do.

My spirits lifted. I could go downtown and be around people. I didn't have to remain here in my empty house, wishing Buster was home.

I started to ping Freddy to ask him to join me. I closed the screen before I entered his entire number. No point in feeding Buster's ridiculous jealousy.

Of course, it would serve him right . . . I quashed that thought.

I changed quickly into my skinny jeans and a screen-printed tee. The night was warm enough that I wouldn't need to carry a jacket. I stuffed some money and my bank card into a small purse and locked up.

Balmy nights were rare in San Jose. Usually cold winds off the ocean kept us in sweaters after the sun went down. Tonight it felt like it was still seventy degrees out. I decided to walk. It was only a couple of miles and I could use the exercise.

I'd pick up the maps at Sonya's office, get a spring roll, check out the exhibits. Maybe I could get Vangie to join me for a little while. I texted her an invite.

I walked fast, now that I had a purpose. My back was sore from sitting at my desk too long and my legs cried for a workout.

Once I crossed under 87, the streets were much busier than I'd expected. People were out walking along San Carlos. I wasn't the only one enjoying the lovely weather.

Traffic was moving but I could hear car horns sounding not too far off. When I turned right onto Market Street, cars filled both lanes. Only those heading south were moving, although slowly.

Ahead of me, a driver got out of his car. "What's going on?" I asked.

"Beats me," he said, standing on his tiptoes. "I've been sitting here for five minutes, not moving."

I ducked closer to the office buildings as a Chevy Tahoe made a U-turn, practically jumping the sidewalk. I would find out faster on foot than he would. I kept going. First Friday had never been this popular. Had I walked into a parade? Was it Chinese New Year? Maybe there was some big convention going on.

Irritation set my teeth on edge. All I wanted was an order of lemongrass chicken. My stomach growled in protest. A sound came from in front of me. I could feel it in my body, like the noise you hear outside the zoo. A muffled roar, the stamping of enormous feet.

I threaded my way through the cars and finally saw the reason they weren't moving.

Plaza de Cesar Chavez was filled with people. The oval park was about three city blocks long and two wide. It was the site of Christmas in the Park and the Jazz Festival but I'd never seen it so full. There was no elbow room at all.

Market Street split at the base of the park, with two lanes heading north and two south. No cars were getting through on either side.

I looked for the reason. Did the police have it blocked off? I couldn't see any signs of SJPD.

Two beach balls flew up in the air, batted by six or seven people. They moaned when it fell to the ground. I fell in step with a young woman who was wearing a blue bandana around her neck.

"What's going on?" I asked.

She smiled and shook her head. "Just going with the flow," she said. "Came here with my band."

She pointed to a trio of longhaired guys. Two carried guitars, one had a block and a drumstick which he knocked together. The tallest sucked on a joint and passed it off to her.

She offered me a toke. I declined. She raised her fist and hollered, "Peace now," before disappearing.

Maybe this was some kind of battle of the bands. In the summer, free concerts were held here. I hadn't heard of anything scheduled for today.

The whole atmosphere seemed kind of impromptu and unorganized.

As I got closer to the fountain, I could see several naked kids jumping through the water. The fountain sent up jets of water at random intervals and the squeals made by those caught in the stream could have been made by the toddlers that I usually saw in there.

Suddenly the water turned off and stayed off. The sprinkler dancers let out an outraged cry but to no avail. The water had been shut off. They melted into the crowd, hopefully to where they'd dropped their shorts.

I backtracked and climbed up the steps to the Art Museum for a better view. The entire area was covered with humanity, mostly young. Looked like college students. The crowd stretched from the Fairmont to the Tech Museum, from the base of Market to San Fernando, overflowing from the park onto the street and sidewalks. There had to be a thousand people milling about.

I approached a guy in a SJSU fleece vest. His hairy arm was outstretched as he pointed his camera phone toward the mess.

"What's going on?" I asked. I had to shout to be heard.

"We're protesting."

"When did this start?" I asked.

He shrugged. "About a half-hour ago, maybe."

"What are you protesting?"

A girl standing next to him leaned over. "It's a human rights violation. Everyone's mad as hell."

I was confused. "What is?"

The man stopped filming and looked at me like I was an idiot.

"Cops, man. See how the cops turned off the fountain? The pigs think they can rule the world."

I must have looked confused because the woman next to him explained.

"The police are all over campus. They're busting everyone for drugs."

"We're not going to take it."

Oh boy, no wonder Buster had to work tonight. Sounds like the Task Force had raided the campus.

The college was only a few blocks from here.

"Is there a plan?" I asked.

"That's not the way this works. We don't need leaders. We want to be heard. And we will." Ironically, he had to raise his voice to a yell by the end of his sentence because chanting broke out a few feet from us.

"What do we want?" a boy in a maroon knit cap yelled.

"Weed!" the crowd answered.

"When do you want it?"

"NOW!"

"What?"

"Weed, weed, weed."

Human rights? Or just the desire to get high? What was driving this crowd? It was quite possible that both items were on the agenda.

The camera guy pointed to a spot in front of the fountain where a man stood on a bench. He was tall and wiry with what looked like curly blond hair. Dangling at his side was a bullhorn that was hooked up to a portable amp.

He held up a hand for me to be quiet. "Hold up. Wyatt's going to speak," he said.

Wyatt? I looked again and recognized the kid I'd seen with Pearl. Was Vangie here somewhere? I tried to look for her but saw only a wall of protesters. I grabbed my purse strap and held it close to my body. These might be peaceful people but it wouldn't take much for it to turn into a mob.

More kids were streaming in from Fountain Alley and from Almaden Way. I saw a news crew walking briskly. I pitied the guy carrying the heavy camera. They must have had to park blocks away.

Wyatt raised his bullhorn high. Had he been waiting for the news crew?

The crowd quieted. At Wyatt's hand direction, they sat. I could see clearly.

Vangie was standing next to Wyatt.

FOUR

"We don't want the feds on our campus," Wyatt shouted into the bullhorn. "We don't need no stinking task force to tell us how to live our lives."

The crowd roared their approval. Next to him, Vangie raised a fist. What was Vangie doing up there? She looked too much like pictures of SLA Patty Hearst to suit me.

Vangie was a hard-working kid who didn't have time for civil disobedience. It took all of her energy to do her schoolwork, work at QP, and look after her family. She was not an activist.

Besides that, she was still on probation from a juvenile arrest for marijuana possession. I could smell weed in the air. Vangie could not afford a night in jail.

I climbed down the steps of the museum and skirted the edge of the crowd. I slipped through between people with hand-lettered signs. "Don't Whack Our Weed" one read. Clever. Another said. "Jonesing for a Toke." These sentiments weren't likely to get a serious hearing from anyone.

Wyatt's voice rang through the plaza. "Today our campus was taken over by thugs. Thugs with guns, tear gas, and battering rams. Thugs who violated our human rights."

Another cheer. Vangie looked up at Wyatt, her face solemn and serious. I knew that look. Adoration.

If she stuck with Wyatt, she was likely to get arrested. The cops would want to take out the leaders. Getting booked into the county jail would probably be a feather in Wyatt's organizing cap.

But for Vangie, getting arrested would be a disaster. She'd promised to stay clean for at least ten years. Vangie still saw a probation officer once a month. Any violation of the law could rescind her parole.

She could go to jail.

Her entire school career was on the line.

I couldn't let her do that. I put my head down and pushed through a line of frat boys carrying 32-ounce beers.

Two mounted San Jose policeman picked their way through the edges of the crowd on the far side, near the Tech Museum. I was glad to see them. I'd thought budget cuts had gotten rid of that division. Buster told me the horses often had a calming effect on crowds.

I cut through the deserted Fairmont Hotel portico, usually filled with luxury cars and uniformed doormen. I could see well-dressed women hanging back in the lobby. Their dinner plans were on hold.

Wyatt turned so he was facing the north end of the square. It was nearly as crowded. "The pigs are going to find out we don't take kindly to narcs on our campus."

He was interrupted by a roar from the crowd. Everyone was back on their feet again, fists pumping.

"It's none of their business if we smoke a little weed now and again. They've got no right to come in our dorms and search our rooms. No right at all to bust us."

I was pretty sure that the police had every right to arrest students for illegal activity.

My phone beeped. There was a message from Buster. "Stay away from downtown. Riot going on."

I put my phone in my pocket. I would get out of here, but not without Vangie. After several minutes of pushing and shoving, I got close enough to tap on her foot. She was standing on the bench with Wyatt, holding two cell phones.

"Vangie," I yelled, as the crowd bellowed its approval at Wyatt's rantings. She looked down, startled to see me.

"What?" She jumped off the bench.

"What are you doing here? Come with me."

She shook her head. "We're making history, Dewey." She held up one of the cell phones. I could see a Twitter feed, the screen seeming to twitch as more entries were posted as I watched.

"Wyatt sent out a tweet asking kids against the drug raid to come to the park. Look what happened," she said, sweeping her hand at the gathering. "It's just like Libya or Russia. People answering the call."

She looked away from me, clapping as Wyatt finished another rhetorical question.

I hissed at her, "What are you thinking? What if you get booted out of school? You'll have to pay back your student loans whether or not you flunk out."

Wyatt yelled into his megaphone again. I was too close—his words were garbled. He reached down for Vangie.

I grabbed Vangie's elbow as she was about to join him again.

"Are you really here so that kids can use drugs? Is that important to you?"

Vangie's eyes narrowed. "Dewey, you weren't on campus today when the bust went down. It was frightening. Seeing armed men on campus, wearing bulletproof vests. It was like an army rolled in. We heard there were going to be tanks. Felt like Kent State all over again."

That was pure Vangie. She'd been born a few decades too late.

"Vang, I'm sure it was scary. But it's over and the kids who were breaking the law have been arrested. The school will be a safer place now that the drug dealers are gone."

Vangie wasn't moved. "We don't know that. We don't know who the FBI was targeting."

Wyatt held a hand out for her to grab.

"Vangie, this isn't your fight. You've got work, and your scholarship to think of."

She frowned at me. "This is exactly my fight. I know how easy it is to be brought up on bogus charges."

I pointed at a duo passing a joint. "These kids don't look like they care about civil rights."

"Not everyone has to believe, Dewey."

"What about your mother? Your grandmother? What about their dream of having a family member graduate college? Are you going to deprive them of that?"

Wyatt wiggled his fingers. Someone had put a stack of pallets alongside him. The top one was higher than the bench he was standing on. He jumped up onto the pallets and reached down for Vangie.

Vangie's eyes narrowed and I knew I had gone too far. Her family was sacred.

"I will never disappoint my family," she said. "My college education will mean nothing if we don't have basic freedoms."

Vangie raised a fist. Her eyes widened as she caught sight of something behind me. She climbed up on the pallets and tugged on Wyatt's sleeve and pointed. I looked over my shoulder.

A police car made its way slowly, poking its nose into the crowd that moved apart only long enough to surround the car from the back. The car was equipped with a loudspeaker.

"Please leave this area. This is an unauthorized gathering. As such, your presence here is illegal. You have five minutes to clear the square. Move slowly in an orderly fashion."

Wyatt yelled, "Everyone stand their ground!"

I grabbed Vangie's hand, forcing her to lean down and listen to me. Wyatt glanced over but returned to his crowd when someone called his name. He was a rock star.

I hissed, "You can't go to jail, Vangie. Your future…"

I was bumped from behind by a surge in the crowd. People were moving forward, trying to get closer to Wyatt.

Vangie wrested her hand from me and linked arms with Wyatt. He jumped down, helping Vangie down. They linked arms with the kids in front of them.

He began singing, leading the crowd in "We Shall Overcome." Vangie sang with conviction, swaying, squashed between Wyatt and a tall black kid in a kente hat. The police car stayed on the edge, ignored by everyone.

An arm landed in the middle of my back and I stumbled, losing my breath and my footing. Someone put a hand out to steady me. I took it gratefully. I tried to thank my rescuer but I was pushed forward, on my feet but caught up in the tide of protesters.

A second police car poked through the periphery, going south this time. His loudspeaker blared its pre-recorded imprecations. "Please disburse. Clear the area."

A ripple went through the crowd. I wanted out. There was no place to go. I was in gridlock with a thousand protesters. Instead of disbursing, the edges of the crowd were moving forward, as if drawn to Wyatt's flame. In the middle, where I was, we were being squeezed from both sides.

My stomach ached. This was bad. If the true believers kept trying to get to Wyatt, it wouldn't take much for things to get out of hand.

I stepped on something.

"Ow!" Someone yelped.

I didn't look to see whom I'd wounded. My chest constricted as the feeling of being overwhelmed grew.

The mounted policeman picked his way past me, slowly moving east. People stepped aside to let him pass. I saw a way out. I scooted close to the horse. One giant hoof came close to landing on my foot. With a small cry, I hopped away.

The horse was conditioned to be immune to human behavior and ignored me. The cop was too busy scanning the crowd to notice one scared woman dogging his footsteps.

I tucked in against the flank. The horse's earthy smell filled my nostrils and I choked. I clamped a hand over my nose and stayed close.

He got me near enough to the edge of the crowd that I could break free on San Fernando Street. I stood outside Original Joe's and panted, my heart pounding at the thought of what could have happened.

From here, I couldn't see Wyatt or Vangie, but the singing had stopped and the crowd was chanting "Freedom Now."

I wanted to see what the police had done. I started toward the college.

I was the only one heading in the direction of the campus. Kids were still making their way to the demonstration, many looking at their phones as they walked.

My phone chirped with messages. The first was from Freddy. "Will you pick me up some maps when you get yours? I'll take a hundred." He sounded so normal.

The second was from Sonya. "My class has been canceled. I'm in my office if you want to come now." She gave me directions to her place.

Perfect. Now I had a real reason to be on campus.

San Jose State campus was eerily quiet. Whatever the task force had done, it had done swiftly and left behind little evidence. So many of the students were over at the park that the campus felt deserted.

Now that I was away from the noise, I thought about the Twitter response. Granted my Quilters Crawl customers were not totally wired-in college students, but I didn't need thousands of participants. Even another fifty would add to our bottom line. The Twitter promotion could be phenomenal.

I found Sonya's office in the art department after taking a few wrong turns. The door to the cramped, dark office was open. A wooden desk faced front with a laptop open. Shelves of books filled the two side walls. Drawings and sketches covered every empty space. Ceramics lined the small window in the back.

There were three names on a small card on the door. I was in the right place. Sonya shared this office with two other teachers. I waited in the hall. She'd said she would be here. With the door open and the laptop in full view, she wouldn't have gone far.

A cluttered bulletin board sat to the right of the door. I was surprised to see that some kids still used it to communicate. Seemed pretty old school. Write a message on a piece of paper, pin it to the board, hope the right person sees it. The notices were eclectic, someone looking for a ride to the Inland Empire for Columbus Day, another offered tutoring services. A tortoise for sale. Helpfully, he came with his own tank.

A bright green paper caught my eye. The brochure was the do-it-yourself kind, printed on 8-1/2x11 paper, folded into thirds. A graphic of a smiling young man behind a lawn mower adorned the front.

The headline read: Need a GrandSon? I held the brochure open. Inside was the pitch.

Do you have an extra room in your house? Are you old enough to have a real grandson? Our GrandSon will mow your lawn, run your errands, take out the trash. Give him his own room, and provide one meal a day. He'll never ask you for money or to bake his favorite pie.

What an appealing idea. Genius, really. The older women I knew weren't sick, they didn't need full-time care. They needed someone to change light bulbs, or clean the fireplace flue. Keep up the honey-do list that had died with their husband. Having someone living in their houses, even a college kid who came and went at odd hours, would be better than living alone.

Before Buster, I'd lived alone. My house was tiny, so having a roommate had been out of the question. After college and sharing a house with three others, I'd been ready to be on my own, but I hadn't been prepared for what that really meant. How quiet the house could be. How staggeringly difficult changing the smoke alarm battery could be in the middle of the night. How long the nights were when all of them were spent alone.

I tried to imagine what it was like for Pearl and others like her. Women who'd been married for decades. Who'd raised kids, and tended to husbands. How empty their houses must feel.

Pearl might benefit from someone living with her. Vangie visited, but she still lived at home.

I helped myself to the brochure.

"Smart, right?" A petite woman came up next to me. I could see a door down the hall swing shut and heard the flushing of a toilet. "Some grad student came up with the idea. I think it was his thesis. He has a stable of young men needing to rent a room near the school. For reduced rent, they do light chores and keep the owner company."

"What an appealing idea. Genius, really. I know a lot of older women," I said. I pointed to my chest. "Quilt shop owner."

"Ahh. Sonya Salazar. I think you're looking for me," she said, holding out her hand to shake.

I took it. "Dewey Pellicano, from QP."

Sonya led me into her office. Her waist-length black hair swayed, nearly overwhelming her frame. She was dressed in complicated layered pieces. Green cabled tights peeked out beneath her

58

long black paisley skirt and were tucked into short tan boots. Up top, an asymmetrical yellow sweater was belted at the waist with several skinny belts. She hitched up a lacy cream shawl over her shoulders. She looked like she shopped in antique shops and boutiques equally. None of her clothes should have worked together.

Oh right, art teacher.

"Find your way okay? The campus was shut down earlier today. Big drug bust."

"I heard," I said. "In fact, I'm still a bit frazzled. I got caught up in a big protest downtown. I was on my way to the First Friday at the quilt museum, but I never made it."

"Oh, First Fridays. I love those. I know a lot of the people who show their work."

She reached into a tote bag behind her desk and handed me a stack of Quilters Crawl maps. I opened one of them.

"Thanks for helping us this year with the map. I really like the new design," I said. "You did a great job."

I pointed at the logo she'd designed. It was a convertible, speeding down the highway, filled with three attractive women and a grinning sea otter.

"I liked that you gave us some quilters with attitude. Those women look more like my customers. My crowd doesn't relate to the stereotype of the pudgy, gray-haired quilter. It turns them off. They don't recognize themselves."

Sonya shrugged. "I just tried to imagine what kind of women would drive hundreds of miles to twelve shops in one weekend. Someone fun, obviously."

"Are you a quilter?" I asked.

Sonya shook her head. "I'd never set foot in a quilt shop before I did the brochure. I'm interested, though."

"Are you an artist?" I asked, kicking myself as it came out. Of course she was. She taught art for a living. "What's your medium?" I said, trying to recover.

She smiled. "In a perfect world, oils. I'm fascinated by the old Italian masters. Some day I'm going to go to Florence. In the meantime, I supplement my income with graphic design jobs and web design. I did that work for the Quilters Crawl to try and find more work."

Surprise must have shown on my face. She flipped her hair back, gathering the long locks in one hand and shifting her entire body to accommodate. "You wouldn't believe how little money I make. The schools only hire part-timers, so that they don't have to put out for pensions and benefits. In addition to State, I teach classes at Mission, Foothill, and DeAnza."

Those schools were all over the map. Fremont, Cupertino, Los Altos. Literally.

"Yikes, that's a lot of driving."

"Like your shop hop," Sonya said. "Only I do it every week."

Talk of driving brought me back to the Crawl. "Let me have another hundred maps," I said. "I'll bring them to Freddy Roman's."

I took the second pile from her awkwardly, adding them to the ones already in my hand.

"You'll need something to carry them in," Sonya said. She dumped the rest of the maps out and handed the tote bag to me. "Here, use this."

The bag was canvas, like the kind readily available at the craft stores for a few dollars. But it was no longer the boring beige generic canvas. Every inch of it had been decorated. Brightly colored swirls, paisleys, flowers made the bag look like it was made from wonderful fabric.

"Your handiwork?" I asked.

Sonya nodded. "I was doodling, testing out some fabric pens."

Some doodles. My most careful drawings didn't look as good. "I'd love to know which ones you use. I'd like to carry them in my store, but am never sure which ones to order. I don't want to disappoint my customers."

Sonya reached into a mug on the desk and handed me a pen. "I love this brand. Take it."

So many gifts. She was the generous sort. "Well, thank you. I hope you can come by during the Crawl. We're giving away some great stuff."

"I'll do that," she said.

———

Once home, I took a shower, changed into my softest pajamas, and crawled into bed. It was only nine o'clock but my body craved my pillow and quilt. A good night's sleep meant I could get up early and get a head start on my busy day.

Comfort didn't come. The weight of the quilt felt stifling and the pillow wouldn't fit the contours of my body. The pj pants rode up uncomfortably. I was too hot.

I sat up, pushing aside the covers and leaning against the headboard.

The real problem was I couldn't shut my brain down. Worry about what was going on downtown popped up like an unwelcome instant message.

I checked my phone. Nothing from Vangie.

I grabbed the laptop to see if the demonstration was still going on. The local news station had live coverage. The reporter was standing near the Fairmont Hotel.

"Now students from other schools have joined the State kids in the protest of the drug bust on campus today. The police will not tell us how many people have gathered, but I would guess there's at least fifteen hundred kids filling the Cesar de Chavez park and the streets beyond."

The camera panned to the crowd. People leapt in front of the lens, throwing up horns and waggling their fingers like they were at a punk rock concert. I couldn't see Wyatt or Vangie from that vantage point.

The news report switched over to a fire in an apartment building in Sunnyvale.

I flipped to other sites, but found nothing. News about the drug bust was sketchy. One place mentioned only that it had happened, with no details.

Buster's ring tone broke through my concentration.

I grabbed the phone off the nightstand. "Hey, you," I said.

"Hi yourself," Buster said, his voice low and tired. "Sorry I missed dinner," he said. "How'd your day go?"

My shoulders dropped. I closed the laptop and hugged my pillow. The sound of Buster's voice seeped into my pores and relaxed every part of me. I would be able to go to sleep after I talked to him.

"Quiet," I lied. There would be time to fill him in tomorrow. I wanted to know only one thing. "Are you finished work? Coming home soon?" I let the questions pour out of me, unedited.

I wanted him home. I didn't care if Buster was too tired to talk or anything else. I just wanted my arms around him, to feel him sleeping next to me. Wake up with him. It'd been too long.

"Not yet," he said.

My hand jerked, knocking my laptop to the floor. Dang it. My own fault. I'd let my hopes soar for a moment. I reached over and pulled it back into my lap.

Buster said, "We've got a lot of people still to process. As usual, we do the grunt work, the FBI and DEA get all the glory. They're off giving press conferences and reporting to the governor. We're stuck here doing input," Buster said.

I made commiserating noises. Buster must be so tired.

Buster continued, "I'll be here for hours. I'll probably go to my place and crash."

That stabbed my heart. Even if I didn't get to see him, I'd rather he was in my bed alone than in his.

My voice thickened. "Try to come here. I don't care how late it is. Truly, I don't. Wake me up when you come in."

He agreed.

I didn't want him to hang up. "Was it a good bust?"

Buster's voice strengthened. "Ridiculous good. We got some bad dudes off the street. Caught at least thirty low-level drug runners and several higher up."

"Any really big fish?"

"Not yet, but these guys will lead us to the fellows at the top sooner or later. In the meantime, it just got a lot harder to score drugs on the San Jose State campus."

"Did you hear about the protests?" I asked.

"Sure did. Makes me think we were on the right track."

"Vangie's one of the demonstrators."

"Really? How do you know?"

Oops. "I was there, too. Since nobody was around tonight, I decided to walk to the quilt museum for First Friday. I walked right into a mess."

Buster was a cop, a protector. He knew he couldn't shield me, but that didn't mean he didn't struggle with his impulses. "Did you get out okay?"

"I did." I got out of the spotlight in the quickest way I knew how. "Turns out Vangie's friend was the one leading the demonstration. Wyatt got on Twitter and called for the students to protest the drug bust. Down with the pigs and all that. I got out of there before it got too crazy."

"I'm glad. Is Vangie still there?"

"As far as I know." I pushed him. "Buster, what if she gets herself arrested?"

"Don't worry. No one was booked. The uniforms pulled a few kids into their cars, but mostly to shake up the group, make them lose momentum."

That didn't soothe me much. "But what if Vangie is caught around drugs?"

"She's a grownup, Dew. She knows the consequences. She'll be careful."

I wished I was as sure as he was.

I heard someone calling, "Healy, you're up."

"Gotta go," he said. "I love you bunches. You get a good night's sleep cause as soon as this is over, I'm going to …"

His promise trailed off and I heard male voices getting closer.

"You're going to what?" I said, lightly. Buster would never be inappropriate at work, but I liked to test his resolve. "Would you please be more specific?"

"Can't. I will say this. I won't fall asleep this time."

I giggled and hung up.

I leaned back against the pillow. Buster was right. I had to let Vangie make her own mistakes. She'd be fine.

FIVE

My phone rang. I pulled myself out of a deep sleep. I knew the ring, but could only think that it wasn't Buster's. I flung a hand on his sheets. Cold and empty. He was still working. I tried to open my eyes but succeeded only partway. They felt glued shut.

I unlocked the phone and muttered something. My mouth didn't want to open wide enough to actually utter a coherent sound.

The person on the other end was having trouble speaking too. I heard guttural noises but nothing I could make sense of.

"What?" I said. "Who is this?" I pulled the phone away but my eyes wouldn't focus on the name on the screen. I put it back to my ear.

"Dewey," I heard. My throat closed up. This was not a random wrong number or drunk dial. That was Vangie's ring.

"Dewey, I need some help." The voice got a little stronger.

I turned on a light.

"Vang..." I said loudly. "Are you okay?"

"Can you come here?" she asked, her voice so low and icy cold, I shivered and pulled the covers up higher. The sick to my stomach feeling doubled. I rubbed my belly to soothe myself.

"Where are you, Vang? What's going on?"

"My car ... Wyatt ..."

"Did you have an accident? Are you okay?"

"I'm okay. But I need you to come. We're ... I'm at Tenth and St. James Street. You'll see my car."

"Hang on. I'll be right there."

I tossed on a pair of jeans and a sweatshirt over my tank top. My fingers hovered over the keyboard of my phone, starting to text Buster to tell him where I was going. But if I told him, and Vangie's trouble was drugs, he would have no choice but to report her.

He wasn't going to be home tonight. He'd never know.

I grabbed an antacid on the way through the kitchen. I knew the pit in my stomach had no physical reason but I needed relief.

———

Vangie was sitting on the curb, her head hung low. Her face was hidden by her curls. She didn't look up. Her car, a fifteen-year-old Chevy Caprice was parked in front of her, the passenger door open, the interior light on. I pulled in behind her.

I approached from the street side and looked inside the car. The keys, dangling from the ignition, caught the streetlight.

Wyatt was slumped in the passenger seat, his dreads spread across the headrest. He wasn't moving.

I ran to Vangie, grabbing her chin, making her look at me. Her face was wet. She wasn't crying now.

"Are you okay?"

Her eyes fluttered shut. I squeezed and she looked at me, squinting as if it hurt to fully open her eyes. Her voice was hoarse. "I'm fine. I didn't know what to do, Dewey. He's not answering me. Is he …?"

Her shoulders heaved. She twisted away from me, and picked at the wet grass on her shoes.

I looked back at the car. Wyatt was not moving. My stomach flopped. This was not good. But I was as worried about Vangie as I was about Wyatt. She seemed out of it.

"Vangie, talk to me." I remembered the smell of marijuana at the rally earlier. "Have you taken anything?"

She snapped her head up. "No. You know better. I don't do drugs."

Vangie stood, shaking off her lethargy. She started toward the car. I followed her.

We were in a quiet residential neighborhood. The night was clear and our voices seemed to carry. I looked around to see if anyone had woken up. No lights were on anywhere except for a porch light on a small house across the street. Wind chimes dangled from the cross post and tinkled in the light breeze.

I couldn't have been more than ten when my grandmother Pellicano had told me to hang wind chimes on the porch to keep my man from roaming. My mother had laughed when I'd asked for a set. She assured me my father wasn't going anywhere. She'd been right. She was the one who left too soon.

Vangie paced.

I heard nothing from Wyatt. "Did he take something? Has he been sick? Does he have allergies?"

He'd looked like a healthy kid a few hours ago, but that didn't mean much.

Vangie moaned, "No. I don't know. I was driving him home. He was having trouble breathing. He threw up on himself, and ... "

Her trunk twisted as if reenacting what Wyatt had been through.

"I tried to save him, but I didn't know what was going on, and then he was gone. Like that."

I realized I'd not been hearing what I expected—sirens. "Vangie, did you call 911?"

She shook her head sheepishly. "My phone is out of juice now."

"Take mine."

I watched to make sure she called, then went to Wyatt. I reached in to feel for a pulse but couldn't find one. His body was warm but he was so very still. His chest wasn't moving, and I couldn't feel any breath.

I felt completely inadequate. I didn't know CPR. If Wyatt *was* alive, there wasn't anything I could do to save him.

He didn't seem alive to me, though.

I couldn't see any blood, although I knew that blood could have soaked into the black upholstery and I wouldn't be able to see it. At least from the front, he didn't have any knife or gunshot wounds.

He might have died of natural causes, but there was nothing natural about dying in the front seat of Vangie's car.

Wyatt had been in the midst of a huge crowd the last time I'd seen him. Now he was alone and dead. What had happened between now and then?

I grabbed a picnic quilt from the trunk of my car and wrapped it around Vangie, pushing her until she was seated again. She clutched at the quilt and I realized she recognized it was one my mother had made. The pink flowers had long ago faded to soft white. It was limp from repeated washings.

Vangie's other hand picked at a zit on her cheek.

What had she and Wyatt been doing since I saw them? I peeled away her fingers to stop the mutilation of her face. "Is there something you want to tell me?" I asked.

Vangie shook her head but I couldn't tell if it was voluntary or not.

The siren noise grew closer and Vangie closed her eyes and rocked on the curb. I put my arm around her. Once the police were here, I'd lose her. She'd be taken downtown and questioned. For hours.

Vangie's long brown lashes were wet with tears. I needed her to wake up and clue me in.

"Vangie," I said, keeping my voice low but finding a serious tone. I sat down next to her. "The cops will be here any minute. Is there something you want to tell me? I promise I won't tell Buster or anyone else if you don't want me to."

Vangie's head slumped farther. I squeezed her upper arm. She brought her eyes to mine but still no sound came out of her mouth. Her hands dangled by her knees. She was in the perfect position to puke. I wouldn't be surprised if she did. I felt my own stomach roiling.

A siren squealed, getting closer until it was cut off in mid-scream. I felt Vangie shudder as a black and white slewed around the corner. A uniformed cop got out of the car and approached us, keeping one hand on his belt near his gun. From our vantage point on the curb, he looked improbably tall and lean.

Suddenly, Vangie pressed something into my hand. Small and round. I looked down. It was a prescription bottle. I squinted at it.

"It's Pearl's prescription," Vangie said. "Take it to her."

I opened my mouth to protest, but the cop spoke first.

"What's going on here?" he asked. He stood at an angle to us, taking in the street, the car and the nearby yards. His eyes didn't rest. I didn't like the feeling of being small and started to rise. His fingers tapped the handle of his gun. "Stay seated, please. Put your hands on your knees."

I complied. No sense making this cop nervous. I closed my fist tight.

Since Vangie wasn't talking, I said, "My friend found her boyfriend in her car. He seems to be dead."

The cop shone his flashlight inside. "How did this happen?"

I looked at Vangie. She nodded. Her voice was rusty at first and she had to stop twice to clear her throat. "I was driving him home, and he had a seizure or something..." she dissolved in tears. Her dark curls spilled over her cheeks, hiding her face.

The officer reached in and pressed his fingers against the boy's throat.

"Were you drinking?"

Vangie shook her head without removing her hands. I couldn't blame her. If my boyfriend was lying dead... I shook off that thought. Buster was in danger all the time. I usually managed not to imagine scenarios like this.

But sometimes in the middle of the night, I couldn't help it.

I hugged Vangie close. She leaned against my shoulder. While my body was hidden, I shoved the pills into my pocket. A second police car rolled to a stop and a woman, looking stuffed into her shirt, got out. She was short, even with thick-soled boots on. I couldn't tell if she was heavyset or if her equipment made her look like a Weeble.

The officer acknowledged the new arrival with a curt nod. She barely glanced in our direction. She waved her flashlight around the car, the light strobing. I turned away so I wouldn't see Wyatt's head illuminated again.

"ID, please," the first officer said.

Vangie and I pulled out our driver's licenses and he jotted down our names and addresses.

"Were you two together?" he asked.

I returned my arm to Vangie's shoulder. She felt so thin and vulnerable. "No. I just got here. Vangie called me. My boyfriend is on the force. Ben Healy."

He gave a barely perceptible shrug. "Don't know him."

So much for goodwill between fellow officers. The thin blue line was very skinny around here. These were patrol officers. There was no reason they would know Buster, who'd only been on patrol a short time before being moved to Homicide and now the Drug Task Force. His attitude made it clear that there would be no special treatment tonight.

"Ma'am." The officer addressed Vangie loudly, leaning down. "I'm going to need you to stand up and answer my questions," he said.

"She's upset," I said. "Her friend died in her car. Can't you cut her some slack?"

He ignored me. Something about Vangie's demeanor had awakened his suspicions. Vangie stood.

"Are you on anything, miss?" He let his flashlight play over Vangie's face.

I caught my breath, hoping her eyes weren't dilated. Hoping she hadn't taken anything.

The officer seemed to be satisfied with what he saw—or didn't see—in Vangie. I felt my shoulders come down a notch.

"Is there anyone else in the car?"

Vangie shrugged. "No."

The officer returned his pad to his pocket. "I'm going to need to search your car, ma'am. Do I have your permission?"

Vangie gulped. She wouldn't look at me. I held my breath as Vangie fought with herself. I was glad now she'd given me Pearl's prescription earlier. She wouldn't have been able to explain to the cops that Pearl was her seventy-four-year-old friend.

She nodded. The cop opened the trunk, letting his light play over the contents. "Clear," he said to the policewoman. "Don't disturb anything but make sure there's no one in the back seat."

I squeezed Vangie's hand.

The ambulance arrived. Two attendants jumped out and hurried to Wyatt. They pulled him out of the car and onto the ground.

The taller one strode over to the patrol officer "Why didn't you just call the ME? This guy's been dead for a while."

I didn't listen for the officer's answer. He was covering his ass. I grabbed Vangie.

"Vangie, how long have you been out here?"

She shrugged. "I don't know. I was scared, Dewey."

They bundled Wyatt into the back of the ambulance and took off.

The silence they left behind filled the space. Now there were lights in the houses around us. Several people in robes and slippers gathered on a front lawn, watching.

"Ladies, I'd like you to come to the station. My sergeant will want a word with you."

Vangie pressed against me and I pulled the quilt closer and tucked in around her armpits. I felt the cold curb against my thighs and was glad I'd worn a sweatshirt.

———

Once at the police station, Vangie and I were separated. I'd known that would happen, but when the officers indicated we should move apart, Vangie clung to me. I patted her between her shoulder blades.

I put my finger on her lips and caught her gaze. I held her eyes so she understood the seriousness of my next sentence. We didn't know how Wyatt died. Even if Vangie wasn't involved—and I prayed that she wasn't—his manner of death might lead to the cops suspecting her of murder. I couldn't have her contributing to their case.

"Tell the truth, Vang. You've got a right to a lawyer. Let them get you one."

She nodded. The policewoman grasped her elbow and started to steer her down the hall.

She got smaller and smaller and I wondered if she would make it through the night.

I was sent home around eight. I intended to shower quickly but I lingered, finding it impossible to leave the warm flow of water. It was a half hour before I felt human again.

Out of the shower, worry about Vangie wouldn't quit. What did Vangie know about this Wyatt? I racked my brain for the first time she mentioned him. She'd met him during orientation a few weeks ago. Or was it in her summer school class?

I couldn't remember. Was he the real reason she got too busy to help at the store and with the Crawl?

I didn't want to go to work yet. I needed someone to talk about what had just happened. Buster was still at work. And Vangie? I couldn't talk to her.

I grabbed a banana and a cup of coffee, the tote bag of Quilters Crawl maps and headed to Freddy's.

Freddy's store opened an hour earlier than mine, at nine. I had to be back by ten to open QP.

I'd given Jenn the week off, and Ursula was working four hours a day this week. During the Crawl, they'd both work ten hours straight. I couldn't afford to pay overtime, so I'd shortened their hours beforehand. It would be all hands on deck during the Crawl.

Once I crossed the threshold of Roman's Sewing Machines, a ding, sounding a lot like my parents' doorbell, let Freddy's employees know someone had entered.

Like Robert Palmer, Freddy liked to hire a type. His sales force was made up of two women, both taller than he was, with broad shoulders and over-arched eyebrows. Rebekah was blond, with clear blue eyes and a Swedish heritage. She looked like she could ski for miles. While carrying a shotgun. Inez was German, with tight curls and a tight mouth to match. They dressed alike, black skirts with black vests and white shirts with low pumps. Both had worked for years for other dealers in the area.

The tallest one, Rebekah, I think, glided toward me. I geared myself to see her disappointment.

She and her counterpart, Inez, hated wasting time on people not interested in buying a sewing machine. I knew she didn't recognize me because she smiled and trailed her hand over the sewing machines seductively.

"Good morning. What are you in the market for?" she asked, stopping by what I knew was a souped-up version of the machine I had at home. Not the most expensive machine in the place, but not the cheapest by far.

This was a rerun of the first time I'd been in the store. That time it'd been Inez who'd tried to sell me a machine. These two were sharks. Customers did not escape their grasp easily. Freddy pitted his two saleswomen against each other, giving out prizes for the most machines closed, the best dollar amount, even keeping track of accessories sold. He ran his shop like selling was an Olympic sport.

I had to nip Rebekah in the bud before she got too far into her spiel. Otherwise she'd be sticking pins in a voodoo doll that looked disturbingly like me before I got out of the parking lot.

I held up the stack of maps. "It's me, Dewey Pellicano. I'm here to see Freddy."

Something like contempt crossed her face before she rearranged her features into a wrinkle-free smile. She pointed to the back of the store. "He's in his office."

Freddy called out. "C'mon back, Dewey."

Rebekah held her hand out. "I might as well take them from you," she said. "He's going to want them on display out here."

I gave her half and took the rest to Freddy.

"You picked up the maps?" Freddy said. He spun around his desk chair. "How were you able to get through downtown? I saw on the news that it was a crazy night in San Jose. Was Buster involved in all that?"

The protest seemed like it had happened days ago.

I looked for a place to sit but there was no extra chair. Freddy didn't believe in paying for space that wasn't being used to sell merchandise. His office was a repurposed closet with the door off. When he worked, he faced the inside wall with the clothing rod still over his head, always watching how quickly he stood up. The desk was high with paperwork.

I nodded. "But that was only the beginning. Vangie was at the protest. Her friend died later. In her car. While she was with him."

"What? That's nuts." Freddy pounded the arms of his chair. "Where is she now?"

I crossed my arms and hugged myself, supporting myself with the doorjamb. "Still being questioned by the police."

Freddy reached for his desk phone, dialing a number from memory. He waited a beat, then left a terse message. "Larry, call me back right away," he said.

"Who's Larry?"

Freddy smiled, the reptilian one. "Did I never tell you about my brother—the defense attorney?"

I clasped my hands over my heart like a heroine in an old movie. "Are you serious?"

"Me? Not so much. But he is. Deadly serious."

———

Back in my car, I noticed the bottle of pills. Pearl's prescription from Vangie. I'd forgotten about them. I spilled a few of the small yellow pills out into my hand and took a closer look. Ambien, the bottle said. I knew that drug was supposed to be a sleep aid.

Insomnia had been Pearl's friend. She'd always said that she was at her most creative in the middle of the night.

Maybe these drugs accounted for some of Pearl's spaciness yesterday. What to do about Pearl?

I remembered the brochure on Sonya's bulletin board.

That GrandSons service brochure that I'd seen at the college might be a great answer for Pearl. Having another human being around would give her a reason to take a shower in the morning. She used to love to cook for Hiro; maybe a GrandSon would bring that out in her again. Any kind of interactivity could do her a world of good.

I'd have to find out more.

I got to QP right after ten, so I opened the front door to the shop, then returned to my desk. I could see the front through the little window that had been put in many years ago. Its original purpose had been to fill orders from the carpenters and plumbers that had purchased their supplies at Dewey's Hardware. For me, it was a view into the retail space that allowed me to work in my office while keeping an eye on the customers.

I called the police station to see if Vangie was still there. The first officer I talked to could tell me nothing. The second told me Buster wasn't at his desk. I already knew he wasn't answering his cell.

I decided to try Roy Sanchez. He'd been Buster's partner and the first homicide detective I'd ever met.

Sanchez owed me. Because he believed quilters were too nice to kill, I nearly got shot. The fact that quilters had fooled even a veteran like him had shattered his belief in his abilities. After that, he and Buster had been knocked down to cold cases.

Roy Sanchez felt like Buster had gotten a raw deal from SJPD because of him.

I hadn't called in that marker but I would now.

"Detective Sanchez," I said. "It's Dewey Pellicano."

Sanchez sighed. "What's the matter? Your boyfriend not keeping you up to date on the local homicides? You getting bored with selling fabric? Want to take the detective test?"

Roy Sanchez was not a jovial guy. This lame attempt at humor was his way of keeping me at a distance.

"Roy," I said. I could practically feel his back stiffen. He was a formal guy. But I'd earned the right three years ago. "Do you remember my assistant, Evangeline Estrada?"

He grunted.

Sanchez was a good interrogator because he knew how to intimidate. I kept going before I lost my nerve. "She was brought in last night. Her boyfriend died in her car. They're questioning her. I'm trying to find out how she's doing, when she might be released."

"Hmmm … I wasn't on last night," he said. I heard him clicking on a keyboard. "That would have been Anton Zorn."

Crap. Zorn had been the lead detective on the case when a body had shown up in the alley behind my store. He had not been happy with me when I figured out what was going on before he did. Add that to a giant chip on his shoulder because Buster was the youngest homicide detective in the history of the department was strike two. Vangie was going to be strike three.

I groaned. "Anton Zorn hates me. I hope he can be objective."

Sanchez said, "I haven't seen Zorn this morning. He must be out working the case. What did the guy die of?'"

"I don't know. Wyatt was the person behind that big protest yesterday. He might be a drug user."

"You suspect he died of an overdose?"

"I'm not sure. All I know is he wasn't stabbed or shot. And he was young and healthy."

"Did you see his body? What did he look like?"

"He looked okay, but Vangie said he had trouble breathing, then had a seizure and died. That could be natural causes, right?"

"Is that why you're calling me? Because you think he died of an asthma attack?"

I was quiet. Young, white men don't generally drop dead for no reason. Most of the time, they have a little help. In which case, Vangie could be in a lot of trouble.

More trouble than just violating her parole. She could be in the middle of a homicide investigation. She could be a main suspect.

And I had the feeling that she wasn't telling me everything. My gut ached.

Sanchez was clicking around on his keyboard. "Wyatt Pederson was checked into the morgue in the middle of the night. That the guy?"

"It has to be," I said. "How many dead Wyatts do you usually get in one night?"

Roy had none of the gallows humor associated with cops.

"Well, looky here. Mr. Pederson had a record. Intent to distribute."

SIX

"Drugs?"

Sanchez said, "Marijuana. A few years back. He got off with probation. The laws were changing and our prosecutor wasn't too keen on pursuing those cases."

"I didn't smell anything on him. Or on Vangie. Early at the demonstration, pot was in the air, but not in the car."

"He wouldn't have OD'd on marijuana. But there are a lot of other drugs out there." It was clear he was done talking.

"So I'm learning," I said. "Thanks for your help, Detective Sanchez."

"Good luck, Ms. Pellicano. I hope your friend makes out okay."

Twitter had been the genesis of the protests. I logged on to see if I could learn anything more about Wyatt. I checked Vangie's feed. Nothing from her since yesterday afternoon. Plenty of tweets about the riot from her followers but nothing that I could recognize as coming from Wyatt.

She followed at least a hundred people. She followed Freddy and Lark, as did I. But then there were many names that I didn't know. She'd told me her teachers used Twitter to put out the latest assignments and she and her lab partners and study groups often used it to keep in touch. I scrolled through.

I got to a familiar name at the end. Sonya Salazar. Vangie must have had her for Art somewhere along the line.

I went back to the top of the page. Vangie's face came up. The picture had been taken a year ago, right after I got back from Asilomar. Vangie had started at the community college and she was happy and excited. Her face glowed. It hurt my heart to realize I hadn't seen that expression for some time now.

When this was over, I had to help her find some balance in her life.

Suddenly a tweet popped up on her account. "RIP, @Wynottoke."

Wynottoke. What? I sounded it out. *Why not toke.* Wyatt. It had to be.

There were many postings like that. Kids had retweeted the original announcement that came in from someone at five AM. "Wyatt Pederson died tonight." News traveled fast on Twitter.

I followed the link to his feed.

Most of the entries were tributes to him. I had to scroll through pages to get his last tweet. At 11:33 PM, he'd written, "*Good job, everyone. We will protest another day. Live free and toke.*"

I moved backward through his feed. So many entries. He had been tweeting every five minutes during the protest. About 10 PM, he was posting pics of the gathering. The pictures were fuzzy and showed a lot of upraised arms and not much else. He might have deliberately obscured faces in case the cops would see them later. If things got out of hand, the pictures could be proof of misdeeds.

This need to put everything online was new to me. I was only a dozen years older than the college students, but I liked to have my private life remain private.

A customer came in so I went up front. While she shopped, I unpacked an order of notions that had come in. I didn't want Ursula lifting the heavy box, so I broke down the order and laid out the pieces on the cutting table for her to put away.

Ursula had lived with an abusive husband for years and her body bore the scars. She was often in pain, but she refused to take medication. She was a valuable asset to QP so I worked around the fact that one of her shoulders was prone to bursitis and her elbow didn't open all the way.

The customer left without spending anything. I gave her one of the Crawl maps and encouraged her to sign up for the Twitter alerts.

For a Saturday, the store was very quiet.

I kept my cell nearby. Vangie would need a ride home from the station. I checked it again. Nothing from her so far.

About noon, the door opened and Buster came through.

"Look what I found," he said, moving aside so I could see. Vangie was bringing up the rear. Her head was down and she was moving slowly. My heart softened. She looked so defeated.

I hugged her tight and her tremble felt like it was my own. I stroked her back, but when I went to smooth her hair she shook her head and stepped away.

Vangie threw her shoulders back and walked off toward our office in the back of the store. Maybe a little work would help. Distract her, keep her busy, make her feel useful.

"Is she okay?" I asked. Buster gave a slight nod. I let out my breath.

Buster said, "Detective Zorn is going to want to talk to her again, but for now, she's done."

Vangie wouldn't be free of this until the police knew what—or who—killed Wyatt.

Buster said, jingling the change in his pocket, "The attorney made himself a pain in the neck. Zorn was happy to get rid of her."

Wow. Freddy had really come through.

I gave Buster a kiss. "Thanks for bringing her here. I really needed to see her."

"She wanted to come here first."

He kissed me gingerly and stepped back. "Sorry, I stink. I haven't been home yet. I'm going to shower and sleep for as many hours as I can."

"I'll wake you when I get home," I said.

"As long as you're gentle," Buster said, whisking his lips past mine. Full of promise. "I don't have a problem with you interrupting my beauty sleep. We need to catch up."

I hugged him close. He was pretty rank, but I didn't care. I was so glad this Task Force investigation was over. The thought of Buster being among drugs and dangerous dealers had never left my mind.

He yawned again, and left.

Vangie was out back, unchaining her bike from the railing. She avoided my eyes. There was something about Wyatt she didn't want me to know. Something she was ashamed of. I could see it on her face. I knew enough not to press her. Vangie always told me the truth, but only when she was ready.

"Are you okay?"

"I'm tired. I need my bike."

"Why don't you let Buster drive you? I can call him—" I started back in for my phone. Vangie's mother's house was at least five miles away, in East San Jose.

She tested her tires, bouncing her bike on the pavement. "I didn't want him to. I could use the exercise."

She hopped on her bike and left.

The store felt empty after Vangie left. Ursula was due in soon to work the afternoon shift.

I wandered the aisles, stopping to straighten a bolt of fabric. I found an empty rotary blades package tucked in between two bolts. I hated blister packs in my consumer life but they did help to cut down on shoplifting in my work life. I liked to believe it wasn't my quilters who pilfered but I knew better. I tossed the empty packaging away.

Vangie's life was going to be turned upside down, unless Wyatt somehow died a natural death in her car. A congenital heart condition would be good. Or an allergic reaction to a bee sting. Something that would show up loud and clear in the autopsy.

I propped open the front door to let the October breeze in. The air was as crisp as an apple. I breathed deep.

I walked back through the store. I loved the way it looked now. It looked more like me.

Six months ago, I'd had a huge sale and sold off all of our fabric inventory. Some of the bolts had been hanging around for years. I got rid of what I could and gave the rest to the guild to be used for their ongoing philanthropy projects.

Then I'd closed the shop for two weeks and Vangie and I painted the entire store in a bright white. Kevin had nearly cried when I'd primed the century-old woodwork. The wall behind the register was filled with tiny drawers that were original to the first Dewey Hardware. I'd painted those too, despite the fact that I'd grown up with tales of how my mother and father had re-stained each tiny drawer front when they were courting.

The result was a space that looked brand-new. Clean, fresh, and modern, exactly the look I'd been hoping to achieve.

I brought in fabrics that spoke to that same aesthetic. I knew there were plenty of quilters my age, in their early thirties, who weren't comfortable around the older crowd. They liked to use full lines of fabric from their favorite designers. They liked traditional patterns but used updated fabrics and colors.

Vangie had been a big part of the change. I didn't want to think about QP without Vangie.

Coming through the classroom, I saw Pearl's ruined quilt and my blackened iron. The quilt was sticky. I tossed it in the garbage. Back at my desk, I grabbed the brochure from the GrandSons. As soon as Ursula came in, I was going to check on Pearl. Maybe there was a solution at hand.

———

"Please let me in," I said again to the closed door. "Pearl, I've got a proposition for you. It's a great solution."

"I don't need anybody but Vangie," Pearl said. "Get Vangie."

"Vangie is not going to be available. You know she's in school full-time now. She needs to study."

Ursula was at the store so I'd come to Pearl's to talk to her.

"You work her too hard."

"We're both going to have to get used to having a little less Vangie in our lives."

Pearl pulled open the door slightly. Her hair was sticking up as if she'd been trying to pull it out by the roots. Her eyes were rimmed red. I had to get inside.

I pushed my foot in and nudged the door open more. Finally, she stepped aside. I grabbed the knob and went in.

A musty smell hit me as I walked into the foyer. A black lacquered table was covered with mail. I slipped on a Kohl's ad, catching myself on the door jamb, scrambling to keep my footing.

She led me through the living room, a study in clutter. Pearl's beloved framed article about her Manzanar quilt was propped on the couch instead of hanging in its usual place over the fireplace.

I pointed at it, and started to speak. Pearl waved a dismissive hand. "I'm redecorating," she said.

The kitchen was worse. A broom leaned against the counter, a pile of dirt still in the middle of the floor. Cupboard doors stood open. I closed one that threatened my head as I entered. The shelf behind it was empty. No wonder. All the dishes were in the sink.

I realized the stale smell was following me. It was coming off Pearl.

I'd had no idea. Pearl and Vangie were both in over their heads. I was going to call the GrandSons. There was no time to waste.

"Pearl, why don't you take a shower? Wouldn't that feel good?"

Pearl scowled at me. "You don't have to treat me like an idiot, Dewey. I don't like showering when there's no one else in the house."

"Perfect," I said. "I'll stay. You take as long as you need."

I stacked dirty dishes, ran the garbage disposal, and loaded the dishwasher. As soon as Pearl turned off the water in her shower, I started it up. It was going to take several loads to get all the dishes clean. Pearl hadn't washed a dish in weeks from the looks of things. Why hadn't Vangie told me?

The kitchen table was a jumble of old quilting magazines and long lists. Pearl's handwriting, cramped and mostly unreadable, filled legal pads with ideas, to-do lists, and diary entries. She was trying so hard to keep it together but it wasn't happening.

I found a large basket on top of the hutch in the dining room and swept everything off the kitchen table into it. There would be time to sort the mess later.

I spotted a postcard of a big ship on the blue Adriatic sea. It was from Ina, Pearl's best friend. She was on a cruise. Ina had written that she was eating too much and reading a lot. She'd be home in the beginning of October, just a couple of days from now.

That was great news. I had no doubt that part of Pearl's downfall was because her best friend was not around. Even so, Ina had her own life to lead. Having a GrandSon around would give Pearl the boost she needed.

I called the number on the brochure.

"This is Ross," a pleasant voice said.

"I'm looking for a GrandSon," I said.

"You found one. For yourself?"

"No, it's for my ... grandmother," I lied. Easier than trying to explain our relationship. She was like a grandmother to me. "How does this work?" I asked.

"Well, I'm a student at State. I will rent a room in your grandmother's home for a nominal amount, usually a couple hundred dollars a month. In return, I'll help her out. Whatever she needs. I mean, not like nursing care. But run errands, weed the garden. I don't mind helping with laundry and such. And I cook a mean omelet."

"I'm intrigued. Can you come over and speak with us now?"

"Umm ... sure. I have class in about ninety minutes."

I gave him the address and went back to sweeping the floor. At least the kitchen would look good.

Pearl came out, her short hair wet and slicked back. She had on a red T-shirt and a pair of jeans. Fuzzy elephant slippers completed the outfit. I would take it. She was presentable.

"Let's sit a minute," I said.

"You made coffee?" Pearl sniffed the air. "I thought I was out."

"I found some in the freezer. Listen, I have a proposition for you."

I gave her the outline of the GrandSons program. "What do you think? This guy named Ross is coming over so we can question him about the kinds of services they offer."

Pearl undid the top button on her blouse.

"Yikes, Pearl, not those kinds of services. That is *not* on the table."

She cackled. "I'm trying to get a rise out of you. If I wanted to satisfy my horniness, it certainly wouldn't be with a ... "

I clamped my hands over my ears. "La, la, la," I said loudly. "I can't hear you."

The old Pearl was still in there. That made me happy.

The doorbell rang. "I'll go," I said, but Pearl jumped up, cut me off, and got to the door before I did. She opened it wide and smiled when she saw what was standing on her porch.

Ross was a five-foot-seven young man, dressed in neat khakis, white shirt, and a skinny striped tie. He'd clearly been coached or given a dress code. He looked more like a missionary or a carpet cleaning salesman than a potential roommate.

Only the sneakers on his feet were what you'd expect from a kid his age. They were trimmed in bright green and looked brand new.

Pearl said, "Come in. We're hanging in the kitchen."

He made a short bow, indicating Pearl should lead the way. I took up the rear. Pearl's small quilts were hung on every surface in the hall leading to the kitchen. Ross stopped in front of one that featured Mt. Fuji. Pearl had beaded it so the snow on the mountaintop was shining.

He reached out, but I stopped him as his fingers were about to reach the fabric. He let his hand drop.

"No touching allowed. Are you an artist?" I asked.

He shook his head. "No. I studied in Japan last semester. I didn't get to Fuji, though."

Pearl turned and clapped her hands together. "Goody! I've been many times. We can have such fun talking about Japan."

She beamed at me. I gave her a look that I hoped would remind her that we were just exploring this idea.

Ross settled into the banquette. I got in next to Pearl.

"Tell us what the GrandSons program is all about," I said.

Ross scooped his hair off his forehead. He smiled. "We are a non-profit that matches up older women with younger guys so that we can serve in a capacity like a grandson. If you give me a room in your home, I will do whatever chores you find necessary."

"I'm not sure what I would need done," Pearl said.

I nearly choked on my coffee, the coffee I'd brewed after scrubbing out the coffeepot with a Brillo pad. My dishpan hands told a different story.

"Do you have CPR training?" I asked.

"I do," Ross said. "And I can take her to all her doctor appointments if you'd like."

"I can drive," Pearl said. "I'm an excellent driver."

Diplomatic, choosing not to answer, he smoothed his tie down over his skinny chest.

Pearl said, "Ross, do you like crossword puzzles? I'm stuck on this week's *New York Times*. That damn Will Shortz. He never met a pun he didn't like."

"I'm a whiz," Ross began.

I held up a hand. "Pearl, let's figure out some other ways Ross can help you. Do you go to school at State full-time?"

"Yes, but I have a very flexible schedule. In fact, most of my classes are at night so I can be available. I can help her with grocery shopping, other errands. Either she can come with me or I'll go myself."

His forehead creased. "For example, my last Granny—that's what we call them ..." Ross explained.

Pearl's lip curled into a snarl. I stifled a laugh. Granny was not her style. "Not me," Pearl put in.

"Okay." Ross's head tilted as though he was puzzled. "Anyhow, my last Granny was very sick," he said. "She had to be driven to dialysis three times a week. Many, many doctor appointments. They know me over at O'Conner Hospital, let me tell you."

Pearl leaned in to him. "What happened to her?"

"She passed a month or so ago."

"How awful for you," Pearl said, her mouth turning down.

Ross said sincerely, "It is a downside of this job, but I prefer to think that I was blessed to have spent time with her. She was a very courageous woman."

We were quiet for a moment, thinking about the people who had passed.

"My husband and I met at Manzanar. Do you know what that is?" Pearl asked, her face close to his.

Ross looked at me for guidance. I sat back. If he was going to live here, he'd hear this story more than once. I wanted to see how he handled it.

"The internment camp, right?" he said. He smiled at her tentatively.

She nodded. "Our families had been taken off their farms. We lived in wooden shacks. I was only four. Hiro was a big boy, about eight."

I watched Ross as Pearl told the story of how the young boy had shared his food with Pearl, and listened to Pearl sing. His eyes never left her face.

I felt myself soften. This kid could be the answer to our problems.

Pearl finished up. "I made a quilt about my experiences. It's won a lot of awards. It's hanging in the Japanese American National Museum."

"I'd love to see it."

"I'll get a picture."

Pearl jumped off the banquette and went down into the living room. There was definitely a spring in her step that had been missing.

I said to Ross, "Do you have references?"

"Of course," Ross said. "I can email you the list."

Pearl presented the framed picture and article. Ross seemed suitably impressed.

"Okay, well, then," I said. "Ross, thank you for coming."

Ross stood up and bowed in Pearl's direction. "*Arigatou gozaimasu*."

Ross started toward the door. Pearl grabbed my arm.

"Did you hear that?" Pearl whispered. "He speaks Japanese. He can move in tomorrow."

Pearl's face opened up in a huge smile, one I hadn't seen in months. Pearl had fallen for this kid hook, line, and sinker.

She stopped in front of her reflection in the microwave and smoothed down her cowlick.

"Okay. Let me check his references," I said.

"He's charming, Dewey. Good job," she said, patting my hand. "You were right. He's just what the doctor ordered."

I lowered my voice. "I'm glad."

She looked better already. Her eyes were shining.

I caught up with Ross at the front door. "Thanks for coming," I said.

"No problem. I've got no place to live right now, so this would work out great for me, too."

When I got back inside, Pearl had climbed up on the counter-top, opening a high cupboard. I could see her lime-green Kitchen Aid mixer on the shelf. That sucker was heavy.

Pearl was reaching for it, kneeling on the Formica.

"Pearl," I yelled, catapulting myself the length of the kitchen. "Criminy, you're going to kill yourself."

I put one hand on her back and the other on the mixer, steadying both. That mixer was so top heavy, I was afraid that one or both of them was going to land on the floor.

"Jump down," I said.

Pearl turned so she was sitting down, facing me, still on the counter. "Chill, Dewey. I've done this a gazillion times before. Just because you weren't here to see me..."

"I'm here now. And I'm begging. Please let me."

She pouted but swung her feet and landed nimbly on the floor. "If Ross were here, he could get down the mixer when I felt like making cookies. And he could fill the bird feeder and..."

I filled my arms with the mixer and set it up for Pearl. She un-wrapped two sticks of butter and plopped them in the bowl.

I kissed her cheek. "All right, all right. I can see you like him. I'll call him and have him come back tomorrow."

The store was closed tomorrow, Sunday. I had to paint the bathroom, but I would have time to help Pearl and Ross settle in.

I let myself out. When I looked back, Pearl was standing in the front window, a measuring cup in her hand. I waved but she didn't wave back.

———

As soon as I got home that night, I could smell the combination of steam and aftershave that meant Buster was fresh from the shower. Yippee, he was awake.

He was standing near the stove, dressed in basketball shorts and a T-shirt with a kitchen towel slung over his shoulder. I loved the domesticated touch on my big and burly guy's guy.

I kissed him hello. I let my cheek linger on his, feeling the sweet vulnerability of his naked chin.

"Hi yourself," he said, returning the kiss. "Have a seat."

He took my laptop case and my purse from me, laying them on the counter. He pulled out a chair at the two-seat kitchen table. We'd found the bar-height table in a dumpster and spent hours sanding and painting the wood.

Buster and I hadn't spent every minute refinishing furniture. One memorable night was forever associated with this piece for me. Running my hands over the smooth top reminded me of Buster's not so smooth hands running over me. I smiled at him.

"Did you put away all the bad guys?" I asked, settling myself. He'd put out placemats, dishes, and silverware already. In the middle of the table sat the souvenir trivet we'd gotten in Monterey. It was a cast-iron sea otter on his back, his paws and feet held up to receive the dish. It reminded me of the Crawl. I put work out of my mind for now.

The trivet meant only one thing. His favorite dish to make and my favorite comfort food—mac and cheese.

"Only playing Grand Theft Auto with your brother," he said. He put on a blue rubbery hot mitt and pulled a bubbling casserole from the oven. I inhaled the sweet smell of toasted bread crumbs that he liked to sprinkle on the top.

"Kevin was here?" I asked. My brother and Buster had been best friends growing up and even though I didn't get along well with my sister-in-law, Kym, I was glad to hear he'd been by.

"He left before you got here."

"That's because he's avoiding me," I said. I didn't even wait for him to sit down before dug my fork into the gluey goodness.

"You're the best," I said, after the first bite. "Boyfriend. Ever." I sighed with contentment.

He dumped the double boiler water and set out steamed broccoli. He put some on my plate and some on his, and sat down, tucking a cloth napkin under his chin.

"Why is your brother avoiding you?" he asked.

I pointed my fork at him. "That bathroom at QP. Still not finished."

Buster spooned a huge forkful of casserole into his mouth. "Still?" he said, around the food.

"And the Crawl starts on Wednesday," I said. "I'm going in to paint it tomorrow. And the tile guys get there on Monday. After that, Kevin tells me it's only a matter of a few hours worth of work."

"I'll help you paint," Buster said. He put more broccoli on my plate. I made a face.

"Thanks," I said. "For the painting, not the broccoli."

He frowned. "You've got to eat your veggies. They're good for you."

"Thanks, Dr. Oz. Not to change the subject, but did you score any playoff tickets?"

He shook his head morosely. The Giants had become too popular since winning the World Series a couple of years back. Now everyone wanted to go to their games.

After dinner, I cleaned up while Buster checked ESPN.

"I'm going to take a bath," I said.

It was the middle of Sports Center, so he had no objection. I pulled off my clothes and sat on the edge of the tub, letting my hand dangle in the water. I could barely wait for the tub to fill up. My hot water heater gurgled and complained as I taxed it to the maximum, asking for the hottest it could give me. I was afraid the old thing would blow up before I got a full tub.

I brought my iPod in and set it to Lucinda Williams, Shelby Lynne, and Rosanne Cash. I needed the plaintive sounds of country music to carry me far from Silicon Valley.

I added bubble bath, and then added more. It had been a two-capful week.

A bubble drifted up and popped. I caught another one on my palm. I imagined Vangie's troubles inside that bubble. When it popped, I felt a little sense of release. I tried it again. Wyatt. Pop.

Barb V. Pop. The Crawl. Pop. Pearl. Pop. Pop. Pop.

Silly but it worked. I climbed into the tub already more relaxed. I closed my eyes and eased back.

I heard Buster come in and sit on the toilet seat. "Feeling better?"

"Getting there," I said, without opening my eyes.

"Can I wash your back?" he asked.

I leaned forward in answer. I let my head and arms fall as he went to work with the scratchy loofah.

"You seem pretty tense," he said. "Vangie?"

"And I'm worried about Pearl. Vangie was sort of looking after her, but now—"

I didn't have to say more. Buster nodded.

I continued, "I heard about this great service. The kids at State set it up. An older woman can get a young man as a roommate. She rents him a room for cheap, and in turn he helps out around the house."

Buster looked skeptical. "Why would a college kid want to live with an old lady?"

"Watch it. Pearl would not appreciate that kind of talk."

"You know what I mean. What's in it for him?"

"Cheap rent, close to school. A home-cooked meal once a day. Wouldn't you have liked that when you were in college?"

"Nope, I much preferred living with four guys, none of whom could boil water and only one of whom hit the toilet with any regularity."

I splashed Buster. "Is that where your neatnik tendencies come from? Frat house trauma?"

He splashed me back. Water dripped from his nose. I brushed it away.

"I was never in a fraternity and you know it. We lived in a condemned public housing tract because it was the cheapest rent we could find."

Buster was the son of a single mom. Money had always been an issue in his life.

"So if there had been a wonderful older lady you could have lived with, wouldn't you?" I leaned back. "I think it sounds sweet."

"Are you sure this guy isn't after her bank account?"

"That would never happen. No way, not after what happened to Tess and Celeste. Pearl is too smart for that."

"What about Hiro's vinyl collection? Isn't that worth some money?"

I sat up straight. "Yeah, but it's not like someone could walk out with hundreds and hundreds of records."

"And you should warn her not to let the guy use her car. There could be expensive ramifications if he gets into a wreck."

My heart sank. Of course he was thinking of problems I'd never dreamed up.

"Buster, you ruin everything. Why do you have to be a cop? You're always looking for trouble."

He shrugged, wrung out the loofah, and set it on the edge of the tub.

It was like asking a cat why it hated dogs. That was Buster's nature.

I closed my eyes. He did have a point. I didn't know much about this kid. I'd been so eager to get Pearl some help, I hadn't really thought it through.

I'd call Pearl in the morning and tell her I'd had second thoughts. Slow it down.

I conceded, "Maybe we'll hold off until I can look into this a little further. Get some references, talk to some others."

"That's a plan."

"As long as you're in cop mode, can you stand a little shop talk?"

Buster groaned and slid as if he was falling off the toilet seat. I took advantage of his vulnerable position and reached under his arms and dug my fingers in, tickling him. He wiggled out of my grasp and sputtered. He slammed his hand in the water and I backed away from the spray, laughing.

"You trying to drown me?" I asked. "Just one question, I swear."

I didn't wait for him to acquiesce. He'd answer my question. He always did.

"I was looking at a Twitter feed today..." I'd keep it to myself that it was Wyatt's. Buster's tolerance had its limits. "And I saw a tweet about Provigil. A kid said he had some and was offering to trade. Do you know what that is? I never heard of it."

Buster squirted soap in his palm. He stroked my arm with the bubbles. He knew how to distract me. I leaned into his touch. I bit my lip to keep my focus.

Buster said, "Provigil is what kids are taking to stay awake. I think it's off use for some narcolepsy drug. He probably wanted something to perk him back up."

"But trolling for it on Twitter? Out there blatantly?" His hands were running up and down my legs. I felt myself begin to loosen. "Aren't they worried they'll get caught? I mean, it can't be legal."

"First of all, we don't have the resources to look at random Twitter feeds. And even if we did, if he's not selling them there's not much the police can do. Yes, it's illegal but those kids are swapping out their meds like we swapped Magic cards."

I turned to stare at him. "You played Magic the Gathering in *college*?"

Buster said, "All the cool kids were doing it."

I laughed. "Yeah, like I buy that. Get in," I said.

He brought his head around to look into my eyes. "You sure? You know what will happen when I get in there. I don't want to interrupt your relaxation."

"Maybe I'm relaxed enough," I said, dropping back, leaning against the back of the tub. I patted the water between my knees.

Buster needed no more invitation. He peeled off his shorts so fast, I giggled. The water level rose precariously as he climbed in. More bubbles popped.

He straddled me, facing me and scooted my hips closer until I was snugged in right against him. I felt his powerful thighs surround me.

He kissed the top of my head and rubbed my shoulders. I cupped my hands and poured water on his chest. I liked watching it sluice through his tightly wound hair.

The tub was an old-fashioned cast-iron type, meant to house an entire family for their weekly bath. Buster and I had searched for months for one that he could fit into. With both of us, the tub was not quite as accommodating. We had to lock our limbs together.

Not that either of us minded.

Buster kissed me softly. He nibbled the side of my mouth and worked his way down to my chest. I sat back and let him do all the work.

The combination of the cool room air and the hot water flushed his face. He thumbed the inside of my knee, an erogenous zone I hadn't known about until Buster. I closed my eyes. The feel of the water heightened Buster's touch. I let my legs fall open and Buster's fingers moved deliberately up my leg. My toes curled in anticipation.

We stayed in the tub until the water had gone cold.

SEVEN

MONDAY MORNING, I WAS at the store early. I opened the window in the bathroom to dissipate the smell. Buster and I'd spent the entire day here yesterday painting.

Ursula had a doctor's appointment about her bum elbow and wouldn't be in until noon. I would be working the floor for those two hours, so I needed to get a head start on the paperwork that kept me in my office. I was behind on bank deposits. I was hoping my order of custom wooden yardsticks would come today. Printed with QP's name and logo, they were giveaways for the Crawl.

First, I needed to track down the shipment from Lark. The books should have arrived by now. She was sending us her newest release. They were coming straight from the publisher because the official pub date was not until next week. We would be the first to have them. They were still in transit. The books were printed overseas and shipped by boat. It took nearly a week for the container ships to cross the Pacific.

I wanted to know where the books were.

Vangie loved this kind of hunt. Follow the paperwork, call the various entities, complain loudly. She always got results. But I hadn't heard from her since she rode her bike home on Saturday.

I left her a long voice mail. "I know the business of QP is the last thing you're thinking of right now, but I could really use your help, what with the Crawl coming up on Wednesday. I can't find Lark's books. I'm way behind on the banking. QP online is bursting at the seams with orders that need to be filled. We've got new fabric that needs to go on the website. I'm trying to keep up, but I miss you terribly. Not to mention I'd love to see you. So come in. If you don't feel up to it, do it anyway. For me."

I hung up and planted my face on my arms. Listing everything that needed to get done made it all real. I had only the next two days to accomplish way too much. It was impossible without Vangie. I hoped she understood that.

I stood, making myself shake off the feeling of being overwhelmed. My mom smiled at me from the picture on the wall. She'd pulled off many of these events while raising four kids. I could do this.

I could see a man standing outside so I opened the doors just before ten. He wanted to purchase a sewing machine. I handed him Freddy's card and gave him directions to Santa Clara.

I called Freddy to let him know. "I'm sending you a hot lead. Can you give it to Rebekah? That might buy me some goodwill with her."

"Lots of luck. She doesn't even like me and I write her commission checks."

"So, have you got all the Twitter baskets together?"

"Waiting on Lark's books," he said. "Everything else is ready to go. I thought that's why you were calling me. Don't you have them *yet*?"

"I know, I know. I'm trying to find them. The tracking number doesn't exist. I tried calling the publisher but they're on the East Coast and evidently the entire office takes lunch at the same time."

"We need those books, Dewey."

"Tell me something I don't know. Like a dumbass, I already put a note out on the Crawl Twitter feed that we had Lark's newest books before everyone else."

"I saw that."

I sighed. "Well, not too many people are following us yet, so maybe no harm."

Freddy laughed, not in a funny way. "Think again. I retweeted to my followers."

I gulped. "How many?"

"At last count, nineteen hundred." He waited a beat to drop the bombshell. "Lark passed it on, too."

I gasped. I didn't have to ask how many followers she had. Thousands. Maybe tens of thousands.

I sank onto the checkout counter, my elbows splayed out, my hands holding up my face.

"Hanging up now," I said.

"I'm going to be an optimist and assume the books will come in," Freddie said. "I'll be at your place tomorrow morning. Nine sharp. We'll deliver the baskets, do our own mini Crawl."

I ducked into my office to check the Twitter account. As soon as I did, I heard the front door open, so I left the computer and went back up front.

"Good morning, Dewey!"

It was Sonya Salazar. Today she was dressed in black leggings, a hot pink fleece, flowing knit scarf, and fuzzy over-the-knee boots. The weather had turned cold overnight but she looked as if she was heading to Alaska. She was tiny and thin, so maybe she felt the cold more than the rest of us. Buster had gone off to work in shorts this morning.

"Hi, Sonya. What's happening?" I slipped in behind the cutting table. She was a welcome distraction.

Sonya reached into an oversize portfolio that was serving as her briefcase. "I have a proposal for you," she said. She laid a piece of paper on the rotary mat in front of me. "I have ideas for a few classes that I could teach here. I think they would be really popular with your customers."

I scanned the proposal. She'd listed three classes with short descriptions.

"Color Vibrations. Pick the right hues for your quilt."

"Art is not a Four-Letter Word."

"You are So Creative."

"The titles are intriguing," I admitted.

"On the back is a detailed class curriculum. You'll see I've laid out lesson plans for each week. Also a short bio and CV to introduce myself to your customers."

Sonya had put a lot of work into this. I glanced at the back. "I don't have time to really study this right now, but..."

"I understand. I just wanted to give you some ideas."

"This week is the Crawl ... and Vangie, my assistant, is out sick." I felt lame making excuses. Sonya was busy with her class load, yet she'd had the time to put this together. None of my other teachers did anything like this. Usually we sat around the kitchen table, talked about their idea or what was needed on the schedule, set up a few dates and put it on the calendar.

If I was really truthful, the professionalism was a little intimidating.

The door opened again. Lois came in, throwing her arms up in a ta-da motion.

"Dew-ey! You called me ..." She stopped in mid-sentence when she saw Sonya. Her feet stuttered and I put a hand out to catch her even though I was not close enough to do any good.

"Oops, pardon me, Dewey. I didn't realize you had someone here. I just wanted my Quilters Crawl map."

"It's okay, Lois. Come meet Sonya Salazar. She teaches at State and designed the map."

"You're the one ..." Lois said, with a spark of recognition. I handed her a map. She opened it. "It's very pretty."

Sonya put a hand out and Lois took it gingerly. "Salazar, huh? What do you teach?"

Sonya said, "Art. At State and several community colleges, too."

"Sonya wants to give some classes here," I said.

Lois screwed up her face. "I probably don't have any extra money for class," Lois said. "I'm on a fixed income now that I'm not working. However, I might be coming into some money. Then I would."

"How about signing up for our special Crawl promotion?" I asked. "You get alerts on Twitter."

At her blank look, I explained. "You would need access to a smart phone."

Lois shook her head. "I don't know what that is."

Looked like Lois was not my target audience.

"Some phones get Internet alerts," Sonya explained.

Lois shook her head. "Oh no. I must have a really stupid phone. All it ever does is ring and most of the time I don't even hear it."

Lois unzipped her purse and showed us the generic flip phone.

"Dewey!"

That voice sent a chill down my spine. A chill of *what now?* I glanced down the hall to the back door. Just as I'd feared, Barb V.

"Pardon me," I said to Lois and Sonya. "I'll be right back."

Barb V was opening the door to the bathroom when I reached her, letting out a grunt of dissatisfaction. Her nose wrinkled in disgust as the smell of fresh paint wafted out. She toed the unfinished floor.

My stomach clenched. Had anyone been thrown out of the Crawl because of an unfinished bathroom?

"Still not completed?" she greeted me.

"Good morning to you, too."

She frowned and nodded to the unfinished room.

"The tile guys promised to be here this afternoon," I said, regretting my words immediately. It was none of her business when my floor got done.

"Something you need?" I asked.

She tore her eyes off the untiled floor and stared at me. "You know what I need. My prize basket for your special promotion."

"Freddy has the baskets. I told you we'd get them to you."

"Yes, well, I don't like to wait until the last minute." *Unlike some people* was the unspoken message.

"You don't need to worry. You will have them in time for the beginning of the Crawl. The Emporium is not on the list for the Twitter thing until Friday anyway."

Barb V would not be put off. "What's the problem? Why can't I get mine now?"

I rubbed my temples and glanced back at Sonya and Lois. Lois was showing Sonya the inside of her purse, zipping and unzipping the hidden pockets. Sonya, bless her heart, looked interested.

"Like I said in my email, the Lark Gordon books are on the boat from South Korea. The publisher promises me I will have them today."

"But they're not here yet. Have you tracked them down? Maybe they're at the UPS depot. You could go pick them up."

"I can't do that, Barb V. I can't leave the store. I don't have any employees here to cover."

I started walking, hoping to force her to back up down the hall. She'd left the door open, and a cold breeze was flowing in. I heard my heating system kick in. Money down the drain.

My ploy didn't work. She sidestepped me. I closed the door, wishing she was on the other side.

"I'll wait here while you contact the publisher. We must have an answer, Dewey."

Didn't she have a store to run? A life to lead? Anything to do besides bug me? At least maybe I could keep her out of my office.

"You worked with Sonya on the map, right? Go up front and say hello. She's in the store."

"She's in your store? Why?"

I wasn't about to tell her about Sonya's idea to teach quilters. I was afraid Barb V would steal her away from me. "She likes to stop by now and again," I lied.

"Well, she should come by the Emporium when she has time," Barb V said huffily. Her chest pouched out like a pigeon's.

She steamed to the front, and I did a quick reconnoiter to make sure no new customers had ducked in while I'd been busy with Barb V. No one. Folks were waiting for the Crawl to go shopping.

I went into my office, rehearsing what I was going to say to the publisher. I didn't know how they were going to make books appear if those books were in the middle of the ocean, but . . .

Vangie was at her desk. How I missed her coming in, I didn't know. The Doc Martens she favored were far from quiet.

I leapt into the room. "Vang, you're here."

She nodded. She looked around the office as if it had been more than a few days since she'd been here. As if she was trying to remember what to do.

"Thank goodness," I said. "You've got to help me. Barb V is hounding me for the books for the Twitter promotion. I tried tracking the shipment. First I had the wrong number, now UPS shows it delivered. What does that mean? It's not here."

"Move over," Vangie said, nudging me out of the way. I gladly gave her access to my computer.

I hugged her as we traded places. It was awkward but I was glad to have my hands on her. She laid her head on my shoulder and I felt her heave once before she got herself under control.

"Are you okay to work?"

Vangie looked distracted. She touched her backpack with her hand as if to make sure it was still there.

I remembered my earlier feeling that she hadn't told me everything. And she still hadn't filled me in on what went on at the police station. I wanted the skinny on Zorn and Freddy's brother, Larry, the attorney. We had a lot to discuss.

Vangie sat down at the keyboard. "My mother and grandmother are hovering so much. And the little kids are noisy. I've got school later but I'm tired of the inside of my room. I needed to feel useful."

"Well, if you can figure out where those books are, you'll be my rock star."

Vangie looked through the little window to the front.

"Do you need to be up front? You've got customers," she said.

"That's Lois and Sonya. They're not buying anything. And I sent Barb V to join the party."

I pointed to the longhaired art teacher. I thought I'd seen her name on Vangie's Twitter list. "That's Sonya Salazar, the teacher. Didn't you have her for art class?"

"That's Sonya Salazar?" Vangie stood and leaned out the little window for a better view. Sonya tossed her hair back, looking like a black waterfall. Her hair shone as if she'd hot oiled the locks.

The screen on the computer changed and Vangie returned her attention to the UPS website.

"Look here," she said. "The books have made it to the local warehouse." She scrolled down. "They're on the truck. We sometimes get a second late afternoon delivery. They should be on that."

I pounded her back. "Thank you."

I had an answer. Not that Barb V would be happy with it.

Barb V was making her way back to the office when I came out to tell her the good news. Her face was drawn and pinched.

"Those two," she said. "I couldn't get a word in edgewise. I don't have time for the likes of Lois Lane. Squabbling about somebody's grandson."

"Squabbling? They just met …"

I looked through the window. I could see how someone might think they were arguing. Lois was throwing her arms around and Sonya was standing very close to her.

Barb V snapped me back to the present. "Dewey, quit stalling. Where's my book?"

"The books will be here later today. I will personally see that the books get out to all the stores by tomorrow."

"Yes, you will."

Barb V started to leave. She turned when she reached the door. "Do not mess this up, Dewey. Not everyone wanted QP back into the Crawl. You're on thin ice."

My face reddened as if I'd been slapped. I looked back to see if Vangie had heard but she had her headphones on. I stood still, wondering who these other people were who didn't want QP in the Crawl.

I saw movement and went on to the store floor. Lois and Sonya had taken their conversation out to the sidewalk. I couldn't imagine what they were still talking about. It didn't seem like they had much in common. That was good, though. It meant Sonya might have appeal to quilters.

A young man came in. I was shocked to see it was Ross, the kid from the GrandSon organization. He hesitated, taking a step back and then glancing over his shoulder before he approached.

"Pearl sent me," he said.

EIGHT

HE STARTED TALKING RAPIDLY. "She said you said she could have the extra paint. From your bathroom? She wants me to fix up my room."

I flushed. "Where is Pearl?"

He pointed and I could see Pearl's Mini parked at the curb. I didn't wait for him to say more.

I raced out the door. "Pearl! What are you doing?"

Sonya and Lois looked up as I yelled. I gave them a little wave to let them know I was okay, and modulated my tone.

She rolled down the window on the passenger side. Ross had been driving.

She smiled smugly. I leaned in.

"What are you doing with Ross?" I had spoken to Pearl on Sunday morning, telling her that I would check Ross's references and get back to her. "We agreed we'd wait until something else came along."

Pearl stuck her chin out. "I didn't agree. You said you thought it was a bad idea. Well, I don't. Ross has been with me since yesterday. We've been having a marvelous time. He loves to listen to my music. He's already mowed the grass and cleaned out the koi pond."

I threw my head back and took in a deep breath. Pearl was so headstrong. I should have known this would happen.

I bent down to Pearl's level. She was smiling brightly, her eyes shining. She turned up the radio and started bopping her hands to "Glad All Over." I knew the Dave Clark Five song was on her favorite British Invasion CD.

She was happy, that was for sure. Did Ross account for all this excitement?

A horn beeped. I looked up as Vangie's mother's car went around the corner. A truck turned in from the other direction. Vangie was gone before I'd had a chance to talk to her. And the tile guys were here. Great.

I turned back to Pearl. "I don't know if you should be letting this kid drive your car. What if he has an accident or something?"

Pearl flipped her hand. "Don't be such a worrywart, Dewey. Ross is a good kid. I spoke to his mother over the phone yesterday. We had a long chat. She's in Sacramento and she's very happy that he has somewhere nice to live."

There was a loud bang as the truck's rear door was opened. Kevin's guys began unloading tile and bags of grout. The bathroom floor had to take priority. I had to go back inside.

I would have to let Pearl be for now. I straightened, feeling my knees complain. I pointed Kevin's men to the back door. As I did, Lois waved goodbye and got into her car.

Sonya seemed to be waiting for me to finish. I guess she wanted an answer about the classes.

I touched Pearl's door and turned to leave.

Pearl called after me, "Don't you worry. I'm a big help to him, too. He needs a little old lady. I'm going to pretend to be one." Pearl cackled.

My heart flipped. I grabbed her hand. "What's that supposed to mean?"

"I'm going undercover. All I have to do is act feeble. That'll be a stretch." She cackled again.

"What are you going to do?"

"Ross has been studying illegal sports clinics. For school." She leaned over the edge of the window. "Did you know there are doctors around here who are giving out prescriptions without an exam? Pain pills, sleeping pills, whatever you want."

I had heard of these places, from Buster.

"Ross says the abuse is nuts. I'm going to be the test case."

"What's the name of this clinic, Pearl?"

Ross was coming out of the store, carrying a paint can. He'd helped himself to the roller with the long handle.

Pearl handed me a torn piece of paper. Ross had written the information on a pink sticky note. "This is where we're headed, right after lunch. I have a two o'clock appointment."

Ross avoided me and walked the long way around to the trunk, around the front of the car. He pushed down the lid of the can before setting it down.

"Thanks for the paint," Ross said as he climbed behind the wheel.

"How about lunch at Bill's?" Pearl said. "I want a tuna on rye."

Ross glanced in his side mirror. I didn't want to see her go off with him.

I glared at the note in my hand. I knew where they would be. Ross pulled into traffic. Pearl waved gaily.

Sonya stood next to me. "Your friend okay?"

I didn't want to get into this with Sonya. She'd thought the GrandSons was a good idea. For that matter, so had I.

A city bus stopped at the corner and Ursula got off. I waited for her to catch up with me and Sonya before going inside. She was holding her right arm across her body, as if it hurt.

"What's the story, morning glory?" I said, surprised to hear my mother's phrase come out of my mouth. But Ursula looked so down, I wanted to cheer her up.

She shook her head sadly. "Sorry it took so long. The doctor saw a lot of people before me."

Ursula went to a huge hospital for outpatient care, seeing a different doctor each time. I couldn't afford to pay her health insurance so she had to pay out of pocket for her expenses. She would be eligible for Medicare in a few years, but in the meantime, her health insurance was her responsibility. One of my goals was that QP could make enough profit to give good coverage to my employees. I didn't see that happening any time soon.

"I'd been hoping he'd recommend physical therapy but all he gave me was a prescription for really expensive muscle relaxants. I can't afford them."

Sonya shook her head in commiseration. "I hear you. I have to pay for my health insurance and it's ridiculous."

"I wish I could do more," I said.

117

Ursula smiled at me. "This is not your fault, Dewey. I'm the one who stayed with the guy who liked to wrench my arm behind my back."

She stopped, although I knew she could say a lot more about her crappy husband. I felt tears in my eyes, but there was nothing to say.

Ursula wouldn't let us wallow. "Let's get to work, shall we?"

"I've got lots to do," I said to Sonya, hoping she got the hint.

She did. "I'm off. Let me know about the classes," she said.

———

I wanted to see where Ross was taking Pearl, but I couldn't leave the store until it was nearly two. The clinic was only a few miles away, in the south end of downtown. A place like that could attract a seedy crowd.

The neighborhood was residential with a few shops, mostly dollar stores and taco restaurants. The freeway loomed overhead, cutting off the sun, a complicated interchange where 87 came in. The houses needed paint, porches sagged.

I found the address on Pearl's note. A plain stucco plaza was set at right angles to a bodega decked out in fake flowers. A large sign at the driveway declared it to be the site of Jordan's Sports Injuries Clinic.

I waited for a dark-haired woman with three children piled on a stroller meant for one to cross before pulling in. The storefront clinic had a banner in the window that claimed in three-foot-high letters: *We Guarantee You Will Feel Better.*

A homemade sign hung low said: *These premises are under surveillance.* The misspelling seemed to fit with the surroundings.

I looked for video cameras on the roofline but didn't see any. My guess was that their clients wouldn't want to be taped.

Vertical blinds clattered as I opened the door. I limped in to authenticate my need for treatment.

I needn't have bothered. No one noticed me come in. The small lobby, painted a hideous gold, was filled with people. All the chairs were taken and several people leaned against the wall.

It was quite a cross section. A family of four with a puppy. An older Asian couple in competing striped shirts and flip-flops. A middle-aged woman, reading a Jennifer Weiner book with a bright pink cover.

No one looked like a dope fiend.

It was after two, but Pearl was still here. She looked up and waved me over. She was seated on a wooden armchair next to a white-haired woman with a walker.

Ross never glanced my way. He was leaning into the open window. The young woman at the reception desk was enjoying his attention. Finally, she looked around him and greeted me perfunctorily.

"Can I help you?" The name badge pinned over a very ample left breast read Ashleigh. Ross recognized me with a start.

Ashleigh sighed and Ross' gaze drifted to follow her rising and falling chest. "Are you new?" she asked. "Fill this out." She picked up a clipboard with what seemed like a ream of paper attached. A pen dangled from a piece of neon-green fuzzy yarn.

"I'm here to be with my grandmother," I said.

She let it drop on the counter and turned her attention back to Ross. They seemed to be discussing the latest episode of the *Real World*. I'd have thought he would be interviewing her for his paper. Maybe he was getting to how the clinic got away with dispensing drugs.

The chair next to Pearl opened up when the reader got up and went through a door next to Ashleigh's desk, carrying her chick lit under her arm. I sat down.

Pearl reached over and squeezed my arm. "Hi cutie," she said.

She was buzzing with excitement. Ross had certainly perked my old girl up. I guess I was grateful for that.

"Have you been in to see the doctor yet?" I whispered.

A look of triumph came over her face. She opened her palm slowly. She was clutching a prescription form. I turned my head to read it.

Oxycodone. Three refills. That was powerful stuff.

"Took maybe five minutes." Pearl said, smiling broadly. She was having a lot of fun. "Easy, peasy, like Ross said. The doctor asked me a few questions and wrote the prescription. I didn't even have to take my clothes off."

"Darn it," said the woman next to her. "I was kind of hoping. At my age, no one asks me to strip anymore."

Pearl grinned at her. "Yeah, he was cute too. Like Omar Sharif in *Funny Girl*."

"Dark and dreamy?" the woman said. "That's how I like 'em."

She and Pearl dissolved into giggles. I didn't think all older women were this randy. Pearl had found her match.

"This is Harriet, by the way," Pearl said, introducing her new-found friend. "I'm going in with her to see the doctor."

I smiled at her. A thought crossed my mind. I leaned into Pearl. "You're not going to fill that prescription, are you?"

She whispered, glancing up at Ross. His attention was on Ashleigh. "Of course we are. Ross needs to prove his contention that these doctors are giving out illegal drugs. He won't have much of a thesis without the actual pills."

"You can't take that medication," I said.

Pearl sniffed, "I would never take this stuff. It's addicting."

Harriet put an age-spotted hand on my knee. Her wig shifted, revealing gray hair underneath. "You're a pretty little thing. Are you hurting, too?"

My heart leapt into my throat. I recognized the voice. That was no Harriet. That voice belonged to Ina, Pearl's best friend, member of the original Quilter Paradiso Stitch 'n' Bitch group. She'd taught at QP for years before retiring.

"You?" I screamed out the word. Ashleigh and Ross looked up. I segued into a coughing fit and they went back to flirting.

Ina/Harriet grinned. She must have wrapped an entire roll of batting around her body to pad her frame. The faded floral housedress she was wearing looked like something the Goodwill would throw out.

"The slippers are a nice touch," I hissed, keeping an eye on Ross. He was still pumping Ashleigh for information. I wondered how much she was giving away.

Ina/Harriet put her arm through Pearl's and pulled her close. "I wasn't about to allow her to do this alone. Why should she have all the fun?"

It was like Spy Kids, only with old ladies. I shook my head.

Ina and Pearl had played good cop, bad cop with me for years. As a high school kid, I'd spent my homework time with them in the classroom. Ina was the tough love type, always loving but taking no guff. Pearl was more laid back. My mother had attributed the difference in their styles to the fact that Pearl had never had children. Pearl thought children would do the right thing if given enough time and love.

Ina knew some kids were just bad.

The door opened to the left of the desk. The entire room watched a couple come out. They were probably in their early sixties, dressed in matching Sharks black and teal gear. She was wearing a bulky orthopedic boot. Her husband held on to her elbow.

"Thank you, Jessie," the woman said to their escort, a young woman dressed in pink scrubs printed with fat kittens cavorting unnaturally with bunnies. She said goodbye to them and called Harriet's name loudly as if Harriet was deaf and two blocks away.

Harriet Tubman, Ina had called herself. I rolled my eyes. These sport folks certainly weren't up on their history. Pearl helped Ina to her feet and they disappeared through the door.

Ross smiled at his lady friend. He said, "Smoke break?"

Despite the arrival of three new clients, she only hesitated a moment. "Sure," she said, rummaging in her drawer, coming up with a cigarette and pink glittery lighter. "Take a seat," she told the newcomers.

"Where's your restroom?" I asked as she raced past me.

"Down the hall," she pointed through the door Pearl and Ina had gone through. "When you're done, come back out here, have a seat and Jessie will take you back when the doctor is ready."

She didn't remember that I wasn't a customer.

I nodded and went through the door. It led to a narrow hallway with rooms on either side. A black and gold sign that said Restroom pointed to the last door.

I started walking slowly. I moved to the first room and listened at the door, keeping an eye out for Jessie or the doctor.

"Make sure you pile it on thick," Pearl was saying. I could hear her pretty clearly.

I looked up. The space had been divided with Flakeboard partitions, not walls. There was a two-foot gap between the top of each office and the ceiling. Noises carried easily through the space.

A door farther down the hall opened, and a short man with a sparse beard and long sideburns stepped out. I froze. I was in the middle of the hall. I took a step forward as if back on my original hunt for the bathroom.

He looked back to say something to Jessie. I took the opportunity to duck into the room next to Pearl's. An examination table sat in the middle. A poster of the human body, all red veins and blue tendons, hung right in front of me. Behind the small desk hung several diplomas and award certificates for Marcus Aldana. I didn't recognize the name of the medical school. It was located in Granada.

This was the wall shared with the next office. I tiptoed over there.

I heard the door open. "Good afternoon, ladies," the doctor said. His voice was smooth and confident but low. I strained to hear him. "Where's it hurting?"

"Where doesn't it hurt?" Ina said gruffly.

"I understand," he said. His voice faded.

Ina said, "I don't think you do. I'm a quilter. My back hurts from stooping over my machine. I ran a needle through my finger and cut my toe when I dropped the rotary cutter. I have a sore elbow from cutting and my knees are killing me."

I stifled a giggle. But I couldn't hear the doctor's reply.

I had to get up higher. I stepped on the desk chair, before I noticed it was on wheels. The seat went skittering out from under me. I landed painfully on the outside of my foot and sat down hard on the floor. I stretched out and steadied the chair right before it crashed to the floor.

I held my breath. I waited for Dr. Aldana to come racing in to see what the noise was.

Nothing. I breathed out. I pulled myself up slowly and put my ear to the partition.

The doctor was murmuring something comforting.

"You want to talk pain," Ina/Harriet said. "Try twenty-four hours a day, seven days a week. Shingles are the worst."

I heard what sounded like acquiescence. The doctor was apparently wrapping things up. After two minutes.

Pearl's voice came through. "Thank you, Doctor. I'll be sure to send all my friends to you. I know plenty of folks who could use your help."

He'd be in here next. I wanted to get out of here before the doctor or Jessie discovered me. I opened the door and checked the hall. I dashed into the waiting room as Ross and Ashleigh came back, bringing with them a cloud of noxious fumes.

I sniffed the air. Had they been smoking funny cigarettes?

Ross pealed off from Ashleigh and greeted me.

"Your charges should be here any moment." I lowered my voice. "Did you get what you needed?"

He nodded, watching Ashleigh take her place behind the desk again.

"You've got two of my favorite people in the world with you." I grabbed his skinny tie. His eyes suddenly locked with mine, his cheeks turning bright pink.

I gave his tie a yank. "You'd better make sure nothing happens to them."

———

When I got back to the store the tile guys were nearly finished with the floor. Ursula said customers had been scarce.

No UPS. Lark's books were not here yet.

All I wanted to do was go home and have a repeat of last night. Bath, Bubbles, Buster. Rinse and repeat. Buster would be up for it, I knew.

I was admiring the slate tiles I'd picked out for the bathroom when Buster came in the back door.

The scowl on his face didn't bode well for another bath night. I left the tile guys to the grouting. Buster followed me into my office. He took Vangie's chair, filling it in a way she never did.

"What's up? Where've you been?"

"Work," he said.

"Not going well?" I asked. He was too quiet. "Everyone from the drug bust make bail or something?

"No." He picked up a pen and tossed it.

I grabbed the pen in mid-air. "Buster, what is it?"

I pulled his chair around so we were sitting knee-to-knee. "Tell me."

"The medical examiner found a needle mark in Wyatt Pederson's back."

"His back?"

Buster nodded grimly, patting a spot near his shoulder. "He was given a fatal overdose. Murdered."

I sat back in my chair. Wyatt had been killed. Vangie would be a suspect. Crap, crap, crap.

Buster nodded. "Freakin' Zorn. He wants a piece of the Task Force glory. The way he sees it, if he can tie Wyatt to the drug dealing, if somehow we missed this big kingpin—"

"He could look like the big cheese."

Buster nodded forlornly. He balled his hands into fists. "Damn that guy. He's the only cop I know who wants the FBI hanging around. He's really sucking up to them."

"But if Wyatt was murdered... how does that fit in?"

"It has to be drug related, right? Wyatt gets killed because he pissed off some other dealer. Or someone wants his territory. Someone who got pinched by the bust. The bust is making a lot of people nervous."

"What about Vangie?"

Buster hung his head. "Zorn's not letting that angle go. He wants to talk to her again. He'll hound her. He's sure she knows something."

I let that sink in. Vangie was not going to be free from this until the real killer was found.

"What does he think? That *she's* some kind of drug kingpin?"

Buster didn't answer.

"Buster?" I said, a knot tying itself in my stomach.

Buster rubbed my knees. "She's not, right? She'll be okay. It was genius that you got Larry Romanski to be her lawyer. He's the most hated defense lawyer in the house. How did you swing that?"

I hesitated. Buster caught that and looked up.

"What?"

"He's Freddy's brother," I confessed.

Buster threw his hands up. "Of course he is. No wonder I couldn't stand Freddy. I knew there was something familiar about him."

I pushed my chair back. "So you disliked Freddy because his brother is a defense attorney?"

Buster stood and shrugged. "Must have been subliminal. Remember that case I had last year? We'd had that dirtbag locked up for the hairdresser's murder in Los Gatos. Remember? Larry the Lip was the one who got him out of jail. Next thing we know the hairdresser's husband shoots the suspect and then kills himself in the movie theater parking lot. Horrible outcome."

I googled Larry Romanski while Buster was talking. I knew the case he was talking about. He'd been really upset when it happened. I got to Larry's website and found a picture of him.

"Huh ... they do look alike," I said, turning the computer around. "So all this time you've been looking at Freddy and being reminded of his brother?"

"Doesn't mean Freddy's not a jerk," Buster said.

I laughed. "You don't give up, do you Healy?"

My phone rang. I answered it while Buster gave me more lame reasons why he didn't like Freddy.

"He's pushy, and never shuts up."

I mimed a duck's beak. "Quack, quack."

127

"Hello?"

"Dewey Pellicano?"

"Yes," I said. How did a telemarketer get this number? I thought cell phones were exempt.

"This is Rita Estrada. Vangie's mom?"

My heart skidded to a stop. I'd met Vangie's mother over the years, but she'd never called me before. Never. I gulped in a breath, and grabbed Buster's hand. Zorn must have arrested her.

"Vangie's mom," I whispered to him. He squeezed my hand. His face was creased with concern. I knew mine was too.

"Vangie was mugged. Someone hit her over the head and took her backpack."

I held onto Buster's fingers. I held the phone away so he could hear. "Is she okay?"

"She will be. She'll be in the hospital overnight."

"Which one? I'll be right over."

Rita said, "You won't be able to see her yet. They've taken her for an MRI."

My throat closed up at the thought of Vangie lying in a hospital bed, hurt.

"When did this happen? She was here this morning," I said.

"About an hour ago. She was walking to school from her parking spot."

"In broad daylight?"

"Yes, she said if it wasn't for a bunch of students who walked by, she might have been hurt more."

Rita's voice caught and I felt my own voice falter. "I'm glad she's okay," I managed to squeak out. Buster stroked my face and I kissed his palm.

"Please give her a hug and a kiss from me. Call me if there's anything I can do."

Buster moved in, enveloping me as I hung up the phone. He held me. I let myself feel the horror of the random violence. His touch did his magic. I felt my heart slow down and the pit lodged in my throat dissolve.

"She'll be okay," he said. "Don't worry."

I pulled back from him. "That girl can't get a break." My tears spilled over.

Buster tilted his head. "You know there is an upside. Zorn will have to leave her alone, at least for now. If she has a concussion, he'll have to wait until she's more alert to question her. Her doctors—and Larry the Lip—will never allow it."

"In that case, I hope she stays in the hospital for a week."

———

A nurse looked up from distributing pills into tiny cups when I got off the elevator at Vangie's floor the next morning. I dodged a breakfast cart and found her room. Her grandmother was in the chair under the window, her head bowed, lips moving, a rosary traveling between her fingers. Her mom fussed, straightening the blankets, tucking in the sides, something Vangie would never tolerate if she'd been awake.

Her mother saw me first. "Dewey, come in."

I walked through the room and embraced her. She let out a little sob. Vangie's grandmother only nodded, her fingers flying. Vangie was racking up plenty of prayers. If Hail Marys healed, Vangie would be better by noon.

"How is she?" I touched the blanket by her knee gingerly. I didn't have much experience with hospital visits. My family was healthy and my mother had died before she reached the hospital.

Vangie's chest rose and fell with regularity but her eyes were closed and she was very, very still. I couldn't remember seeing her so unmoving. Vangie was always a bundle of energy. "Is she unconscious?"

"Whatever they gave her knocked her out," her mother said, swiping a hair from her daughter's cheek. "She needs rest, according to the doctor. They're worried about her brain swelling."

That sounded awful. My throat tightened.

The room smelled like overly starched linens. The other bed in the room was empty with blankets and sheets piled on the end. A whiteboard on the wall at the end of her bed had Vangie's name and today's date on it. Her nurse this shift was Concheta.

"Have you two been here all night?" I asked.

Rita nodded. "I tried to get Mama to go home, but she refused. We wouldn't have slept at home anyhow."

I put my arm around Rita. The circles under her eyes were dark and deep. "Why don't you go take a walk? Get some breakfast? Better yet, go home. Change your clothes. I can stay with her until you get back."

Rita gnawed at her cuticle. Like mother, like daughter. "I did want to get Vangie some of her own pajamas and the hand cream she likes. Her skin is getting dry."

She rubbed Vangie's arms. Vangie stirred but didn't wake up. "We won't be long," Rita said in a lilting tone to her daughter. "I just washed your favorite pajamas. I'll bring them right back."

"Thank you," she said to me. "I know Vangie will be glad you're here. She was asking for you last night."

The pair left, although Grandma didn't let go of her rosary, her lips moving as she walked.

I took in a deep breath. I walked to the window and looked out over the parking lot. Beyond, I could see the hills in the distance, brown with waving grass. In another month, when the winter rains began, the hillsides would start to turn green.

Vangie was in trouble. I didn't think it was a coincidence that she'd been mugged the day before. Something was going on.

She'd been hanging around Wyatt and he'd been murdered. The police were looking at him as someone involved with drugs. My heart ached at the idea that Vangie might somehow be involved, too.

Behind me, I heard a groan.

"Vangie?" I rushed to her side. "Are you in pain?"

"I'm okay," she said hoarsely. I grabbed the water glass and pressed the straw near her mouth. She turned her head away.

She opened her mouth again. Nothing came out but a croak. She reached up and touched the big bandage that covered her head. Vangie's eyes widened in fear.

"You're okay," I said, pulling her hand away and rubbing it. "Your mother and grandmother were here. They went home for a few things."

She blinked. "Friday," she began. Her voice was weak. Her throat must be rubbed raw from some tube or another.

I held the straw steady and this time she drank.

"Wyatt—" she stopped and turned her head away from me. A tear trickled down her cheek. I wiped it away. She clawed at me.

"Vang ... save your strength. We can talk later."

"Listen. Drugs."

Each word was a struggle. She was getting agitated, and noises came off her machines like annoyed birds.

"Lay back, Vang. Please. I know about Wyatt and his drugs."

Vangie sank against the pillows. Concheta, the nurse, came in. She was a tall blonde.

She said, "Someone is awake, is she? It's about time." She set to work on the things Vangie was connected to, moving them to a mobile tether. "Okay, darling. Now that you're up, we have plans for you. Tests and more tests. I know, nothing but fun around here."

She moved quickly with authority. There was no room for debate. I stepped away as she came to my side of the bed.

She said to me. "You're welcome to wait, of course, but she will be awhile."

I was able to get in a quick squeeze of Vangie's hand. I smiled at her, stretching it out. "I've got to get to work, but I'll be back tonight."

Vangie's face was crumpled. "I'm sorry, Dewey. Sorry."

The nurse hoisted her up into a wheelchair and the two of them went out of the room.

Why did I feel abandoned?

NINE

FREDDY WAS AS GOOD as his word. He arrived at my QP right at nine. "Tell me the Lark Gordon books arrived."

I shook my head. "UPS never came last night," I said.

He frowned. "What have you got?"

I led him into the classroom. "Felix Scissors Company sent me a batch of special fabric snips. They've got blue plaid handles and are as cute as a button. What every quilter needs next to her sewing machine."

I knew I was overselling, but I needed to believe we had good prizes.

Freddy said, "I've got twelve baskets in the car that contain threads and tape measures. That's not going to cut it."

"I stopped at Costco and bought some pens and sketch books. And dark chocolate Dove Hearts. That'll fill the baskets up."

Freddy glanced at his complicated watch. I was pretty sure he could predict earthquakes with one of those dials. "We need to get on the road."

We loaded Freddy's car with the scissors and Costco stuff. "Jim, my UPS guy, will be here soon," I said, collapsing into the passenger seat. "He's never later than 9:15. Then we can get moving."

Freddy stood outside his car, tapping his fingers on the roof.

"I didn't tell you what happened to Vangie last night," I said. "She got mugged."

"That's horrible. Where was she? At school?"

"On her way to a class."

"Is she going to be all right?"

"She has a concussion. They're worried about her brain swelling."

"I heard they have good drugs for that. Vangie will be okay," Freddy said. He was as anxious as I'd ever seen him. He couldn't stop looking at his watch.He was making me nervous. We did have a lot of ground to cover.

"Get in," I said. "If UPS won't come to us, we'll have to go to UPS."

I directed Freddy to make a U-turn. I looked up and down the Alameda and didn't see the brown truck. I sighed. We needed Lark's books. They were the best prize we had.

"Turn here," I said, directing Freddy down Naglee. I looked down the streets at the stately homes. Nothing. We drove past the junior high and the library. At Bascom, I told him to turn back.

Why did Jim change his route? Today of all days. We cut over on Race and got lucky.

"There!" I pointed behind a Mexican restaurant. I had my door opened before Freddy pulled into the parking lot, the Jag scraping the bumpy driveway.

Jim was surprised to see me, but gave up the shipment. I ripped open a box while Freddy rearranged his trunk to accommodate the new stuff.

"Score!" I yelled.

"Let's go," Freddy said. "Where's the nearest freeway ramp? We'll go to the farthest-away shop first and work our way back. Give me the address. I'll feed it into my nav."

I pulled out the cheery map and read off the street and the numbers. The nav went to work. According to it, our drive to Pacific Grove would take an hour and a half, meaning we'd get there around 11:00.

I studied the map. Now I was getting nervous. "We'll never make it back to Half Moon Bay," I said. That was miles north of here and we were heading south.

"I told you we had to get on the road earlier."

"We must get to Barbara the Damp's in Fremont. She's up first thing tomorrow for the Twitter. And we'd better get to Barbara V's before five. She's already called twice."

Freddy snorted. He checked his mirrors and changed lanes. "I say we leave Barb V to last. She's pissing me off. Let her stew all day."

His car hugged the guardrail. The Lexington Reservoir was low. I could see grass and the concrete remnants of the old road that had been abandoned when the reservoir was built.

"Are you sure we should be leaving her books until last?" I didn't want to tangle with Barb V.

"She needs to be taught she doesn't rule the world. We promised she'd have her Twitter basket in time for the Crawl. And she will."

I leaned back in my seat. We were heading up into the Santa Cruz Mountains now, and the trees were getting denser and taller. Older. The treetops whizzed past. I let the fancy leather upholstery envelop me.

If we weren't in such a time crunch, I could have enjoyed this break in routine. Freddy's hands rested lightly on the wheel confidently. His eyes flitted from the side mirror to the rear view. He eased in and out of the lanes, slotting his Jag behind whoever was moving the fastest.

Route 17 was ten miles of climbing roadway with switchbacks and dangerous curves. It was the quickest way to the Santa Cruz Boardwalk and the Pacific Ocean. I hadn't been allowed to drive this road until I turned eighteen.

"When it's my turn for the Twitter promotion, I'm going to cause a riot," Freddy said, raising his voice over the roar of the engine as he downshifted. I'd never been in a car that rode so close to the ground and went this fast. Freddy's driving was making me slightly giddy.

"Excuse me?" I said, trying to catch my breath as he steered through the treacherous Big Moody Curve. I was starting to understand the race car driver's love of speed. I felt like I'd left the astral plain. Worries about QP, the Crawl, even Vangie, darling Vangie, were lifted off my shoulders and snatched by the wind.

I fought the urge to giggle as Freddy gave the gas pedal a goose. I leaned into the curve of the roadway.

"I've downloaded this software that allows me to send out a tweet every sixty seconds. I'm going to blast my followers with notices about the special prize basket."

"You can't reveal that you're the shop until the hour starts."

"I know, I know. I promise not to do anything until the clock strikes the top of the hour. It'll be like Easter morning, waiting for the okay to start looking for eggs. No early birds allowed."

We were on the downslope of the mountain. The road widened and straightened. My heart rate returned to normal. I wanted to go back to San Jose and do it again.

"I'm not going to be happy until there are two hundred people in my shop."

Every available inch of floor space in Freddy's store was taken up with merchandise. "Two hundred? Twenty people would be crowded in your place."

"I figured that out, too," he said. "You know I've got a big parking lot out front. I'm going to rope it off and keep the folks contained. My buddy is coming to make balloon animals and Inez will play the accordion."

I had to laugh. "Party at Freddy's," I said. The man knew how to make a spectacle.

"You got it," he said. "Too bad you're going to miss it."

"Yes, well, I do have my own shop to tend to."

Freddy turned south on Route 1 and set the cruise control at 80 mph. The nav adjusted our estimated time to 10:45. Freddy was doing the impossible, making time fly.

I caught my breath when the Pacific Ocean came into view as we hurtled down Highway One. The clouds thinned out and the blue sky lost its intensity, diluted by wisps of fog. The air coming in was cold and wet but felt restorative. I breathed deep.

Forty-five minutes later, the nav told us we were arriving at our destination. *On right. On right.*

"Hustle," Freddy said. "Hustle."

I grabbed a basket and a book. "All right," I said. "I'll run in and drop these off."

I ran inside, but was quickly stymied. The sole employee was with a customer and wouldn't let me interrupt. She ignored my attempts to break into their conversation. I unloaded my burden on the long counter near the cash register.

I looked for a piece of paper. I'd leave a note for the owner.

I grabbed a pen from a mug and a yellow flyer and turned it over to the blank side.

"Twitter promotion basket," I wrote. "Thx." I added "XXXOOO" to help mitigate the abruptness.

Freddy had turned the car around and was entering the info for the next place, in Monterey, ten minutes away. I flung open the door.

He threw the car in first and roared away from the curb. I was thrown back against the seat and scrambled for my seat belt.

We arrived at the second shop seven minutes later.

"Ha!" Freddy said. "Take that, nav. You're not as smart as you think. Beat you by two minutes."

The handoff went smoother that time, with the owner being not only present but grateful. I got back into Freddy's car. This time I got my seat belt connected before he took off. Cookie's shop was forty minutes away, heading north again.

"Yikes. I forgot to call Lark to let her know the books got here in time," I said.

Freddy turned off his satellite radio. "Use my phone and put her on speaker." He leaned into his dash. "Call Lark," he yelled.

"Hey Lark," I said when she answered. "It's Dewey and Freddy, flying down the highway."

Lark laughed. "That's a bad road movie waiting to be made. Pellicano and Roman on the Road to Mandalay."

"Technically, we're on the road from Monterey," Freddy said.

I talked to the display. "Actually, it's more like Bonnie and Clyde. If you ever want to rob a bank, I can recommend Freddy. He drives a mean getaway car."

"I would say I'd like to be with you two, but I remember how that movie ends. Try not to get shot," Lark said.

"As long as Barb V is unarmed, we're safe," I said.

I told Lark that the books had arrived and thanked her for saving my life. When I disconnected by yelling, "Hang up" six times, Freddy was quiet.

"What's up? Lark say something?"

"You had to bring up Barb V. That bitch ..."

"That's not news."

"Wait till I tell you the latest," he said. "I got a call from my shop when you were inside."

Freddy's eyes were slits as he avoided a minivan that pulled from a fruit stand onto the highway without looking. The Jaguar seemed to slide around the bulky van onto the shoulder and back into traffic before I had a chance to notice.

"I don't care if Barb V doesn't like me personally. That doesn't give her the right to go after my business."

"What is she doing?"

"Remember the trouble I had with those bad CDs a couple of years ago?"

Did I remember? I'd thought Freddy had committed murder over those embroidery discs. He had purchased a huge amount of CDs used in high-end sewing machines. Turned out the foreign discs were cheap for a reason, and wouldn't work in American machines. Freddy had spent thousands on useless bootlegs.

"She's telling everyone that the CDs I sell now are knockoffs. That my CDs are no good. Rebekah said a customer came in, complaining that her eight-thousand-dollar machine would be ruined if she used a design disc she bought at my place."

"That's terrible." Reputation was key to any business, but a sewing machine store didn't have much else. The machines were the same wherever you bought them. My mother had always told her customers that you bought the dealer, not the machine.

If Barb V managed to trash Freddy's rep, he'd be out of business.

"How do you know it's her?" I asked. Even Barb V deserved a fair trial.

"One of the machine company representatives told me. They nearly believed her. The company was getting ready to pull their brand from my store. When I grilled her, she said she heard it from Barb V."

We turned off onto the Aptos exit and entered the darling downtown that sat on the cusp of the forest and the ocean. Freddy slotted the car neatly into a parking spot right in front of the store. Even the good parking karma didn't improve his mood.

Before I got out of the car, I said, "We've got to stop her."

"Believe me, I will make sure of that," Freddy said.

Twenty minutes later, we arrived at Quilts Up, in Santa Cruz, our fourth stop in less than two hours. Summer greeted us as she bounded out of the shop, her braids bouncing on her chest and her long skirt nearly tripping her.

"Dudes!" she said.

She hugged me around the neck. "You're the best. This is going to be so much fun. I can hardly wait until tomorrow."

Summer's enthusiasm was infectious. Freddy and I both cheered up. It looked like we might make it to all the shops before they closed.

Barb the Damp's shop in Fremont was next to last on our list. We pulled up into the parking lot as two women were pulling the front door shut. The shorter of the two had her keys in her hand when I raced up with the basket in hand.

"Excuse me, I'm with the Quilters Crawl. This is your basket for tomorrow. Can you put it inside?"

The two women looked at each other.

"Where's Barb?" I asked. I looked into the store. The lights were out. "Is she working tonight?"

"No, she didn't come in today," the woman with the key said. "She's under the weather."

The other woman raspberried her lips. "Is that what they're calling it these days?"

The key woman shot her a look and grabbed the basket from me. She opened the door and turned on a light. She marched into the depths.

"Thanks," I said. I was happy to get away from that atmosphere.

I got back into the car. Freddy was fiddling with his radio. "Last but not least, Barb V."

TEN

FREDDY AND I GOT back to QP around seven. Buster's big truck was parked out front. Freddy pulled in front of it and put his car in neutral.

"I won't come in if that's okay with you. No sense incurring the big man's wrath."

"You must be tired," I said. "Pissing off Buster is one of your favorite pastimes."

He laughed.

I patted his hand that rested on the wooden gearshift. "No matter. We're off to the hospital to see Vangie anyhow."

———

Vangie was sitting up when we got to her room. She smiled at the sight of Buster and waved us over. Since last night, she'd gotten a roommate, a thin older woman who barely looked at us, despite Buster giving her his best smile.

"How's the noggin?" Buster asked. We gave Vangie a kiss on opposite cheeks.

"Hurts," she said. She frowned. She looked far healthier than last night. The bandage on her head was much smaller. Her complexion was not as sallow and her eyes had some of the spark back in them.

I gave her hand a squeeze and she smiled at me.

Buster rubbed her back vigorously. "You resisted, didn't you? How many times have I told you not to fight back? Hand over the damn backpack or whatever they want. It's not worth it."

"It was a reflex," she said. "My whole life is in that pack. My schoolbooks. I can't afford to replace them."

Vangie moved away from his touch. He was a bit too zealous. I got between them.

"Hey," I said with pseudo cheer. "Speaking of books, Lark's books finally arrived."

"Was that just yesterday that we were tracking them down? Feels like a month ago to me," Vangie said.

"Me, too," I agreed.

I filled her in on my road trip with Freddy. She laughed when I told her about chasing down Jimmy, the UPS guy. "In the end, we made it to all eleven stores."

"CHP must have been on vacation," Buster said. "Freddy had to have been over the speed limit ninety percent of the time."

"Seventy-five," I said. Buster gave me a baleful look. "Okay, maybe eighty."

"Next time, give me a heads up. I'll make sure Freddy has a little company on his ride." He winked at Vangie, who laughed. She knew how he felt about Freddy.

Buster's phone buzzed and he looked at the readout. "I've got to take this," he said.

"You won't get reception. You'll have to go outside," I said.

"Thank you, Officer Cell Police." He kissed Vangie on the cheek again. "Get better soon. It's your move in Scrabble."

He tried to kiss me too but I dodged him. He'd pay for the cell police crack and he knew it.

Vangie and I watched him go. She laid her head against the pillow.

"Hey, you're in your street clothes," I said. The top she was wearing wasn't her pajamas, it was a blue Henley T-shirt. "You going home?"

She nodded. "As soon as the hospitalist gets here to sign off. His office said he had an emergency but promised he'd be in tonight. I can't sleep another night in this hospital."

She leaned over and whispered. "They brought her in at two in the morning. She snores, and if she's not snoring, she's crying. I've got to get home."

I looked out the window and saw Buster on the sidewalk. One hand held the phone up to his ear, the other kept pace with his stride. He didn't look happy.

"I bet he's going to have to go back to work," I said. "Dang it."

Vangie made a commiserating noise. I settled into a chair at Vangie's side, glancing up to see what was on the TV. The woman in the next bed startled when the *Jeopardy* music morphed into people yelling, "Wheel … of … Fortune."

Was Vangie up for the heart-to-heart we needed to have? I snuck a peek at her profile.

I started to speak but she interrupted, "Dewey …"

Vangie picked at a thread that was loose in the blanket. "I hope you don't mind, I told my mother that you would bring me home."

I hadn't told her I was coming to visit her tonight. I didn't know myself I was going to make it until Freddy and I hit remarkably light traffic coming down from Fremont.

She took my silence as a plea for more information. "My mother had to make dinner for the little kids, and Grandma was napping…"

"Hey, it's no problem. You know you can count on me," I said.

"I just did," she said. Pat Sajak was smarming his way into a commercial break.

I gave her a questioning look.

"I just counted on you. And you were here."

Vangie smiled her broadest smile, the one that made her eyes crinkle up. Pearl had warned her against grinning, said she'd regret the wrinkles later, but Vangie didn't listen, thankfully. Her smile went straight through to my heart.

There would be time to talk tomorrow.

We watched the next segment of *Wheel*, both of us guessing "Saddam Hussein" before the contestant. Buster still wasn't back.

I got up, stretched, and went to the window again. Buster's hands were at his sides. No phone in sight. He was talking to someone standing in front of him. That person was smaller than he was, and shorter. I only caught a glimpse of a leg and a man's dress shoe.

Buster threw up his hands and took a step away. I could see who he was talking to now. Anton Zorn. Uh-oh. "Vangie," I cried. "You feeling okay? For real?"

"Fine," she said. "The doctor said there was no reason I couldn't go home. He just needed to see me one more time..."

"Then come on, let's go."

I pulled back the closet door. "Do you have anything in here?"

"Mom took everything home earlier. Except the hand lotion," she said, reaching for the drawer next to the bed.

"Leave it," I said. "I'll buy you a new one. Follow me."

I glanced out the window. Judging by his body language, Buster was reading Zorn the riot act. Thank you, Buster.

"What's going on?" Vangie asked. She climbed off the bed.

I pulled back the curtain so she could see.

"Zorn."

Vangie's eyes grew wide. "Is he going to arrest me?"

"Not if he can't find you," I said.

I opened the door to the hall. The lone nurse at the desk looked up. Her phone rang and she turned away. We did a speed walk toward the elevator. My car was parked in the back lot. Luckily, Buster and Zorn were out front.

"Hurry."

We ran down the hall.

I had no idea if Zorn was on his way himself, or if he'd sent patrol officers to pick Vangie up. A blue shirt with epaulets gave me a skipped heartbeat. Turned out to be a teenager in faux military garb.

146

Vangie put her hand in mine. It was slippery with sweat. Hair was plastered to her forehead.

"Are you okay?" I asking, squeezing her hand.

She nodded, then put a hand up to steady her head as if she was a bobble head about to go out of control. "Get me out of here."

"Through here."

We went past the gift shop and out a door. I glanced around the corner but didn't see Buster or Zorn. I pushed Vangie in the direction of my car. I pulled through the doctor's lot and a gas station on the corner, bumping into the side street, scraping the bottom of my car.

Vangie lurched in the seat next to me. "Hang on," I said a little late.

I glanced at her head, half expecting to see blood. Nothing yet.

A few blocks from the hospital, we were stopped by a red light. I glanced in my rear view for the hundredth time. Nothing.

"We're okay," I said. Vangie grabbed the dashboard and blew out a breath.

"Thanks," she said. "I really don't want to talk to him."

"You can't go home," I said. "He'll find you there. I can't even take you to QP. He's been there, he knows you work with me."

"Where am I going to go?" Vangie cried. She cracked her knuckles loudly. I grabbed her hand.

"I've got an idea."

A few minutes later, we parked in front of Pearl's. The lights were on in the living room, and I could see Pearl seated in front of the TV. *Wheel of Fortune* was still on. That seemed impossible.

"What do you think? Can you hole up here? We'll stash you at Pearl's and call your attorney. Zorn can talk to Larry the Lip."

Vangie looked at me questioningly. "Larry the what?"

"Don't ask," I said. "Let's go tell Pearl she has another room-mate."

I knocked gently on the door. Pearl answered, carrying a small quilt, *Wheel of Fortune* theme music playing behind her.

She clicked the TV off when we came into the small living room. The magazines were gone from the coffee table and some-one had recently dusted. Pearl looked good, too. She was wearing a clean pair of yoga pants and a T-shirt from QP's twentieth anni-versary sale.

"Sit," she said, taking her place in the small recliner. The bigger chair—Hiro's—had a sci-fi novel cracked over the arm. Ross had made himself at home.

Vangie and I sat side by side on the couch. Vangie leaned back and closed her eyes.

"What's wrong? You two look like someone died," Pearl said, stabbing her needle into a saucer full of beads.

I cringed at her choice of words.

"We were hoping you could put Vangie up for a couple of days."

Vangie's breath steadied. I patted her knee and she made a murmur that let me know she was okay, but out of juice. The es-cape from Zorn had taken its toll on her.

Why was Pearl hesitating? She and Vangie were as close as two unrelated people could be.

"Ross is in the spare room," Pearl said, her little chin coming up defiantly.

So that was it. I'd forgotten. I was the bad guy when it came to Sir Ross. "I'm not here to kick Ross out," I said. "You can make your own decision about him."

I gave Pearl a look that I hoped conveyed how I felt about the idea that she would choose a total stranger over Vangie. Pearl stabbed the needle into the quilt, affixing an azure blue bead in place.

I decided to appeal to her renegade side. "The police want to talk to her. She doesn't want to talk to them."

"The police, why?"

I realized Pearl knew noting of Vangie's last week.

"A boy in her class died of a drug overdose, and the cops think she knows something."

Vangie didn't open her eyes. "I can sleep on the sofa in the sewing room, Pearl. Please."

Pearl watched Vangie. "What happened to your head?"

Vangie placed a hand on the bandage. "Like my new hat?" she said.

"She's okay," I said. "She had a little accident. Doctor says she'll be better in no time. She could use a little of your TLC."

Pearl ignored my plea, watching Vangie intently. "Of course you can stay."

"Thanks," Vangie said.

Once the decision had been made, Pearl switched gears.

"How about some tea, Vangie? I have that special green one that you like. A few cups of that and you'll be up and around in no time."

Pearl dashed off to the kitchen. I followed her. The dishwasher was humming, and the counters had been wiped down. Having Ross around had put a spring in her step, I had to admit that.

"Where's Ross?"

She glanced at the clock. "Class. He'll be back soon."

"You will take care of her, right?"

"Of course I will, Dewey. What do you think I am?"

"I understand you're mad at me. Don't take it out on Vangie."

Pearl made a pfft noise. I went back into the living room. Vangie was lying on the couch, her hand thrown over her forehead. I hoped she wasn't hurting too badly.

My phone beeped and I saw a message from Buster. Buster's voice came through the small speaker. I put it close to my ear so Vangie wouldn't hear. "I'm sorry. I tried to stop Zorn from coming upstairs. He doesn't care that Vangie is hurt. He's determined to question her about Wyatt's death. I'm going to work for a few hours. The Task Force is calling us in. I'll look for Vangie at the station after I'm done. I'll try to bring her home."

Pearl clattered in her kitchen, something metallic falling to the floor. "I'm okay," she hollered. "I'm going to put some cookies in the oven. I have dough left over. Vangie loves my butterscotch chocolate chip."

Vangie shifted when she realized I was standing there. I sat on the end of the couch and Vangie laid her head in my lap. I stroked the hair out of her face.

"Does your head hurt?" I asked.

"Not really. I feel kind of sick to my stomach."

"Probably the result of too much adrenalin running through your system. I'm sorry you had to go through that."

"Not your fault that Anton Zorn is such a jerk."

My fingers on her cheek were wet. I looked closer at her face. "Why are you crying?"

"Wyatt was murdered, right? I saw it on the news earlier."

I rubbed her temple. "He was. The cops are saying that he was given an overdose."

She cried quietly, turning her head to the back of the couch. "He was not a druggy, Dewey. He wasn't."

"I know. The medical examiner found a needle mark on his back. He didn't put it there."

I pulled her upright. Her arms were tightly crossed against her body. "Tell me about that night, Vangie. Come on."

She rocked, hugging herself. "I don't want you to think badly of me."

"Vang, something is eating you up. I can tell. You'll feel better if you spill. I love you no matter what."

She pulled her feet underneath her and glanced into the kitchen. Pearl was still fussing. I heard the oven go on with a whoosh.

"Did the protest go crazy? I heard it was a riot," I said.

She sighed, a sound that racked her body. "Not at all. The protest was amazing. By the end, people were chill. We sang. Everyone was very mellow. Very sixties."

Highest form of praise coming from Vangie.

Her forehead creased. Her gaze shifted to the past. She said, "Wyatt and I got separated. One minute he was behind me, then when I turned, he was gone. I looked for him but I couldn't see him in the crowd. I texted him. He didn't answer."

Vangie rubbed her eyes. "I made my way back to where I'd parked earlier, my usual spot in the lot by the school. The streets were so crowded, it must have taken me half an hour to get over there.

"When I got there, Wyatt was already in my car. I guess I'd left it unlocked, I don't know, but he was sitting in the passenger seat. He was exhausted and wanted a ride home."

Vangie pulled her fingers through her hair, catching a large knot. I untangled her fingers gently. "To tell you the truth, I was kind of excited. I never knew where he lived. His student ID still had his first dorm address on it. He was very private."

The house was starting to smell sweet as the chips in Pearl's cookies began to melt. Her teakettle was whistling, and it shut off abruptly. I wanted to get to the truth before she came back in.

I interjected, keeping my voice low. "Did he seem high?"

"No, he seemed like Wyatt. Really, he was stoked. He kept talking about how cool the response to his call on Twitter was. Then he kind of wound down, stopped talking. I thought he was tired. He told me where to turn and stuff. When I parked, he started choking. He couldn't catch his breath. I didn't know what to do."

Vangie's tears spilled over. "It happened so fast. I went around to the passenger side to help him. I stopped at the trunk to get my quilt, figured he might be cold."

Her gaze came up to me, then drifted. The worried look returned. "A gym bag was in the trunk, the zipper open. Inside were pill bottles, lots of them. I could see prescription labels."

She picked at her face. "There were maybe thirty bottles of pills inside. I grabbed the blanket and went back to Wyatt, but he was so still. Drool dripped from the side of his mouth and his eyes were empty. Empty. He was gone."

"Dewey," she began. Her chest caved in and she slunk back against the couch. "I—"

I squeezed her hand. "It's okay, Vangie. Whatever happened. It's okay. We'll figure it out."

She rubbed her temples. Her voice got louder.

"I had to get rid of the bag. We were right by Wyatt's house. So I went through the gate. There was this garden bench thing with a lid. I dropped the bag in there."

"That's when you called me about Wyatt? And you didn't tell anyone about the drugs?"

She shook her head. "Who was going to believe me that they weren't my prescriptions?"

We sat quietly. I held her hand. So Wyatt was into dealing drugs. What other explanation was there? Poor Vangie. Clearly she had really liked him.

She sighed heavily. "I went back for them yesterday. I figured I would give them to Buster. That's when someone hit me over the head."

My head snapped around. "The drugs were in your backpack when you got mugged?"

"No, that's the thing. I didn't find the drugs, they weren't there."

"Where are they?"

She shrugged. "I don't know. I didn't know any of Wyatt's friends. I swear to you I didn't know he was dealing drugs until that night. Whenever I saw him, he was sober, and sweet."

"What about the pills you gave me for Pearl?"

Vangie looked up. "Oh no, that was legit. Pearl had given Wyatt her prescription earlier that day from the doctor, and he'd filled it for her."

Pearl came in when she heard her name.

"What's the dealio?" she said. "Why are you crying, sweetums?"

Vangie shook her head.

"It's a long story," I said. "Right now, Vangie needs to rest."

"After tea and cookies," Pearl said. "There's nothing tea and cookies can't fix."

I stared at Pearl. This was not a side of Pearl I'd seen before.

At least Vangie would be safe here.

ELEVEN

THE FIRST MORNING OF the Quilters Crawl, I got to the shop early and walked through the front door. I used my mother's old trick, pretending to be a brand-new customer, coming in for the first time. I closed my eyes and opened them again.

Thank goodness Jenn and Ursula had stayed late last night, dressing the place. The first thing I noticed was Jenn's latest QP Original, a Christmas block of the month hung under the loft. It was a good choice. The odd colors, not your usual red and green but lime green and pink, drew my eye right into the middle of the store.

I checked out the walls. All the current samples were hanging. The projects were colorful and enticing. Most importantly, the name, dates, and times of the class were prominently displayed. Getting butts in our chairs was a high priority. Classes added to our bottom line.

The Quilters Crawl was an opportunity to market QP to new people. I expected some locals who had never been to the store, but from what I'd heard, quilters from southern California, Oregon, and Washington State came, too. Rumor was that one large family from Massachusetts with several generations of quilters had made it a family tradition to vacation during the Crawl.

Vangie was at Pearl's. They could keep an eye on each other until the Crawl was over and I could figure out a more permanent solution. No harm would come to Pearl while Vangie was there, and Vangie was hidden from Zorn.

I could concentrate on the Crawl and not wonder why thirty bottles of pills had disappeared.

The store was clean. No pins on the floor. Threads were notoriously hard to pick up with the vacuum but I didn't see any. Every bolt of fabric had been pulled tight, no loose ends flapping. The shelves had all been dusted, and the countertops shone. Rotary cutters were lined up for use. Fingerprints on the monitor had been vanquished.

I walked to the back of the store to where the books and patterns were. Our QP Original patterns had their own easy-to-reach display with plenty of extra inventory. Jenn had made several signs that let the customer know these patterns were only available here. Unique to the store, get 'em while you can.

Signs had always been Vangie's favorite chore. Jenn's were okay but were missing Vangie's special touch. I'd called Vangie before when I came in. Pearl had picked up. She was taking her nursing duties to heart. She said Vangie was still sleeping and admonished me to leave her be.

Ursula called for me from the kitchen.

"Be right there," I hollered. I had one more thing to check out.

In the hall, the welcome station had been set up. On the advice of the other shop owners, we'd situated the card table in the back so that the customers had to walk through the shop to get their stamp.

The QP yardsticks had arrived and were standing behind the table, the box top ripped open for easy access.

I straightened the passports, our special palm tree stamp and inkpad. Each customer who began at QP would get a pre-stamped passport. Others would have their passports already and just need a QP stamp. In order to be in the running for prizes, the hoppers had to get their entire book stamped.

My father would be our greeter. All he had to do was sit at the table, welcome the customers and stamp their book and hand out yardsticks. He'd done it many times before when Mom was alive. He'd be a welcome sight for many of my older customers. His energy was always upbeat, even—to my dismay—flirty.

Ursula was making punch. She poured the contents of three different kinds of juices into a fluted crystal bowl. My mother had bought it at a garage sale for these occasions. Generally it resided in the cabinet above the fridge.

"Can you get out the fruit?" she asked.

My Costco trip had paid off. The cookies looked homemade. We had trays of veggies. I pulled out the cut-up fruit and plated it, fanning out pieces of pineapple.

The classroom would serve as a break room. Ursula and Jenn had set out paper plates, cups, and napkins last night. The customers could get a drink and a snack before moving on. Later, we'd be putting out cheese and crackers, hummus and veggies. And cookies. Lots of cookies.

The hope was that if we fed them, the participants would get renewed energy and head back into the store to spend some cash. I was balancing the options. Didn't want to overload anyone with too much sugar. That meant a nap in the car, not a foraging trip down our aisles.

Ursula dug bagels out of the Panera bag and cut them into quarters. We had cream cheese for the early birds. I speared pine-apple with toothpicks.

"You and Jenn did an amazing job on the store," I said. "The place looks wonderful."

She nodded. Praise was not easy for her to take. She took ref-uge in small talk. "Perfect weather," Ursula said. "Not too hot, not too cold. No rain in the forecast for three days."

"Just right," I agreed. "I'm getting excited. There's been so much going on, I haven't been able to concentrate on the Crawl. Now that it's here, I'm beyond."

"We're going to have a great one."

She put up her fist for me to bump. I obliged and laughed.

"It's you and me for the first hour," I said. "After that, Jenn and Claudia and Florence will be in. My father will be manning the greeting table."

My phone alarm went off. Nine o'clock. Time to open the doors.

"Ready?" I asked Ursula, smiling at her. I was surprised to feel butterflies.

"Ready, boss," Ursula said, wiping her hands on a paper towel. She put on a clean QP apron and tied up the back.

I opened the front door and flipped on the open sign. I'd barely turned my back when our first Crawlers arrived. Ursula stamped their books and they scooted out, eager to get to the next shop. The early birds were not the kind to linger. They felt it was their duty to get to as many shops as they could in the first day. A few would even push themselves and hit all twelve shops, driving hundreds of miles in ten hours. After yesterday, I knew what a grind that was.

There was no prize for finishing early. Customers could use all four days to get to complete the circuit of shops. But for some it was a badge of honor to be first.

My hope was that the Twitter prize basket would lure them back to the store. I gave them each a sticker with the Quilter Crawl's Twitter address.

"Be sure to sign up," I said cheerily, waylaying them at the door, ignoring their obvious need to move on. "Special prizes will be given out each day only at the Twitter shop."

For ten minutes, we were busy greeting and stamping the early birds. After that first flurry, the traffic died.

As in no customers. Not one. We were used to slow times at the shop, and generally had plenty of work to do to fill up the empty time. But we were so ready for the Crawl that there was nothing to do. The shop was clean. The remodeled bathroom was sparkling. All the new fabric was displayed.

When Florence and Claudia came in, I didn't know what to do with them. I went back into my office so I didn't have to watch them standing around.

Ursula was in the kitchen. I poked my head in.

"You're not cutting up more bagels are you?"

She smiled. "Actually, I thought I'd put some in the freezer. No sense in them going stale."

"Because no one is here to eat them."

Ursula pointed at me. "Don't go all doom and gloom on me. Business will pick up. Besides, the Quilters Crawl is not about one day, remember?"

"Okay," I said, pinching one of the crumbs she was making between my fingers and eating it. I didn't even have the energy to fight with her. All of the fun seemed to have gone out the door.

"Besides, we're the special secret Twitter shop this afternoon, aren't we? That's going to cause a ruckus. Here," she said, handing me half of a cinnamon raisin bagel. She knew those were my favorite. "Cheer up."

When my father arrived at eleven, we hadn't had a single customer since the last early bird. He took his spot at the greeting table, rearranging the stamp pad and the pile of passports. He liked to do things his way.

"Hi, Dad," I said.

"I can't be here tomorrow," he said without preamble.

"Dad! You have to," I said. "I don't have anyone else. I'm short handed."

He held up a hand. "Don't worry, I found a replacement for myself. She'll be able to work all day."

She. The back of my neck tingled with anxiety. There was only one "she" that my dad talked to regularly. Kym, my brother Kevin's wife.

I'd have thought rescuing her from certain death would have changed Kym's attitude toward me. She'd changed all right, but not for the better.

Kym had given up the idea of taking over Mercedes' retreat business at Asilomar when she realized that would mean being away from Kevin for twelve weeks out of the year. And that she might have to face another mountain lion.

She'd tried selling dishware and online advertising. For one dreadful month, she'd answered the phones at Pellicano Construction.

She'd given up quilting completely. She couldn't get away from associating quilting with the dangers of being held hostage.

Much as I didn't like Kym, I didn't want that for her. I wanted her to enjoy her life. But I'd fired her from QP and I didn't want her back. Even for a weekend.

"Dad, not Kym. Please say it's not Kym."

"It's not Kym."

I could tell by the look on his face that he thought he was being funny.

"Seriously?" I whined. "You asked Kym?"

Dad frowned. He didn't have a lot of patience for whiny me. "Of course, it's Kym. Do you think I have a Rolodex full of available women to call?"

My mind was flipping through possible replacements. There was no one. I'd called in all my markers to staff up.

"Step aside, Dewey."

The door had opened while we were talking and several women were lined up behind me to get their passports stamped. He beckoned them forward. I stepped aside.

A woman with a prominent jaw bumped the redhead who'd cut in front of her with her hip. "I was here first," she said.

I glanced up. Uh-oh. Now that we had a few customers, were they going to fight with each other?

The redhead straightened up and frowned.

My heart sank.

Then she grinned. "Are you following us?" she said. "I swear we just saw you at the Emporium."

"What took you so long?" the leader of the other pack said. "We've been here for at least ten minutes."

Two groups, who'd clearly met up at a different shop. Strangers before today, now friends. Or at least friendly enough to tease.

"You have not," the redhead exclaimed. They all laughed.

Dad stamped their passports. The leader of the pack said, "See you at Roman's."

"Not us," Blondie said. "We're heading south now."

I asked, "How many of you have smart phones?"

All eight nodded their heads except for one quilter who looked to be about my age, thirty. She reached in her bag and pulled out an iPad.

I grinned. "Even better. Follow the Quilters Crawl on Twitter. We're going to announce special prizes."

The women gathered around each other, entering info into their phones and checking their Facebook accounts. Two decided to become friends on the spot.

Jenn came rushing through the back door. She had a large bag slung over her shoulder. Jenn was the queen of homemade bags.

"Sorry to be late," she said. "My son broke his arm after school yesterday. Fell off his skateboard. Last night, he insisted he didn't need the Vicodin the doctor had prescribed. This morning he changed his mind. I had to get to Walgreen's before coming here."

"Is he okay?" I asked.

"He'll be fine. This is not his first. He broke his leg last year. I wish he'd take up skiing or extreme snowboarding. Something with less probability of breaking every bone in his body."

She dropped her bag in the office and pulled on her apron. She went up front, calling out to Ursula as she did that the cavalry had arrived.

I wished we needed the cavalry. The two groups went out the back door without buying a thing.

I went back into my office. Why wasn't this working? I checked the Crawl's Facebook account. Summer had posted a picture of her display of quilts based on Roman architecture. Customers liked her note, giving her thumbs up. Maybe I should take a picture of the shop, and put it up.

I went over to the Twitter account. @Quilters Crawl had gained some more followers.

I surfed over to Wyatt's account. After hearing Vangie's account of the night he died, I was sure there was more to him than I'd thought. Someone was probably looking for those drugs. That person might even have been the one who killed him.

He must have stashed the drugs in Vangie's car earlier. She had an assigned spot in the parking garage. Her car was always in the same spot. The drug bust probably had many of the drug dealers on the run, doing things that they wouldn't have considered. Like hiding drugs in Vangie's car. Or killing other dealers.

I read through the tweets that had come up after he died. I didn't see anything as blatant as the kid looking for Provigil.

———

Dad left his post about twelve-thirty and wandered into my office for the fifteenth time. He wanted to grouse about how different this Quilters Crawl was than the last one he worked, nearly six years ago.

"Still not much action?" I said, not quite succeeding at keeping the exasperation out of my voice.

"Nobody's coming. Did you guys advertise this thing or what? You gotta advertise," he badgered. "Take an ad in the paper. I used to do that all the time. What about the Yellow Pages? You in the Yellow Pages?"

I sighed. There was no point in arguing with him. I could never explain Twitter to him.

He needed something constructive to do. I handed him a stack of sandwich request forms. "How about going to Zanutto's and getting lunch for everyone?"

That could get rid of him for a good hour. Florence alone could spend twenty minutes with the menu making up her mind between Jack and American.

I checked the boxes that would get me a turkey sandwich on whole wheat with cranberry sauce and mustard and handed my form to my father. "We've got plenty of snacks and drinks here, so we only need sandwiches. Take my credit card."

He pulled his hand away as I tried to give him my plastic.

"I got this," he said gruffly. He shuffled up front. "Lunch wagon," he called.

I brought my laptop out to the greeting table and settled there.

Jenn came back, holding our Twitter prize basket aloft. "You like?"

"It's fabulous," I said.

She'd taken the basket that Freddy had brought and gussied it up. Glittery silver ribbon wound through the handle. Lark's book was featured prominently; the scissors were nestled on a bed of candy and silver confetti. She'd attached silver balls on matching pipe cleaners. If I'd done that, the result would have been Martian. Hers was chic.

Of course, if we'd had more business this morning, the basket would have remained unadorned. I would have been okay with that.

"Have you been checking the tweets?" she asked.

"I'm about to," I said, opening the laptop.

Jenn pulled her phone out of her apron pocket. "This friend of mine is tweeting as she goes from shop to shop." Jenn said, "She's funny. Snarky."

My heart did a little flip. This was the part of Twitter that was nerve-wracking. Instantaneous judging. "Has she been here? What did she say?"

Jenn looked down at her phone. "Not sure. She's not specific. She probably doesn't want to get sued. Listen to this, though. I bet you can tell which shop this is. *Expect puppies and rainbows to fall from the ceiling. Sweet overload. Specializes in twee florals.*"

I had to grin. That was the perfect description of Barbara the Damp's shop.

"How about this one? *Surf's up, dude. If a quilt shop can be righteous, this is it. Every fabric has a peace sign on it.*"

Ursula joined us. I looked behind her. I couldn't see one customer on the shop floor. Business was slower than our slowest day this year. The Quilters Crawl had probably scared away our regular customers. And no one was crawling here.

"Oh, that's definitely the Santa Cruz shop," Ursula said.

"*Type A. Not a speck of dirt anywhere. No fun either.*"

We all said in unison, "Barb V!"

We laughed.

Jenn said, "She's going to keep it up all day today. Her husband drives and she tweets."

"Is she following the Quilters Crawl Twitter feed?" Ursula asked. I looked at her in surprise. Ursula was not known around here for her technological prowess.

"Hey, I'm figuring this out," she said. "I signed up for an account myself last night. I'm following David Boreanaz, the guy from *Bones*. He tweeted a picture of his cool socks. Red and black argyle. Very hot."

I looked at her in amazement.

"What?" she said. "It's not rocket science."

"Go, Ursula," Jenn said, giving her a fist bump. Florence looked up questioningly from where she was straightening the bookrack, trying to follow the conversation.

I got up and gave her wrinkled hand a pat. "Nothing to worry about, Flo. Today, I only need you to cut fabric and chat up the customers, making them feel at home. Making them want to spend more time here. You're the best at that. No wi-fi or plug-in required."

I sat out front while Flo, Jenn, and Ursula ate lunch in the classroom. My father was telling them stories and I heard plenty of laughs and giggles. At least he'd found his audience.

The store remained quiet. I told myself the hoppers were all out to lunch.

166

Finally, it was time for our Twitter event. I had the laptop open and Jenn came back from lunch with her phone at the ready.

At the stroke of two, Freddy sent out his tweet. "Special prizes at these two Quilters Crawl locations, QP on the Alameda in San Jose and Quilts Up in Santa Cruz."

"This is it, ladies," I said to my staff who trickled back in from lunch. Dad frowned. "And gent. Get ready. Jenn and I will take the doors. We'll give a special ticket to everyone who comes in. The winner has to be here at three o'clock when the prize is awarded, so all the participants should be mingling for the entire hour. Be sure to tell them there's food in the classroom."

I got their nods. "And point out the QP Originals, please."

"Let's go," I said.

"Wait," Jenn said. "We need a picture."

Ursula said, "I'll take it."

Jenn handed over her phone. She and I stood holding the Twitter basket.

"Smile like you mean it," Ursula said. "This is an historic moment. The first Twitter event in the history of the Quilters Crawl."

Claudia and Florence clapped as Jenn and I posed. I didn't have any trouble smiling genuinely. My staff was trying really hard to cheer me up. They wanted the best for me and that felt good.

I raced to the back door. Dad was at his station.

"Be ready, it's Twitter time," I said. "We are going to be really busy for the next hour."

He cracked his knuckles in response. I stopped to give him a quick hug.

"Hey, what was that for?" he said, straightening out his Mr. Rogers-type sweater.

"I'm glad you're here for the fun. This Twitter thing was my idea, mine and Vangie's, and it's happening."

The wind had died down and the sun had heated up the afternoon. I stood outside on the tiny porch, ready to greet anyone who came by.

The back parking lot was small, only holding about a dozen cars. We shared it with Mrs. Unites's burrito shop but her lunch crowd had come and gone, so there was plenty of parking. Customers had no excuses not to stop.

It was too bad Vangie wasn't here. I pulled out my phone to call her. Not now. I'd wait until after the Twitter event and let her bask in the glow of the success. Maybe I'd call her when we pulled out the winning ticket. That would be perfect. She could be in on the big moment that way.

A bird sang heartily from the pine tree in the neighbor's yard. People in this neighborhood loved their bird feeders, so the array of songbirds was always wonderful.

I wanted to hear a different kind of bird, though. The kind that tweeted online.

I paced. A car came around the corner. I took my place at the door, threw my shoulders back and smiled. The car continued past the driveway into the neighborhood beyond. Dang.

I walked some more and forbade myself from looking at my watch. Or the phone. I wasn't going to check the tweets. I wouldn't drive myself nuts.

I glanced in the back door even though I knew I couldn't really see the shop floor from here. I could see Dad. He was reading the paper.

Jenn had to be doing better. People must have parked on the street out front.

Forty minutes went by without one customer coming in the back door. I went in and put the roll of special tickets next to my father.

"What's this?" he said, folding the sports section.

"Make sure anybody that comes to get their passport stamped gets one," I said, not pausing. I headed for the front door.

"I thought we were going to get busy," he said after me.

Three customers holding pink tickets were gathered by the cutting table. They were looking through the prize basket.

"Pretty sweet," an apple-cheeked blonde said. "This is Lark Gordon's newest book."

Her friend pumped a fist. "One of us is bound to win," she said. "The odds are really good."

"Do we have to hang around until three?" her friend whined.

Ursula said, "Those are the rules."

My heart sank. I crossed the shop to skirt around them, avoiding eye contact. I couldn't make small talk right now. I went out to Jenn.

"Is that it? Three people?" I asked as soon as the door had closed behind me.

She nodded. "That's all. What about you?"

I shook my head. "Nobody. Let me see your phone."

She held it away from me. "Freddy followed up a minute or so ago."

There was something else. Some reason she wouldn't let me see her phone.

"What?" I demanded. "You know something. Tell me."

169

She looked away. We were both hopeful as a PT Cruiser went past, but the driver didn't stop.

"*Quiltsaplenty* is at the Santa Cruz shop. She says there are at least thirty people there."

"Damn!" I said, kicking an empty soda can. It landed noisily in the gutter. I fetched it and put it in the recycling bin.

I looked up the street. "Do you think the freeway ramp is closed for construction again? Maybe there's an overturned tractor trailer that we didn't hear about."

Jenn shrugged, without looking at me.

"Are we hard to find? I'm sure our address is correct on the map. Where are all of our customers?" I cried.

Jenn put a hand on my shoulder. I could tell she wanted to tell me something.

"Tell me," I said. "What am I doing wrong?"

Jenn frowned. She suddenly looked like a mother about to give her kid some vile-tasting medicine. I straightened my back. I wasn't sure I wanted to hear the answer to that question.

"Do you really want to know?" Jenn asked.

Jenn and I had had a bumpy relationship. She had been Team Kym when I'd fired Kym. When I brought Ursula back with me from Asilomar, Jenn had nearly quit in protest. Ursula had been the one to bring Jenn back into the QP fold, with her gentle persistence. She'd informed her that she was counting on Jenn to teach her the ropes. They'd bonded over the correct way to fold a fat quarter and cash counting techniques.

But Jenn had always remained a little cold to me.

She found her voice. "You've been making a lot of changes around here. You don't have the kinds of fabrics that your mother used to carry. I think your customer base has eroded somewhat."

"Quilting is changing," I protested. "Besides, sales are up."

She held up a hand. "I'm not saying you're doing the wrong thing. First of all, it's your shop. You're in a transitional phase. I think your new quilters are not the type that go on shop hops. They're at work on Wednesdays. Maybe we'll see them on the weekend. But today, it's a lot of traditional quilters who have eleven other shops to pick from. They'll get here eventually."

"But I promised that this Twitter promotion would be a good thing for everyone. And here it's sucking for me."

"It's a smart idea. You may be a little ahead of the curve. I guarantee you by next year, using Twitter will be the norm. Every other Quilters Crawl is going to copy you."

I hugged Jenn and went back to my post in the back.

Right at three, Jenn took a picture of me with the apple-cheeked blonde. She'd won the basket.

TWELVE

I'd been closed for at least twenty minutes when there was a knock at the back door. I heard the handle jiggle. Oh, no. Was it an errant shop hopper? I had the slowest day in QP history and now someone wants to come in?

I collapsed against the counter. The Quilters Crawl dictated the hours all the shops were open. I didn't have the energy to deal with someone who thought the rules don't really apply to her.

I wanted to go home. Home to Buster. And bubbles. I needed to erase this day from my memory bank.

The knock came again, louder this time.

I went down the back hall to see who was banging at the door, preparing a speech about how I had to obey the rules or I'd get thrown out.

Through the glass I could see Freddy smiling at me. He was holding a bottle of wine up like an Oscar.

"Got cups?" he said, when I threw the deadbolt and let him in.

"You bet," I said. He followed me into the kitchen, collapsing on one of the retro red-vinyl-covered chairs.

I pulled out two of our best QP logo mugs, giving Freddy the biggest one.

"Ice?" I asked, pausing in front of the freezer door.

Freddy's brow furrowed. Nice to see he was laying off the Botox. "Don't be gauche. This is a robust red. Best at room temperature."

"We're drinking out of mugs, Freddy," I said. "Gauche is something to strive for."

He poured.

"What a day," Freddy said, rubbing his scalp vigorously. He'd let his bald spot take over and cut the remaining locks short. I liked it so much better than the ponytail combover he'd been sporting.

"I'm telling you, if I had to give directions to Barb V's shop one more time today, I was going to shoot myself right in the kisser. Every single hopper seemed to be going from my place to hers. Why do women assume I know how to get places? Number one, I just moved up here. And number two, I'm a dude. I navigate by the stars."

I laughed and took a big swig of the wine. Freddy was like a straight hairdresser or ice skater. Always trying to prove his masculinity, he liked to err on the macho side.

I was glad Buster was at home.

"Number three, you hate Barb V," I said. "Did you have a good day?"

He glanced at his phone. "I think so. It seemed busy. But I'm not in this for the daily numbers like you. I want these quilters to remember Roman's Sewing Machines and find their way back when they need a new machine."

I was hungry, so I pulled out some cheese and crackers and put them on the table. Freddy poked at a slice.

"Has this cheese been sitting out all day?"

"Geez, no!" I said. "Do you think I'm trying to kill you?"

Freddy smirked. "Don't play like you never thought about it."

"Who hasn't?" I said. He stuck his tongue out at me. "Don't worry, this is the cheese for tomorrow."

"I'm honored," he said, biting into the little sandwich he'd made, spreading cracker crumbs everywhere. He pushed the rest in his mouth.

"So my Twitter thing was a total bust."

Freddy had more free time than I did. I knew he would have checked in with the other shops during the day.

Freddy stuck his finger in the condensation puddling on the tabletop near the wine bottle. He drew little paisleys on the metal. "I heard."

"Hey," I said, punching his arm. "You don't have to agree with me."

"What did you think was going to happen? A flash mob? A couple of hundred quilters rocking out to Bon Jovi's 'You Can't Go Home'?"

I could hear the song in my head. Now it would be stuck there all night.

Freddy liked the idea. His smile grew. "I can see it. We could film it in Cesar de Chavez Park next to the dog poop statue. Tons of middle-aged white women doing the Hustle, fist pumping."

He sang a few notes.

I said, "Hey now, I'm not middle-aged, nor are my quilters. My customers are not all white, either. And you need to respect the Quetzalcoatl statue."

Freddy wasn't listening. "We should totally plan one of those. I've got a customer who's a choreographer. She would help. I bet it would be great."

Freddy drained the bottle of wine. I was surprised to see that it was empty. I hadn't noticed him refilling my glass. I'd thought I was still nursing my first.

I didn't care. The wine was relaxing. I felt the concerns of the day fade away.

"So my brother called," Freddy said.

I sat up straight and felt the tightness return to my shoulders. I nearly got whiplash from the jolt. Has Zorn caught up with Vangie?

"And?"

"The police are looking for Vangie. She's not at the hospital anymore, but she's not at home either."

At least she wasn't in police custody. I relaxed a little, and shrugged my shoulders at him innocently.

"Larry's concerned. He hasn't heard from her."

"Are you asking me if I know where she is?" I asked. I picked at the label on the bottle. It was an estate Cab from Duckhorn Vineyard in Napa. Freddy didn't mind spending sixty bucks for a few drinks.

Freddy frowned. "Larry wanted me to tell you to tell her it would be better for her if she returned his calls. He can't protect her otherwise."

I shrugged. "If I see her—which I'm not saying I will—I will pass on the message. I think Vangie should be talking to her lawyer, too. That would be the smart thing to do."

Buster's ring sounded on my phone, playing "Hammerhead Stew." The Delbert McClinton song was the tale of a guy who protected his girl to the extreme of making mincemeat out of Jaws. Truthfully, it made me a little nervous that he'd picked that song as his ring tone.

Freddy reached for the phone. He'd had enough wine to make him think it would be a good idea to answer and say inappropriate things. I snatched it away from him, letting the call go to voice mail. I texted Buster instead, telling him that I was on my way home.

I stood. "Time to go," I said.

I rinsed our mugs and the plate in the sink, and we walked outside together. Freddy waited as I locked the door from the outside, jiggling the handle to be sure.

"Here's to a Twitterific day tomorrow," he said with a jaunty wave. "If you hear from Vangie, tell her to call her lawyer."

"Got it," I said.

———

"Dewey!" Kym yelled from the back of the store. She really had to holler to be heard. I took a breath. Kym was here because I didn't have anyone else to work the table, I reminded myself. If we were going to be busy today, I needed her.

It was the morning of the second day of the Crawl. After yesterday, my expectations had definitely come down a notch. So far though, attendance had been steady and there were at least a dozen people in the store.

I walked back to where Kym sat at the greeting table. "Please lower your voice," I said. "Don't shout for me. It's not cool."

"You told me to stay put. How was I supposed to let you know you had a phone call? You can't have it both ways, you know."

"You can use the intercom feature..."

She thrust the portable store phone at me. "Did you find a purse?" she asked. "This lady lost her pocketbook."

"What?" I said, looking at the phone in my hand.

"I don't know. Talk to her."

Kym worked a nail file over her thumbnail, her business with me complete. I walked a few steps away, into my office. "This is Dewey," I said.

"Dewey, thank goodness. Kym said you found my purse."

I glared at Kym, but she had picked up a *Fabric Trends*. The latest edition, of course. I had plenty of older magazines on the sale rack, but she had to have a new one. I cringed as she licked her figure to turn the page. After she got done with it, I wouldn't be able to sell it.

The woman was speaking rapidly "I was so afraid I'd lost my wallet. My credit cards are in there, my license. I don't want to go to the DMV..."

"Hold on, I didn't find anything. Start at the beginning. Who is this?"

"This is Lois Lane. I've called every other shop I went to yesterday. I should have started with you."

Looking for lost items was a hobby of many of my post-menopausal customers. We kept a big box of stray eyeglasses, keys, and even a sex toy under the cutting table. No one had ever claimed the toy. Ursula had thrown it out.

"None of my employees have told me about finding a purse. Sorry."

Lois said, "You don't have it? You remember what it looks like? Remember that fabric I bought last week?"

"Of course," I said, picturing the purse she'd brought in earlier in the week. "Lois, don't worry. I'll go look for it right now."

I handed the phone back to Kym. I smiled at the five women who had just had their passports stamped. They were moving into the store. Yippee. I could see more people parking their cars out back. One was a large minivan. This morning was much busier than yesterday, thank goodness.

"Someone's purse was stolen?" Kym said, her voice carrying. Panic colored her tone.

"Please lower your voice," I said, whispering. The stamped Crawlers went into the classroom for a snack, but they were still within earshot.

Kym flipped a page of the magazine so hard it ripped. I bit my lip. Money down the drain. The cost of doing Kym business.

"I bet someone walked off with it," she said.

"Kym, please."

She looked up, eyes wide. "What? Think about it. The Crawl is purse-snatcher's paradise. Distracted shoppers with cash. Crowded spaces, plenty of jostling."

She was getting louder, not quieter. The back door was opening. I couldn't have her scaring my customers. Even the rumor of a thief working the Quilters Crawl could affect business. No one was going to have fun if they were worried about their belongings.

I wanted quilters with their purse strings loosened, not tucked under their arms.

I leaned on the table, hoping to shut her up. "Lois probably laid her purse down somewhere and wandered off. Most likely, I'll find it in a jiffy."

Kym nodded her head knowingly. She couldn't stop herself. "I'd look in the dumpster if I were you. Her purse is probably there. Of course, without her cash or her credit cards."

I walked to the back of the table, and pulled on her chair, unseating her. "Kym, take a break," I said.

"I don't need …"

The minivan had disgorged seven women. Each was carrying a large tote bag. These women meant to shop.

"Seriously, Kym. Take five. Now."

She huffed up from the table and stomped to the bathroom. I prayed that five minutes repairing her eyelashes would put her in a better frame of mind.

"Welcome to QP," I said, smiling brightly. "Everyone having a good day?"

I let Kym stew until a text came from the burrito shop next door, telling me lunch was ready. She wouldn't look at me, but sat down when I asked.

"You need to use the bathroom?" Mrs. Unites called out when I walked in. She knew the work had finally been finished, but she loved to tease me.

I shook my head. "Maybe. For old times' sake."

She cackled and reached for the bag that held my order. I gave her the store credit card.

"How's Mr. Handsome these days? You hiding him from me? You afraid he will like me better than you?"

She guffawed and ran my card through her reader. For someone who had been standing on her feet ten hours a day for the past thirty years, Mrs. U was cheerful.

"He's been working a lot. He'll be in for lunch next week, I promise."

"Good. I feed him and make him so happy. What about Miss Vangie? You didn't order her enchilada? Is she not working today?"

I shook my head. "School," I lied. I didn't have time to explain that Vangie was hiding out at Pearl's.

Mrs. Unites beamed proudly. "She is a good student."

"Yes, she is."

Vangie had texted me several times. She was bored silly. I could have used her help today but Zorn was likely to find her here.

I checked my phone as I walked back. Vangie had stopped flooding my phone. Maybe she was napping.

Freddy's tweets had started to go out. Special prizes. Don't miss the excitement at Roman's Sewing Machines. Fun starts at three sharp. Must be present to win.

He followed that up with *Come one, come all. If you're short or if you're tall. Roman's Sewing Machines is the place to crawl.*

I retweeted his exhortations to my followers and to the Crawl followers. I hoped he'd have a better day than mine had been yesterday.

THIRTEEN

AT THE BACK DOOR, I shifted my bag of burritos and held the door open as a pair of women approached the shop. "Come on in," I said.

"Having a fun day?" I asked. These two weren't familiar to me and I wanted to make sure they felt welcome. The one in the red sweater pulled her passport out of her homemade holder looped around her neck.

"Is this the line for stamps?" she said warily. "Where do I go?" She stood on her tiptoes and peered into the hall.

"Go on in ..." I pointed to the front of the hall where the greeting table was. I let my hand drop. I looked around her. The stamping station was invisible, even to me and I knew where to look. My skin tightened.

I saw nothing but a crowd of women.

Giggling women. The same women who'd been there ten minutes ago.

"Hold on," I said to my new customers.

I marched to where the bottleneck was. Just as I expected. Four of Kym's cronies from the appliqué club were gathered around. Kym had been their leader when she worked at my shop two years ago. They were having a grand time.

Meanwhile, hoppers weren't getting their books stamped or if they were, they were being greeted perfunctorily at best. No one liked to walk into a gaggle of women with their heads together. I had to break this up, pronto.

I reached past the duo wearing denim vests decorated with crocheted doilies, trying to grab the stamp and pad. I couldn't reach.

The blonde to my left wore a button that read, *"Hand is not a four-letter word."* Their manifesto to the joys of sewing without a machine.

"Hi, Dewey," she said.

I said a cool hello. None of these women had shopped in QP after I'd fired Kym. They were only here today because the Crawl required it. Running into Kym was an added bonus.

I leaned in, putting myself between them and Kym. "You gals having a good Crawl?" I asked. "On your way out?"

Kym's eyes flashed.

"We haven't seen Kym in a dog's age," the button-wearer said. She must be their designated spokesperson. "We were discussing all the changes you've made here in the store." It was clear from her tone she disapproved.

"Lots of changes," I agreed. "Kym's got work to do, so if you don't mind …" I looked significantly at the back door.

Two took the hint and moved off, but button-wearer and her buddy did not. They must have mistaken their denim vests for body armor.

I motioned for the red-sweatered woman and her friend to move forward. They looked tentative but wanted their passports stamped.

Kym did a quick swipe at their passports and the duo hurried off. It would be a long time before they returned to QP.

Kym's friends were still here. I moved so they would have to take a step back.

I smiled the fakest smile I could muster. "SO nice to see you again. Don't be strangers."

I waved, a soft beauty-queen wave I knew they could relate to. Elbow, elbow, wrist, wrist.

The button-wearer snarled but she backed off. "Bitch," I heard her mutter as she hooked arms with her friend and sidled away.

I turned back to Kym. "You're not here to socialize. Either do the work, or go away."

"I'll stay," she said, not looking me in the eye. It probably had more to do with not wanting to invoke my father's ire than mine, but I'd take it.

The smells coming from the bag of burritos were overpowering and starting to sicken me. I went into the kitchen. Jenn followed me.

"Houston, we have a problem," she said. She was carrying a fresh stack of fat quarters from the supply in the classroom.

I pointed my chin at her burden. "Fabric's flying out the door? That's the kind of problem I like. I'll be out there as soon as I put these in the frig."

"That's not it. We're busy, but we're handling it. No, the problem is people are arriving for Pearl's Advanced Color class," Jenn said. She nodded her head toward the classroom across the hall.

"Pearl doesn't have any classes scheduled," I said. The smell of cilantro was overwhelming. My throat got dry.

Jenn said, "Yes, she does. I checked."

She pointed at the class calendar on the bulletin board. There it was. Pearl's Colorings from 1–5 PM today. The class, like many of our classes, had been scheduled months ago. Before Hiro died. Before Pearl went a little nuts. Even before I'd signed up for the Crawl.

I dropped the bag of burritos on the counter. Jenn began to unpack them, righting them so that the label showed. Two bean and cheese, three chicken. I'd split a vegetable with Ursula.

"I canceled it. I know I did," I said. As soon as the words came out of my mouth, I realized I had given the task to Vangie to do. I had assigned her the job of removing the class from the website and notifying those who'd already signed up.

I asked, "How many students are here?"

"At least twelve."

"Yikes." Pearl's classes were always popular.

What was I going to do with a dozen students expecting to take a class from Pearl this afternoon? I could refund their class fee, but some would still be unhappy. It was not just that they'd been looking forward to the day but they'd already spent additional money on their supplies.

It was like buying a fancy dress for a wedding, having already spent a hundred dollars on some casserole dish from the Macy's wish list, and then having the bride and groom break up two days before the ceremony.

Miserable quilters were often vocal ones. I could guarantee there would be at least one quilter who'd insist on trashing QP's reputation. Loudly.

Not today. Not in front of total strangers.

I needed to isolate the group to contain the damage.

"Jenn, send them up to the loft classroom. I'll get the checkbook and come up and tell them the class has been canceled."

This was going to hurt.

By the time I went upstairs, twelve women were seated at the six tables. Pearl's students were our art quilters, and their creativity showed up in their clothes and accessories. Homemade totes of varying hues were scattered on the tabletop. Many wore jackets or vests that they'd made.

They were settling in, unpacking supplies and laying out notebooks and the special colored pencils that Pearl required. A brunette with a huge smile was showing off the pencil holder she'd made. The fabric looked hand-dyed and was stamped with a turtle motif.

They looked up expectantly, smiling.

"I'm afraid I have to tell you that the class has been canceled," I began.

A disappointed sigh rippled through the room. I smiled in empathy.

"I know, I'm truly sorry," I said.

"The class was on the website," a woman with a Heidi braid on the top of her head said. Heads nodded in agreement. "I checked this morning." She folded her hands on the table, as if the class would begin if she waited long enough.

Murmurs of discontent begin.

I looked at Heidi directly. The only way to do this was to let them all in on the troubles QP was facing. No Vangie. No Pearl. And hope for some understanding and sympathy.

"I do apologize. We're having a little trouble staffing. Vangie, my assistant, is carrying a heavy school load as well as working here. She made a mistake. As some of you know, Pearl's..."

The brunette interrupted. She wasn't smiling now. Instead her large mouth was twisted in anger. "Are you kidding me? Do you know what I had to do to get this day away from my family? The kids had a minimum day. My husband wanted to play golf today and I told him he couldn't. He's going to be pissed."

The murmurs grew louder. I glanced over the railing to the store floor below. It was crowded with people. People I didn't want to hear about QP's screw-ups.

I held up a hand, hoping to stem the tide of anger.

"Pearl isn't feeling well..." I started again.

"This is b.s.," Smiley said, picking up her pencil holder and slamming it into her purse. "Total disorganization."

I raised my voice and held up the checkbook. "I will refund your class fees," I said. "Right now. As soon as Pearl returns, I'm sure she will schedule more classes..."

Smiley wasn't finished. "I've driven for forty-five minutes. Are you going to pay me for my time? Do you know how much gas costs these days?"

I didn't have an answer. "It was my understanding that the class had been canceled over a month ago and that you'd all been notified. We dropped the ball. All I can do is apologize."

Heidi raised her hand, peering around the unsmiling brunette. "What about the email?"

I shook my head, not understanding.

"I got an email from Pearl last night."

"Me, too."

"So did I."

Now I was stumped. I'm sure it showed on my face. Smiley-face stopped packing up her stuff and looked at me, waiting for my answer.

I didn't hear anyone coming up the stairs but suddenly their faces brightened. I turned and Pearl was at my elbow.

"Hi everybody. Sorry I'm late. I stopped at Costco for gas and the line was way too long, but I was on E-E-E and I never would have gotten here without filling up. You'd have found me on Santa Clara Street, thumbing it."

She grinned at her charges and mimed hitchhiking. "Not that I haven't traveled that way before. Did I ever tell you how Hiro and I got to Woodstock?"

Pearl looked good. Her hair was combed and shiny. Her jeans had a deep cuff and her stylish ballet flats were red. She was carrying her quilting teaching bag. I could see she had handouts ready for her students and had an assortment of her pieces for show and tell.

Smiley-face grinned. She unrolled her pencil roll and sat down. The others sat back in their seats and waited.

"Thanks, Dewey. I can take it from here."

Pearl waited for me to leave. I had to be sure she was okay. Still, she sounded fine. I looked over the classroom. These women were happy to see her. My job was to keep my customers happy.

"Okay," I said. "Enjoy your day."

I walked down the stairs slowly, listening to the voices in the loft turn happy and light. Before I reached the last step, Pearl had them laughing, telling them how she and Hiro had hitched a ride on the Hog Farm bus, and doing a dead-on imitation of Wavy Gravy.

Jenn was straightening a row of blenders. "What happened?" She raised her eyes.

"You hear that?" I said.

She listened, then nodded. "Sounds like they took it okay."

I shook my head. "They were not happy. But Pearl showed up, bright-eyed and bushy tailed, ready to teach."

"She seems like a new woman," Jenn said.

"Fingers crossed," I said. "Let's all try to keep our ears open, okay? Let me know if you hear anything I should know about."

A customer grabbed my attention. She was looking for a special gift for the friend who was the designated driver on the Crawl. We snuck around to the display of Jim Shore figurines and she picked out an angel. I wrapped the gift and was rewarded with a big grin. This day of the Crawl was so much more fun.

Jenn called out, "Dewey, check this out."

Two women in matching jackets were smiling at me. I walked over and said hello.

"Turn around," Jenn commanded. They obeyed like models on a runway.

The back of the jacket was a blow up of the Quilters Crawl map.

"Nice!" I said. "You printed the map on fabric?" The sea otter was flying down the road.

They nodded. "Do you like?"

"Awesome," I said. "I wish Sonya could see that. She's the one who designed the map graphic, made it so cool."

"Someone call my name?"

Sonya peeked around a large man in a blue polo. I grabbed her by the upper arm and dragged her over.

"Take a look at this," I said.

Sonya oohed and aahed. "How did you do that? That is too cool."

The jacket people explained their technique and were rewarded with hugs from Sonya. They moved on and I noticed Sonya was carrying a passport.

I was surprised. "You're doing the Quilters Crawl?"

"What can I say? That map I designed really worked." She laughed, and tossed her long hair back.

I agreed. "So what do you think of the event?"

Sonya tilted her head pensively. "It's interesting, isn't it? I mean, all these women—mostly, although I saw a couple of men—charging from store to store. There's a great female energy. Sisters doing it for themselves. They seem to have left all their cares behind."

That was a pretty good description. Of today, at least. "How many stores have you been to?"

"Yours is the fourth," she said. "I think. It's a bit of a blur."

She took out her passport and showed it to me. She'd started at Barbara the Damp's shop in Fremont.

"Each store has its own personality, don't you think?" she said. She leaned over the table and lowered her voice. "I like the atmosphere here the best. You have all the funky modern fabrics, and your staff is really friendly. I feel welcomed here. I think that's what's important."

"Thanks." Sonya had a trained artistic eye. Her opinion meant a lot. And she could be a valuable source. I could always use help with the displays. "After this is over, I'd love to pick your brain."

Out of the corner of my eye, I saw Ursula about to grab a stack of four bolts. "Don't lift that," I admonished her. There was a lot of fabric that needed to be reshelved. I knew Ursula was trying to be efficient but she could hurt herself.

I took the stack from her. "I'll put them away."

Sonya followed me as I returned the bolts in their proper place. I slotted the latest Amy Butler with its matching coordinates. My customers liked the new fabrics in a collection to be kept together. Some made a quilt using every piece in a line.

"Ursula still hurting, eh?" Sonya said, holding open a spot between two bolts.

"I'm afraid she'll always hurt," I said. I didn't want to say more. Ursula's past was her business.

Sonya's big eyes widened. She tched in sympathy. "That's not right. Listen, have you given any thought to me teaching?"

A sound like a group moan came from the loft. Sonya and I both looked up. She glanced at me questioningly. The noise was quickly followed by a giggle. I'd been monitoring the class as best I could from down here. It seemed to be going okay.

"There's a class going on," I said. "On color."

Sonya looked up as if she could see the students through the floor. "Color? See? There's something I could teach. Man, what I wouldn't give to have students who are actually interested," Sonya said. "I'm so sick of entitled twenty-year-olds complaining about being awake at noon."

I started to protest on behalf of Vangie and other not-entitled students but a commotion in the back caught my attention.

A backlog was forming at the stamping table again. Kym's voice came through.

"And then I told my husband . . ."

I turned to Sonya. "Excuse me. I've got to go deal with someone."

Sonya looked up the stairway to the loft. "Mind if I go upstairs?" she asked "It would give me an idea of how you do things."

"Be my guest," I said. I pushed the last bolt into place, and went to police Kym.

She caught my gaze and lowered her voice. She stamped the books quickly, greeting the customers and encouraging them to go shop. As I stood there, I remembered I'd never looked for Lois's purse. Poor thing. She was probably going nuts without it.

I'd been so busy since she called, I hadn't had a chance. I walked up front. The last customer went out the door and the store was empty. We'd hit a lull. At least I hoped it was only a lull.

Ursula was refilling the small baskets near the register. I kept them stocked with low-cost items that might entice a buyer into an impulse buy. We sold fifty one-inch rulers a month that way.

"One of our customers called. She lost her purse. Has anyone turned one in?" I asked.

I was a little afraid that Kym was right. That I should start my search in the dumpster outside.

She shook her head. "Not that I heard."

Jenn who was chewing on a granola bar piped in. "Nope."

"Did you get lunch?"

They both shook her head.

"Go now," I said. "I'll stay up here."

I scanned the floor next to the cash register and the cutting table. People stood in those spots the longest, waiting in line to get fabric cut and then waiting again to pay.

No sign of a purse. Should be easy to spot.

I got the carpet sweeper from the hall closet and poked underneath the toe kicks to make sure nothing had fallen behind. I ran the sweeper under the fabric displays. I might as well freshen things up while I looked.

QP definitely had a slightly worn look now. The spit and polish of yesterday morning had been replaced by a limp atmosphere as if every bolt of fabric had been touched and moved out of place.

I was glad. That meant we'd had plenty of action.

Pushing the sweeper in front of me, I moved to the back of the store. The bookrack was a mess. We carried nearly two hundred titles, divided by subject matter and then alphabetical by title. I'd been wondering lately if that was a smart way to spend my inventory money. I'd noticed some of the shop owners on the Quilters Crawl carried very few books.

Six copies of Lark Gordon's appliqué book were in the paper piecing section. I grabbed them, smoothing down the covers. One had gotten bent, which would make it a tough sell.

When I did, Lois's patchwork purse dropped out of its hiding spot.

I recognized it now. I loved the fabric she'd used. I opened the zipper. Inside as Lois had described, was her bejeweled cell phone and a small wallet containing her ID, a credit card, and her Quilters Crawl passport.

I tucked the purse under my arm and continued straightening the books. I'd call her in a minute. I'd never get back to this mess if I left it now.

My foot kicked something. A small white lid was at my feet. I picked it up. It was the childproof top to a prescription bottle.

We used that type of bottle to contain our sharps—pins that were bent and unusable or old sewing machine needles from the classroom. It wouldn't be good if the lid was missing. Sort of defeating the purpose.

Jenn came on the floor, drinking from her neon-pink water bottle. She settled behind the cutting table.

"Jenn, is our sharp trash container in the drawer there?"

Jenn opened the drawer. She picked up the old prescription bottle and shook it. "Right here, boss."

"Okay, thanks." I tossed the extra lid in the garbage.

According to her passport, Lois had hit five shops before losing her purse. I called the number she'd given me the other day. Her phone went straight to voice mail. I left a message.

"Did you find that lady's purse?" Jenn asked.

I held it up. "I did, but her phone is going straight to voice mail. She sounded so panicked. I'm going to call around to the shops and see if I can't find her."

I struck out. I called Freddy.

"You calling to wish me luck?" he asked.

I glanced at the clock. It was ten minutes to three. I pulled my cell phone out of my pocket. I had missed fifteen tweets from him.

"Yeah, go with that," I said. I doubted he'd be able to find Lois Lane in his excited state anyhow. "Good luck."

"I'm getting lots of replies and retweets. People are really getting behind this."

"A day late for me," I whined.

"Put a cork in it. You'll reap the benefits next year."

"It's going to be off the hook," Freddy crowed. If he ever gave up selling sewing machines, Freddy would make a great late-night infomercial host or a hawker of expensive blenders at Costco.

"I've been sending out messages all day. And then when the first people arrive, I'm going to make such a big effing deal, that they're going to be tweeting all their friends to join them. I want a crowd, baby."

"Don't forget you only have an hour. From three to four. You've got to award that prize promptly."

"I will, don't worry. But for that hour, I'll be going bananas."

I laughed. "Not that I'd expect anything but."

Freddy let out a howl that sounded vaguely like a wolf. "Gotta go. Rebekah and Inez are freaking out."

"Call me when it's over," I said.

I hung up. I had a sick feeling and realized I was jealous of Freddy. I shook myself. There was no point in envying Freddy's success. It hadn't even happened yet.

I called Lois's phone again. Calling the shops would be futile.

———

Four o'clock came and went. I didn't hear from Freddy. He must have a lot of customers still in his shop. Maybe he was selling a machine or two. Good for him.

My business had slowed. I had faith that it would pick up again after Freddy released his share of the hoppers.

Buster came in. "Hey, babe," he said. "Need me to do anything?"

"I could use a bank run," I said.

Buster scanned the shop. His cop eyes were always on the lookout for anything out of place.

"You're having a good day?" He knew I didn't take money to the bank unless I'd had a very busy day.

"Up until an hour ago, when Freddy had his Twitter event. He seems to have sucked every customer into his orbit."

"Kind of like a creepy vampire."

Jenn giggled from her post.

"Not at all like a creepy vampire," I said, handing him the bag full of money.

He kissed me and headed out. He offered to pick up coffee and tea for Jenn and Ursula as he sallied out the front door. He never forgot anyone. No wonder they loved him. No wonder I loved him.

As I headed back to my office, Sonya was coming out of the bathroom.

"You still here?" I asked, surprised. I thought she'd gone hours ago, after she looked in on Pearl's class.

"I hope you don't mind," she said, wiping her hand on a paper towel. "I've been having so much fun with Pearl and her students, I decided to hang around."

"I didn't realize." I felt guilty that I hadn't been up to check on them. I'd meant to but every time I started up there, something or someone downstairs needed my attention.

"I feel kinda bad. I mean, it's not like I can pay you—" I stammered. I was grateful for the help but I couldn't afford any more outlay.

She waved off my concerns, turning to toss the paper in the trash behind her. "Are you kidding me? I'm having a blast. Your customers are so cool. Pearl's a hoot."

I walked with her up the stairs to the loft. I waved to the students. "Everyone doing okay?" I asked.

I was happy to get nods of agreement. Sonya looked over the work of the brunette who'd been so vocal earlier. I felt a rush of relief when she broke into a big smile as Sonya complimented her work.

Pearl looked up from her notes. She was standing next to the wooden lectern. It was nearly as tall as she was. I could see her pages were in disarray.

"You're back?" she asked.

"I've been here all along," I said.

She frowned at me. Was Pearl losing it again? She had to be tired, having taught now for several hours. Sonya caught my eye and smiled. I relaxed a bit.

A noise went up from below. From the loft, looking down, I could see a crowd had gathered. A man and a woman had commanded the attention of several shop hoppers near the front door. I heard the timbre of harsh whispers flying back and forth. A hand flew up to a mouth and a woman emitted a small shriek. This didn't look like ordinary gossip. I started down the stairs.

I felt a hand on my arm and looked back to see Pearl. Her eyebrows were knotted and her lips tight.

"I don't need a babysitter, you know," she said. She was angry. Oh dear. "First you stick Vangie in my house, now this witch."

"Sonya's not your babysitter," I said, working on sounding convincing. That's sort of what she had been. I didn't want to admit that to Pearl.

"You shouldn't have sicked that woman on me. She was so disruptive, with her comings and goings. I didn't like it one bit."

"Pearl, I'm sorry. But this was your first class since Hiro died. I didn't know if you could make the entire session."

She tched. "You have no faith in me. Get out of here. I've got to get back to class. Don't bring me any more sitters."

Before I turned away, I got a small smile from Sonya. Whatever Pearl thought, I was glad Sonya was here.

I went downstairs. Just as I'd hoped, the store was getting busy again.

As I got closer, I heard someone mention Lois Lane. I relaxed a little. This was about a lost purse, nothing more. Sometimes I was amazed by the amount of turmoil generated over the little things.

"Do you know Lois?" I asked, glancing around the group to see who'd spoken. "Where is she? I've been trying to reach her. I have something she left behind yesterday."

The couple front and center exchanged a look. They were either brother or sister or long-time marrieds. They each sported a short spiked hairdo. They must buy hair gel by the bucket. Her hair was a bright yellow and his was gray. Both wore the identical grave expression, mouths drawn down in a U-shape.

"Didn't you hear?" she said, her hand, seeking her mate's.

"She's dead," he said.

"Dead?" I asked. "She died? What happened? How?"

"She got trampled to death at one of the quilt shops," the woman continued, her eyes flashing a bit with self-importance when she read the shock on my face.

I fought to catch my breath. Dead because of the Crawl? That couldn't be. I was sorry I'd sent Buster away. I needed to lean on him right now.

"Which one?"

He answered. "That sewing machine shop on El Camino."

My heart plummeted. Freddy's place. A cold chill settled on the back of my neck.

I thanked the couple and pulled my phone out of my pocket and raced outside. I dialed Freddy's cell but he didn't answer. I tried the shop but no one picked up there either.

I had to get to his shop. Freddy would be beside himself. I looked back at QP through the plate glass window. The crowd had dispersed. Jenn was packing a customer's purchases into one of the special Quilters Crawl bags and Ursula was cutting fabric, her ears cocked to hear the story her customer was telling. Everything normal, except that Lois was dead.

I could hardly believe it.

I looked at the time. Four thirty. QP had to remain open until six. There were at least fifteen customers in the store. How could I leave now?

I clicked off the phone and went back inside. I found Buster being cornered by a contingent of quilters in matching pink T-shirts and high heels. They seemed to be determined to prove that the Crawl could be done in six-inch stilettos.

I crooked my finger at him. He finished stamping their passports and followed me into my office.

He swiped his forehead theatrically. "Thanks for the rescue. One of those women is a badge bunny. She hangs around the office and brings coffee and donuts to the cops. She loves any guy on the job. I thought I was free here."

I smiled but saw that I wasn't fooling Buster. He knew the difference between a real smile and a fake one.

"What's going on?" he asked. He took my hand and kissed the palm.

I blew out a breath. "There's been a death at Freddy's shop. One of my customers got trampled or died of a heart attack. I don't know, but Freddy's not answering his phone and I need to go find out what happened."

Buster squeezed my hand. "I'll drive you."

I shook my head. "I need you to stay here. Jenn could use help at the register. You need to make sure Kym doesn't get wind of this and start spreading rumors. Don't let Ursula lift anything heavy."

Buster studied my face. I knew he was struggling. He didn't want to tell me what to do, but I could tell he didn't think I should go.

"Look," I said. "Freddy's my friend. I want to make sure he's okay, but I'm doing this for the Quilters Crawl, too. If he goes nuts, he's going to scare a lot of people away. I can soothe him over and make sure he keeps things in perspective."

"That a dead body doesn't have to be the end of things?"

I felt anger rise up in my throat. "That's not fair," I said. "It's not really my fault that I've had some experience with this. I can help him understand what's going on."

He struggled and then he relaxed. He knew I was going to do what I thought I had to do.

"I'm asking you to hold down the fort here for me for a couple of hours," I said.

"I can do that."

I threw my arm around his neck and pulled him close. "That's what I love about you. You're so damn versatile. Busting drug dealers one day, wrassling quilters the next," I said.

"What an exciting life I have," he laughed. "I don't know how my heart stands up to it."

I touched his chest. "Because you have the biggest heart in a man that I've ever seen."

I was doubly glad now that Sonya had stayed. I could leave Pearl alone with her in the loft. I'd have to remember to send her a gift certificate. Or maybe a copy of Lark's autographed book.

"I won't be long," I promised. "There's a class going on that'll be over in a few minutes. If you could help the students out with their stuff, that'd be great."

"Bye, sweetie. Go. We'll figure it out."

I barely heard Buster as I rushed out to my car.

FOURTEEN

FREDDY'S STORE WAS IN a strip mall. The façade had recently been overhauled to enhance its Spanish style, with fake timbers and buttery stucco. Freddy had purchased the entire strip when he'd moved up north.

His place took up three of the nine storefronts. He had sewing machines in the window, alongside large posters from the manufacturers, extolling the virtues of their latest innovation. The windows gleamed invitingly. Freddy managed to inject an air of excitement into the somewhat staid world of machine sales.

The parking lot was empty. The special pink raffle tickets littered the ground. A crushed pen gave credibility to the hundreds of rushing feet. Balloons tied to the street lamp were flat.

There was no sign of Lois. No sign that paramedics had come and gone. No indication that someone had recently died here. All of a sudden, the shrines that crop up on freeway ramps made sense to me. I understood the need to mark the spot. If I had a teddy bear or a silver vase of flowers, I'd have laid one down.

I pulled open the door, hearing the bell ring to let his staff know I was there, but no one came forward.

"Freddy," I called out. I headed to the back of the store where I knew his office was.

"Back here," he said.

He was leaning against a shelving unit that held boxes of unsold sewing machines. Rebekah and Inez were standing, watching him. I wasn't sure of their loyalty. Would something like this make them quit?

I gave Freddy a sideways hug and settled in next to him, feeling all the bumps in my spine as I leaned against the metal shelving. I worried for a moment about boxes of machines avalanching.

"What happened? Are you okay?"

Freddy shook his head. His speechlessness worried me. A silent Freddy was not one I'd seen before.

Rebekah answered, "There was a rush and this woman fell in the middle. She couldn't breathe."

"No, that's not what happened. Let me tell it," Inez said.

Competition was the glue that bound these two. They didn't let go of their natures easily.

Freddy held up a hand. They both quieted. "Truth is, none of us saw what happened. All I know is that the Twitter thing was going great. We had a huge line of people waiting to get their raffle ticket. I swear, there were at least two hundred people out there."

Rebekah said, "We thought we had a good system going. I was stamping passports and Inez was giving out tickets," Rebekah said. "But we fell behind. The line kept getting longer and longer. Freddy got on the megaphone, telling everyone that they would get a ticket."

"Did you see Lois?"

Freddy shook his head. "I don't know a lot of the customers here by name yet."

I looked at his employees. Inez and Rebekah had been around for years, working in other shops in the Bay Area. I was pretty sure Rebekah had sold my mother her last Bernina ten years ago. The machine I used now. They knew a lot of locals even if Freddy didn't.

Inez was shaking her head. She had a tone that broached no argument. "She's never been here. We don't know her."

"I met her the other day," I said. "She was nice."

Freddy closed his eyes. I felt a shudder run through his body.

Inez and Rebekah were looking down at their shoes. Freddy was their boss, not a friend. His discomfort was nothing to them. I wouldn't have been surprised if they weren't mentally rewriting their resumes right now.

After a long pause, he swiped a hand over his face. His complexion was gray and the skin under his eyes sagged. I'd always thought of him as my contemporary but he was in his mid-forties and today he looked all of that, and more.

"Then, a limo pulled up," Freddy said. "Can you believe it, a freakin' limousine. Who thought that was a good idea?"

Freddy's face darkened as he remembered the scene. "There was no place for them to go, so the driver double-parked on El Camino. Not smart. I was sure the cops were going to come and shut us down."

I could picture the scene. What a mess.

"The doors opened and at least a dozen women came out. It was like a clown car."

Except way bigger.

Freddy pinched his chin and I wondered if he was missing the goatee he used to sport. Something to rub. "The girls in the limo had had champagne. They were a little tipsy and very loud. They started toward the front of the line, not realizing everyone else was waiting."

Rebekah looked up. "That inflamed the crowd. All of sudden, people were pushing and shoving."

Freddy nodded. "Next thing I know, women are screaming. The noise was awful. People were hollering even though they didn't know what they were yelling about."

He stopped, and when he spoke again his voice was shaky. "There was a ripple effect, women backing up in rings, doing anything they could to get away from Lois, who was on the ground. I couldn't see that of course, just an open space where everyone was fleeing from."

"I thought she had heat stroke," Rebekah said. "Fainted."

Inez snorted, "It wasn't warm enough for that."

"She was in the middle of a lot of people," Rebekah said. "It could have been very hot."

Inez tched.

"A guy came forward, and started doing CPR."

"Was Lois conscious?" I asked.

Freddy shook his head. I could see he was rattled. "I don't know. I called 911. The paramedics came and took her away."

The softer side of Freddy, the rescuer, was not one I encountered very often. It was something he kept hidden. I thought I saw tears in his eyes, but Freddy blinked and they were gone.

He pulled himself away from the shelves. "I'm closing up."

"It's against the Quilters Crawl rules," I said before I had a chance to think.

He frowned at me. "Screw that."

"Sorry," I said.

He turned to his employees. "Rebekah, Inez, go on home. I'll see you tomorrow."

The pair left, stopping in the break room to gather up their purses. Both carried enormous expensive leather satchels that I knew Freddy gave out as a reward for selling over one hundred thousand dollars worth of machines.

We followed them out to lock the front door. The Quilters Crawl basket sat on the counter, mocking the event with its perkiness. Freddy fingered the ribbon.

"This happens to you, not me," he said. The whine in his voice told me he was going for self-pity. "You're the one who finds dead bodies."

"It's awful, no matter what," I said. "It's not exactly a competition."

"Yeah, but, you're the one who knows how to handle this. I don't."

"That's why I'm here. To hold your hand."

"Does your boyfriend know?" Freddy asked. He couldn't resist a little mischief.

"Of course. He was at the shop. I told him before I left."

"Oh," Freddy said, his voice cresting with disappointment.

I stepped away from him. I didn't like the direction this was headed. "Freddy," I said, warning. "You know there's nothing between us. We're friends."

"I know," he said, stroking his non-existent goatee again. "It's just—"

I knew what was going on. Times like these make you lonely. Life looked vast and loomed with too many empty places. Freddy had no one at home, preferring his girlfriends to be many, with minimum commitment.

The first time I saw a dead body, I'd had to go home to an empty house. It was too much to bear and I recruited Buster to keep me warm that night.

This was no time to be alone. "Come on," I said. "Isn't there a bar nearby? I'll buy you a drink." I could use one, too.

He brightened. "You'd do that for me?"

"I'll stay until you're feeling better," I said, making sure I wasn't promising more in his eyes.

"That might take quite a few drinks," he said. We went out the back door. His car was parked under a sign that read "*Parking for the King. Anyone else will be beheaded.*"

"Get in my car," I said. "If you're going to get good and drunk, you're not driving. I'll take you home later."

Freddy looked a little too pleased with himself as I texted Buster and asked him to lock up. I promised to be home by eight.

———

"I feel a little guilty," I said. "I mean, the Twitter thing was our idea."

"We never intended anyone to get hurt," Freddy said, sipping his fourth scotch. After downing three straight shots, he'd finally ordered one with water and was nursing it. For all the alcohol he'd consumed, I couldn't see any change in his demeanor. No slurring, no glassy eyes. He had a greater tolerance than I did. After my first drink, I'd switched to tonic water. I had to drive home.

"I know, but..." I pushed a finger through the condensation from my glass on the bar.

Freddy tipped his glass and watched the amber liquid move. "It's human nature, Dewey," he said. "I mean, for crying out loud, they were there for a gift basket with maybe a hundred dollars worth of stuff in it."

He turned to me, his eyes flashing with scorn. "Those women probably spend more than that on fabric every week. This wasn't about the prize."

Maybe the alcohol was having an affect after all. Freddy's eyelids drooped.

"People like giveaways," I said. "We use them all the time to lure people into our shops."

Freddy put his forehead against his glass. "You didn't see it, Dewey. They were like animals, clutching and clawing."

He looked at me. His eyes were filled with tears. "Truly awful."

"I'm sorry it got out of control."

His shoulders sagged. "Promise me you'll find who did this."

"Ouch. Could you sound any more like an extra on *Law and Order*?"

He closed his eyes. He drained his glass and held it up for a refill. The bartender obliged. The bar was empty except for Freddy and me. It was early for most partyers.

"We need to figure this out."

Freddy leaned in to make his point. The eau d'scotch was overpowering this close.

That last drink had been the tipping point. He was over the line. He leaned further. His butt slipped off the barstool and he landed on my shoulder.

I stood and planted my feet. Freddy was taller and fifty pounds heavier than me. I couldn't handle him if he was too drunk to walk.

I pushed him into an upright position. "Seriously. Let's go. You'll feel better in the morning."

Freddy's eyes darkened. He straightened his spine and sat down. Any vagueness in his eyes disappeared. "I'm not kidding, Dewey. We must find out what happened to her. Otherwise, you and I are going to hell for our part in this woman's death."

He burped. "Another, barkeep," he called out.

My phone rang. I held it out so the Budweiser sign illuminated the name of the caller. The readout said it was the San Jose Police Department. I couldn't ignore this.

Anton Zorn launched as soon as I said hello. "You quilters have the worst luck, don't you? I heard about your buddy, Miss Lois Lane. Too bad Superman couldn't help her."

He chuckled at his lame joke. "I want you to know that I see a connection, Ms. Pellicano. A direct link from Wyatt Pederson to Lois Lane. And that is you. You."

He paused dramatically. I didn't even breathe for fear he would take that as an acknowledgment that I was listening.

"I will let my colleagues know about you. I will help them make the connection back to you."

He hung up without saying more. My stomach roiled. I gulped in the bar air, but it only filled me with the smell of alcohol and stale men. I closed my eyes against the onslaught on my innards.

When I opened them, Freddy was staring at his scotch like it held some answers. His phone rang. He reached into his shirt pocket. The phone caught on his pocket and he pulled hard, knocking himself in the nose.

I grabbed for the phone, but he held it away from me. I wasn't sure if he actually got it shut off with his fumbling, or if the person on the other end gave up, but the phone stopped ringing. He placed it on the bar in front of him with the careful, exaggerated movements of a drunk.

My phone rang. Barb V. I glanced at Freddy's phone. Sure enough. Missed call from Barb V. She must have heard the news.

I held a hand over my right ear. "Hello?"

"Hello," Freddy answered. I shook my head at him, and gave him a shush a librarian would have been proud of.

I got up from the barstool and walked to the short hall where the bathrooms were located. The din from the bar faded.

"Dewey?" Barb V's voice, as sharp as a broken beer bottle, came through loud and clear.

"Yes, Barbara."

"Did you hear? What are we going to do?"

We? What was with the "we"? She surely wasn't going to drive over to console Freddy. I looked back at the bar. A woman had taken my spot and he was leering at her. She was smiling in a way that suggested she might be for hire. I doubted that was what he needed tonight, but if Freddy thought that was a good idea, who was I to stop him?

"Yes, Barbara. I heard. I'm with Freddy now."

"Good, I was trying to reach him. We need to call off your silly Tweeter thing."

"No, Barbara, that's not the answer."

"Dewey, I'm not going to argue with you."

Freddy was leaning over, looking down the woman's shirt. A line of drool was ruining his sexy vibe. No way was he getting lucky tonight, even for a price.

"You can't unilaterally decide that. We need to talk to the other shop owners."

"I'll call an emergency meeting tonight."

"Tonight?" That wasn't going to work. Not with the shape Freddy was in. The bartender was looking at me meaningfully. I had to get him out of here.

"We can't let this wait," Barb V said. "We all have to work tomorrow."

"Tell you what. How about we meet very early at my place?" I didn't give her time to say no. "I'll call everyone and let them know. Seven AM. I'll have coffee and bagels."

She started to protest.

"See you tomorrow, Barbara." I clicked off the phone.

I hung up before she could argue further and headed over to the bar. I gave the hooker a look and she slid away. I took the stool.

"That was Barb V," I said.

"Vomit," Freddy said.

I jumped up to avoid getting splattered. But Freddy hadn't moved, slumped over, his body relaxed and not heaving.

He pushed his face off the bar and said, "Vertigo."

That was all I needed. A dizzy Freddy.

I waggled my fingers in front of his face. "Are you okay?"

His mouth moved before the sounds came out. "Barb V, V for Vise."

"Jerk," I said. A drunken version of Name That Barbara. "I thought you were getting sick."

The door opened and a man who looked a lot like Freddy if Freddy favored suits and ties over polos and jeans walked in. Could this be Vangie's lawyer?

"Larry!" Freddy called, waving his arms so widely, he tipped himself off the stool. His brother took three long strides and caught him in mid-air.

I waited for Freddy to right himself before offering my hand. "Dewey Pellicano. You are Larry?"

He nodded. "Can we get some coffee?" he asked the bartender.

Freddy flopped his arm between me and Larry. "Larry, Dewey. Dewey, Larry. This is Vangie Estrada's boss."

I wanted to tell him about Zorn's call, but not with Freddy listening.

Larry said, "Tell Vangie to call me. Now, what's up with him?" gesturing at Freddy.

"You know, brother ..." Freddy slurred. "When you moved up here, I thought we would spend more time together. Why don't we?"

"Did you call your brother?" I asked Freddy.

He pulled out his phone from his pants pocket. "Guess my butt did."

"I'm flattered," his brother said, scrolling through emails on his phone.

"Well, I'm glad you're here. Freddy's had a rough time. A woman died at his store."

"Are you going to be sued?" Larry said, putting his phone away. "Negligence?"

Freddy shook his head, moaning at the effect that had on him. I could practically see his brains sloshing around.

"I've got to be getting home, so I'll leave him to you. Freddy, we're having an emergency Quilters Crawl meeting at my place early tomorrow morning. Wicked early. I'm going to call you at six to wake you up. So sober up. Quick."

Freddy caught my gaze. Something in his eyes chilled me.

"What if I killed her with my tweeting?"

I didn't have an answer for him. "See you in the morning," I said lamely.

I left as Larry poured Freddy a big cup of coffee.

———

Having the meeting at seven at my place meant getting out of bed before six. Buster had the day off so he went for bagels and cinnamon bread after I drove us both to the store.

I made coffee. My mother's old twenty-cup coffeepot was getting quite a workout these days. The familiar gurgle now felt like a death knell.

The garbage was pungent so I pulled out the bag and twisted the top. The wastebasket in the classroom was full of used paper plates and cups, so I gathered it too, and heaved both bags outside.

I had pushed the dumpster back when Freddy pulled in, followed by Buster. I went to the car to help him with the goodies for the meeting. Freddy went to the back door and held it open for us.

"Good morning," he said slowly as we approached. As we got closer, I saw his eyes were red-rimmed and his skin was pale under his fake tan.

"Rough night, cowboy?" Buster said.

"Yeah, well, it's not every day a customer dies at my store," Freddy said. "Not like here."

"Nice," Buster said. "That was a low blow."

Freddy draped an arm over my shoulder. The fumes coming off him stung my eyes.

"His eyes *are* amazingly blue," Freddy said nodding at Buster's back. "I've always heard that but never really noticed."

Freddy's hangover had dulled his senses but not his urge to needle Buster.

"Someone is still feeling no pain," Buster said. He held the door open for Freddy and me to pass through, then let it slam shut.

Freddy's body jerked and skipped a step at the noise. I shot Buster a dirty look and got an innocent one in return.

They followed me into the kitchen.

"I did have a rough night," Freddy said. "Why aren't you out there detecting?"

Buster said, "Not my case."

Freddy's voice was high-pitched and whiny. I grated my teeth. I tried to quiet him with a look but he wasn't looking my way. He was right behind Buster, who'd laid the bags down on the kitchen table. Buster turned and glowered. Freddy stared back.

"You're the super cop, right? You must know people. Make a couple of calls, will you?"

I didn't need this this morning. Having these two in the same room was like putting a food dish between two stray cats. Someone was going to lose an ear.

I grabbed the cinnamon bread from Buster and dumped the contents into a wicker basket. "Thanks, honey."

"There's more in the car," Buster said. He tried to get past Freddy who didn't move aside.

Buster said, "Dude, you're in the way. Step aside."

Freddy said, "You're not the boss of me."

Why didn't they just mark their territory? Part of me wanted to yell "Dudes, pee on the floor, already."

I whirled around with the serrated bread knife in my hand. Buster took a step back. Freddy closed his eyes as if the motion was too much.

I used the knife to point at the pair.

"I'm sick of your silliness," I said. "A sweet lady died last night."

They both looked at the floor.

"I need help today. From both of you. This committee is coming here to ream me for my Twitter idea. To give me hell for getting Lois killed and jeopardizing the Quilters Crawl. I could use some ideas on how to mollify them."

Buster grabbed my free hand and squeezed it. "I'm here for you."

"Me, too. Sorry," Freddy whispered painfully. My yelling had done his headache no good, but too bad.

I lowered my voice and slowed down. "I can't afford for the promotion to be a failure. I promised Lark her books would be given away this weekend. That has to happen or my credibility with her is shot."

"Me, too!" Freddy agreed vigorously. Too vigorously. His eyes squinted against the pain his outburst had caused. He squeezed his temples.

"I pulled in some favors, too," he said quietly. "My friend the thread vendor will not be happy."

I said, "Not to mention … if my idea goes down in flames, I'm not going to be welcome on the Quilters Crawl next year or any year thereafter. I want to salvage this."

"I've been thinking," Buster said, his eyes narrowed in the way that meant he was concentrating hard. I loved that look. "What if you gave the customers a longer time frame to report to the Twitter shop? That would help spread out the arrivals."

Freddy stroked his chin. "Hmm … part of the problem *was* that people were frantic to get their ticket within the allotted hour."

Buster nodded. I got a little tingle seeing these two actually agree on something.

Buster said, "Crowd control is essential. The last thing you want is mob mentality to take hold. People lose their minds when there's enough of them."

"Buster has a good point," Freddy said. "If I'd gotten those folks in and out fast, that scene would have never happened."

Buster continued. He'd given this a lot of thought. "That 'must be present to win' requirement has to go."

"No way!" I held up a protesting hand. "That was the best part," I wailed. "The winner was so excited when I gave her the basket. I love seeing that."

"You'll see their happy, smiling faces when they come back to pick it up," Buster said with the good logic of a cop. Facts is facts.

Freddy was nodding so hard, I thought his neck would snap. There was a boys' club forming in my kitchen right in front of my eyes.

I didn't want to let the prize go. "But remember, Freddy, how we talked about building the excitement? I mean, that's the whole point of Twitter. People feel like they're in on something special. Watching someone else walk away with your prize is part of that."

Freddy sneered. "Really, Dewey? You want the rest of the crowd to feel bad?"

I tilted my head. Where had my friend Freddy gone and who replaced him with this guy?

Buster and Freddy bumped fists. The boys' clubhouse was complete. All they needed to do was hang the sign that said, "no girlz aloud."

I knew how to be gracious in defeat. "I'll give up the idea of being present to win, if you two will clean the classroom. Vacuum and dust."

Two heads nodded as one. Freddy threw up a fist in victory. "Bring those witches in here, we're ready to go."

Freddy's face went pale, and then turned a sickly shade of green. The fist pump had done him in. He put a hand to his mouth, his fingers long and delicate. "Oh, boy," he said.

He stumbled to the bathroom. Buster shook his head as we heard the door slam shut.

"Looks like he did a lot of damage last night. Maybe you shouldn't have let him drink so much."

This was my fault? I couldn't believe my ears. I swung around to see if Buster was kidding. He wasn't. He was gazing at the bathroom door like Robin waiting for Batman. Unbelievable.

"I seem to recall someone complaining about Freddy being around too much."

Retching noises came from inside. I stepped away. I didn't need to hear that.

Buster shrugged. "Aw, Freddy's okay."

I pulled the vacuum out. "Make sure you get under the shelving units, too."

He saluted. "Yes, ma'am."

I reached out to swat Buster's behind. He cocked his hip so my blow landed sharply.

"Thanks," he said. "That was exactly what I needed to get going."

I shook my head. "I think you're the one who needs to spend less time with Freddy."

FIFTEEN

BARBARA V ARRIVED FIFTEEN minutes early. I was still wiping down the kitchen table and had a handful of crumbs in my wet hands when she steamed into the kitchen. I hadn't heard the back door open over the noise of the vacuum. I could only hope that the vomiting noises were over.

Despite the hour, Barb V was feisty. "Dewey, what are we going to do about this? I didn't sleep a wink last night."

Lack of sleep didn't show on her face through the antediluvian layers of makeup she'd applied. Her eyes were bright and shiny. She licked her lips.

I could feel waves of tension coming off her. She was carrying an old leather briefcase, which she set on the tabletop. Right in a wet spot. I handed it back to her and swiped at the table with a towel.

"I'm not quite ready for you. It's not even 6:45," I said.

"I know, but we must get on top of this," she said. She flicked an errant crumb off her briefcase and cradled it.

"I agree, Barb. It's really terrible. Did you know Lois?"

She shrugged. "I don't think so." Her gaze shifted away from me.

I rinsed out my sponge and put it in its holder. I checked on the coffee, but the old machine wasn't finished brewing yet.

"She was one of my mother's customers, but she'd stopped quilting for several years. The Quilters Crawl was going to be her entrée back into it."

Sadness filled my chest. I looked at Barb V but there was no comfort there. She didn't seem to have sympathy at all for this quilter who wouldn't be quilting again, ever.

Her shoulders were taut, her strong jaw pointed in my direction. Barb V was dealing with Lois's death by taking care of business. She clicked open her briefcase.

"I have created a checklist of potential problems. Everyone at the meeting needs to get one of these. May I use your copy machine?"

The noise stopped in the classroom. I heard Buster stowing the vacuum.

Her stoicism was getting on my nerves. "There's one in the classroom. We're going to meet in there. I'll be in as soon as I pour the coffee…"

"I hope this meeting doesn't take too long."

She gathered up her things and moved away, her sensible shoes making no noise as she glided across the floor. She seemed to move under a power that was not visible. I heard her greet Buster. The door opened and several shop owners come in.

I went out in the hall and knocked discreetly on the bathroom door. "Wrap it up, Freddy," I growled. I kept my voice low. "I need you out here. Now."

The toilet flushed. This was no day for him to be under the weather.

He looked a little better when he came out. At least there were two spots of color on his otherwise gray face.

"Barb V and a couple of the others are here already. Get in there and schmooze. Act contrite."

"I am contrite."

I smoothed the collar of his shirt, bypassing the wet spots. "Yeah, well, it doesn't always show. Put your tail between your legs and beg their forgiveness. I need you to claim responsibility for this. This never would have happened if you hadn't tweeted every two seconds. Tell them that."

Freddy straightened his shoulders. Buster, looking on from the hall, gave him a thumbs up. Freddy gave him a half bow as if he was going into battle.

"Get a breath mint," I called after Freddy.

Buster touched my arm. He leaned in and whispered. "I'll go holler at my buddy at Santa Clara PD," Buster said. "See if they've figured out how Lois died yet."

I got up on my tiptoes and gave him a kiss. "Thanks for all your help this morning."

He let his hand slide down my back slowly. I tamped down the shiver of delight that threatened to make my mind go fuzzy. We split up, Buster going outside to make his cell call, me into the kitchen.

I poured coffee from the big urn into a smaller carafe and took that into the classroom, along with a plate of bread. Paper cups, utensils, and plates were still stacked on the side tables along with small cups of flavored coffee creamers and packets of cream cheese. No one would have had time for breakfast this morning.

The classroom was buzzing with the owners catching up on what happened yesterday. Most of the owners on the Crawl were here. The four with shops down south were going to call in.

"Good morning, everyone," I said. "I'm glad you could all make it."

The greetings were quiet and subdued. The phone rang and I placed the phone in the middle of the table and put it on speaker so the absentees could hear everyone. While I was occupied with getting them online, the room quieted.

"Let's get started, shall we?" Barb V said without a glance in my direction. "We all have time constraints."

"Understood," I said. "Freddy and I have some ideas on how to prevent what happened yesterday from ever happening again."

"How did she die? Do we know?" Cookie asked.

I looked at Freddy. He acknowledged me with a small nod. His face was lined with concern. I didn't have to worry about him acting remorseful. The creases on his forehead said it all. I felt bad for doubting him.

He spoke. "We don't know exactly. But I want to say it was because I allowed the crowd to get out of control. I have spoken to the police—"

He had not. Did he mean Buster?

"And a lawyer," he continued.

His brother. At the bar. After six straight shots of scotch. Oh, Freddy, king of spin. Politics lost a viable candidate when he decided to go into sewing machine sales.

"We have come up with some ways to prevent this type of tragedy from ever happening again," he continued, remorse dripping.

He explained Buster's suggestions for lengthening the time and allowing the customers to leave before the drawing.

Most heads nodded. Barb V was staring at her hands folded on top of the table. Unlike everyone else, she hadn't helped herself to coffee and food. Barb V must run on bitterness.

Gwen, the owner of Half Moon Bay Quilting, spoke. "Let's think about this. There have been six Twitter events over the last two days. Six shops, including mine, have not had a chance to do this. I want that chance. Otherwise, it's not fair."

I chimed in, "I had mine the first day and it was a non-starter. But I'm okay with that because this is the kind of thing that needs time to build."

Gwen said, "Maybe not build as much as Freddy did . . ."

Cookie said, "The two dozen or so that came at the Twitter time liked the promotion. They felt a part of something special. Dialed in. Modern and . . ." She curled her fingers into air quotes, ". . . with it. Many of them told me that they'd been meaning to start following our shop on Twitter."

Summer from Santa Cruz spoke up on the phone. "Our event was very successful. We had about forty new people in the shop. We fed them and played games and had a blast. The feedback was very positive. I had sales in that hour equivalent to an entire day on a non-Twitter day. I loved it."

I smiled. "Thank you. I'm glad."

Around the table, shoulders were starting to come down and people were smiling. Sales were up. That's all they wanted to hear.

Barb V cleared her throat and all eyes went to her. "Nevertheless, we should stop this promotion all together. Just because one store had a good experience does not make up for the debacle at Freddy's. A woman was trampled to death."

Freddy flinched. The drinks he had last night were keeping him off kilter. "We don't know that," he said lamely. "We don't know how she died."

Barb the Damp said, "All I know is that the risks outweigh the benefits." A rivulet of sweat trailed down her cheek. "There can be no doubt that the Twitter promotion is far too dangerous."

I exchanged a look with Freddy. The Damp could be counted on to spout the party line.

Freddy directed his comments to the phone. "I can tell you this much. There was a wonderful atmosphere outside my place before..." Freddy searched for the right words. His synapses were not working well. "*It* happened. The customers were happy, having fun."

Wendy pushed on her elbows and lifted up her butt to get a better sight line to the co-chair. "Barb, you were there. What did you see?"

"What?" Barb V's head swiveled. She glared at Wendy. "Me? At Freddy's? Why would I be at Freddy's?"

Barbara the Damp leaned in to get a look at who asked the question. Wendy glanced around the table, her voice unsure. "My sister was there when Lois died. She said she saw you."

Barb the Damp said, "Your sister needs to get her eyes checked."

Barb V made a tight face and shook her head. "Let's stick to the important thing here. A woman died because of the promotion."

"We don't know that," I said. "If we adjust the timing..."

Wendy protested. Gwen talked over her. The speaker crackled with voices from the coast. The voices mingled until no one could be understood. I couldn't understand what anyone was saying. I sat back in my seat.

I needed a new tactic. Freddy and Buster's ideas could lead to a solution that would take care of the problem but no one was listening.

"Ladies," Barb V said. The chatter continued.

Barb V looked at me. She leaned toward me. I moved closer in order to hear her over the din.

"Your mother would be so disappointed in you," she hissed softly. My head snapped back. How dare she invoke my mother.

"This is not what she envisioned when we started the Quilters Crawl," Barb V continued. Her lips were wet and she was spitting.

I tried to stand up. I wasn't going to let Barb V get away with this. My mother was off limits.

Two hands were on my shoulders, seemingly friendly but restraining me. I craned my neck to see that it was Freddy holding me back. He was shaking his head, and making comforting, murmuring noises. Like I was a horse that needed to be stilled.

Barb V had not taken her eyes off me. Her chin was up and her arms folded tightly across her chest. Her face was triumphant.

All she wanted to do was maintain the status quo. That's all that was important to her. That nothing changes. Ever.

I felt Freddy loosen his grip. I stood, kicking my chair back. But Freddy had let go for a reason. Buster was right behind me.

No one noticed. The shop owners were still squabbling. Freddy took a step away from me as if respecting Buster's territory.

Buster handed me a note. He whispered in my ear. "Lois overdosed."

I felt my face twist in disbelief. Freddy moved closer and saw the note in my hand. He picked it up and waved it like a cape.

"It wasn't the Quilters Crawl that killed Lois," he crowed. "She took too many drugs."

The chatter ceased immediately. A disembodied voice said, "Hello?" from the phone.

All eyes were on me. I looked to Buster. He had plenty of experience giving people bad news. His face was neutral. He squared his shoulders to the group.

Buster took the piece of paper from Freddy. "All we know for sure is that she had drugs in her system that killed her. She might have taken the wrong combination or had a bad interaction with two or more drugs."

Freddy was instantly chagrined. "I'm sorry, man, that's not what I meant. I'm just happy because I didn't cause her death."

"I get that, dude. I totally do. It's okay." Buster clamped a hand on Freddy's shoulder and squeezed.

The bromance continued.

Everyone started talking at once again. I shut it all out. I wondered if that was all there was to it. Perhaps she had mixed up her medications, but there was another possibility. Zorn had suggested that she was murdered. Like Wyatt.

Buster held up a hand and the group quieted. "The police are investigating," Buster said. "I know the detective in charge. He's a good man. He'll figure it out. I wanted to let you folks know that the Quilters Crawl had nothing to do with Lois's death. You should be fine to carry on. I recommend making the changes Freddy suggested."

Freddy beamed.

Barb V had gone rigid, her back straighter than before and her lips so thin that they were barely visible. Barbara the Damp was watching Barb V's expression closely.

Cookie stood. She clapped her hands together. "We all have to get back to our stores. Let's do what he says. Scale back the Twitter promotion. The remaining shops should be able to get their chance at it. We'll implement the changes. No time limit, don't need to be present to win. Dewey, can you email those to the stores that are affected, outlining the new rules?"

I nodded. Barb V pushed away from the table. She stuffed the handouts that she'd copied and never handed out back into her briefcase and walked out without another word. She'd lost this round.

Barbara the Damp followed. She stopped next to me. She pinched my upper arm hard. "You'll regret the day you made an enemy of the Barbaras."

SIXTEEN

THE MEETING BROKE UP quickly with the owners needing to get to work. Buster walked Freddy out and went home. I had an hour before opening.

What had really happened to Lois? Zorn was trying to link Vangie with Lois.

I opened Lois's purse. Her passport would tell me where she'd been. The QP stamp was there, along with five others. I pulled out the Crawl map from under my laptop. I got out a Sharpie and put a red X next to QP.

It was impossible to tell where she went next, but logic would dictate the most direct route. Tracing her steps might tell me something.

I marked an X by the Half Moon Shop. She'd gotten there. I wondered if she took time to drive to the ocean. The bluffs there were a great place to walk. It was sad to think her last days on earth had been spent driving around to quilt shops. I hoped she'd at least taken a glance at the ocean.

She'd been to the San Mateo shop, Barb V's in Redwood City. All the local ones. She hadn't ventured over to Fremont or over 17 to the coastal shops. She was sticking close to home.

And Santa Clara. A stamp from Freddy. The day before she was killed. She had to have returned to Roman's Sewing Machines for the special Twitter prize.

I called Freddy. "Listen to this, I said. "Lois was at your place on Wednesday."

Freddy sighed. "Okay, but so what? I told you I didn't recognize her. Neither did the Ikea twins. She must have come back for the Twitter event. A lot of people did."

"But she had a stupid phone."

Freddy was driving, listening to an obnoxious drive-time crew. He turned off the radio.

"Huh?"

"Listen to me. She was in my store last week. I tried to set her up on Twitter, but she didn't have the right kind of phone. Her cell was a basic one. She bought minutes by the month. She didn't have a data plan, couldn't get on the Internet. So how did she hear about the Twitter promotion?"

"Maybe she heard about it at another shop."

"She'd have had to be close by. But she'd already gone to all the local shops the day before."

"I don't know then."

I had another idea. "Maybe someone directed her there."

"Buster said she overdosed. I'm going with that."

I bit my lip. I wasn't going to tell Freddy about Zorn's theory linking the two deaths. "I'm not saying she was killed, but if she was, it was by someone who knew about the Twitter promotion and your plans."

"You don't think my Ikea twins did it, do you? I know they're cutthroat, Dewey, but really..."

Freddy was enjoying teasing me.

"Gotta go, Freddy."

"Wait..."

I hung up before he could harrass me some more.

I called Wendy. Her sister had been a witness. After a greeting and a word about the meeting, I said, "You said your sister was at Freddy's the day that Lois died."

"She was. She can't stop talking about the near riot. She was scared to death."

"Poor thing. Would she talk to me, do you think?"

"Sure. I feel so bad about Lois. I hope she rests in peace. She was in here the first day with her route all written down."

That was Lois. She couldn't even go online without her grandson. There was no way she was savvy enough to understand Freddy's Twitter promo. Someone sent her there.

Wendy said, "My sister texted. She's actually doing the Crawl with a couple of friends. I'll text her and tell her to talk to you."

When Jenn and Ursula came in, they were chattering about the busy day yesterday.

"Ready for another one?" Ursula asked.

"Maybe," I said. I filled them in on the meeting. "We'll see what happens."

"A lot of people are talking about Lois on Twitter," Jenn said. "Someone even made a memorial page on Facebook."

"So sad," Ursula said. "So sad."

Wendy's sister and her friends were our first customers. Wendy's sister looked like Wendy, a big woman with a head of curly hair. I pulled her aside and asked her about being at Freddy's when Lois died.

"Oh, Dewey, honey. It was truly terrible." She laid a hand on my arm and I felt her tremble. Her broad cheeks flushed.

"I'm so sorry. I'm trying to figure out what happened. Did you see Lois go down?" I asked.

"I did not," she said.

"But you saw Barb V?"

Her eyes opened wide and she nodded. "Right after it happened. I know her, I've been in her shop plenty of times. She was walking quickly away. Most people were milling around for a while. That's why I noticed her. She just took off."

"Well, thanks. I wanted to be sure. Barb V says she wasn't there."

She snorted, her curls bouncing. "Of course she would. She was up to something, I'm telling you. She was up to no good."

I thanked Wendy and stamped her passport. She rejoined her friends in the Amy Butler aisle.

Barb V acting weird wasn't exactly proof of anything. I needed more. I needed Barb V with drugs in her hand. At the very least, I needed Barb V with a reason to kill Lois.

Maybe Lois wasn't the target. Was Barb V so determined to keep the Quilters Crawl as is that she would kill anyone? How much did she want the Twitter thing to not succeed?

Perhaps it didn't matter who died. She might have poisoned a random person in that crowd. Sprinkled ground-up drugs in someone's coffee, and waited for them to die. Lois could have been in the wrong place at the wrong time.

First, I needed to know for sure that she was there. I pulled up Barb V's picture off her website and printed it out. I would show it around and see if she was anywhere else she shouldn't have been.

Freddy's was the place to start. That's where Lois died.

My store was quiet. Ursula, Jenn, and Florence could handle things.

Rebekah was standing by the side street, smoking. As she saw me get out of my car, she quickly dropped her cigarette, grinding it out with her black heels.

I walked toward her. Getting her alone was a bonus. Trying to talk to her with Inez present was tough. Those two couldn't stop baiting each other and proving the other wrong long enough to give a straight answer.

"Rebekah, hey."

I moved quickly, intercepting her, standing between her and the side door. I glanced inside. This entrance led to the embroidery machine section. A giant machine was punching a design into a baseball cap. No sign of Inez or Freddy.

"I need to have a word with you about yesterday."

Rebekah's forehead creased and she shook her head. Her short hair didn't move. "I don't want to talk about it. It's very disturbing, and I refuse to think about it."

"That's too bad. Inez will talk to me, but I believe you know more than she does."

Rebekah sniffed as if the wind had brought us an unpleasant smell from the bay. "She knows nothing. Don't listen to her. She didn't see what happened. She was in here, selling a Quilt Expressions 3000. Against Freddy's rules. There were to be no sales during the Twitter hour."

Her mouth closed and her lips thinned.

"Just let me ask you one question. Not about Lois," I added hastily. "I'm trying to find out if this woman was here during the Twitter promotion."

She turned away, making a move to get around me and get to the door. "Dewey, there were two hundred people here. How can I pick out one?"

"Give this a quick look." I held up my picture of Barb V.

Rebekah glanced my way reluctantly. Her face flooded with recognition. "Barbara Victor? Why would she be here? Her own place was on the Quilters Crawl, no?"

I pulled the picture back and looked at it myself. Rebekah grabbed the door handle and yanked it open. The noise from the embroidery machine got louder. A movie princess was appearing on a baseball cap.

"Barbara *Victor*?" I said.

"Of course. I used to work for the family. Victor's Sewing Machines. Before Freddy moved up here, they were the number one shop in the Bay Area."

I wanted to be sure we were talking about the same person. "This is the owner of Barb V's Quilting Emporium?"

Rebekah relaxed, now that we weren't talking about the Crawl. "Yeah, when she started out years ago, she didn't want to cash in on her family's success. They're close, really close, but professionally she's always been known as Barb V."

The chime sounded. A customer was in the store. Rebekah's body tensed and she leaned toward the front door. She was finished with me.

"I've got to get back to work before Inez steals all the good customers."

I let the door swing close, and stood on the sidewalk outside Freddy's shop. Was that Barb V's motive? To ruin Freddy. Lois may have been a casualty in the sewing machine wars. Barb V might not even have meant to kill Lois. She might have only been trying to cause a scare.

One that would put an end to the Twitter promotion and Freddy, and return the Quilters Crawl to its former glory. And put Freddy out of business.

I drove away from Freddy's without going inside. I had to do a lot of thinking before I could accuse Barb V of murdering Lois. No one would believe that such an outstanding member of the quilting society would kill for profit.

At the shop, Ursula was alone at the cutting table. She had the contents of the communal drawer out, a job usually reserved for rainy winter days. She'd sorted the junk into piles. Strips of fabric, paperclips and rubber bands, scribbled notes all got their own pile.

"How's business?" I asked.

Ursula shook her head, testing out a ballpoint pen. She tossed it into the trash next to her. "We were busy for the first hour, but then traffic died."

Dang it. I'd been hoping this was more of a temporary lull.

Jenn was studying her phone. Her usually sunny expression was dark. She scrolled through, her finger never leaving the screen.

I went to her side. "What's up?"

She showed me the screen. "There are dozens of tweets about Lois's death. They're getting ugly."

I looked over her shoulder. The comments were running along the lines of the one posted by @QuiltsGalore. *Stay away from the Quilters Crawl. It's jinxed.*

I scratched my head. "That's it then. The Crawl might as well be over. It's dead."

Jenn patted my back. "Let's wait and see. It might not affect business. After all, haven't we been told over and over how our customers are not online?"

I frowned, feeling the drag on me like a real weight. "I guess. This is bad, though."

Really bad.

I couldn't stand sitting around doing nothing. Again. Florence had set up a machine in the classroom and started sewing a block she'd brought from home. Kym stood by the greeting table, attempting to twirl a yardstick.

I'd nearly made it to the back door when it burst open.

"Dewey, you've got to do something about Vangie."

Pearl was in my face, keys dangling from her fingers. I was suddenly glad we had no customers. She looked a bit crazed, her eyes unfocused and glaring.

She was so loud and shrill, my ears hurt. "Pearl, could you keep it down?"

Vangie came in behind her. "She's incapable of moderation right now."

Pearl cast her a mean glare. "You are not my friend, anymore."

"Oh, but Ross is?" Vangie sniped.

Kym had stopped twirling and was leaning in. She wasn't even hiding the fact that she was eavesdropping. If we went into my office, she'd hear everything.

"Let's take this upstairs."

I led them to the loft classroom.

'What happened?" I said, shooting for some levity. "Vangie leave the toilet seat up again?"

This time the glare came from Vangie. I could get cut from all these sharp glances.

Pearl tossed her keys on the nearest table. I hadn't been up here since yesterday. One of her class samples was still hanging on the wall. I was a little sad to see it was her second Manzanar quilt, the one she'd made to replace the one in the museum. Her life had been so rich when she'd made that.

"What's going on?" I looked from Vangie to Pearl. Vangie had her arms crossed in front of her chest.

"Are you going to tell her?" Vangie said. "Or should I?"

"I've got nothing to say," Pearl said. She crossed her own arms. They faced off like a pair of hip-hop dancers. Attitude galore.

Maybe it was a sibling rivalry thing. Vangie didn't like Ross living with Pearl. Pearl and Vangie had always been more like family than friends.

This was Family Feud.

"Well?"

Pearl thinned her lips as if she would never talk again. Vangie sighed and reached into her back pocket.

She tossed a bottle of pills on the table. They rolled in front of Pearl who snatched them up, holding the amber vial close to her body.

"What are those?" My heart thudded as I remembered the clinic and the prescription. Was Pearl taking those powerful painkillers?

"She's taking Ritalin," Vangie said.

Ritalin? The boy in front of me in fifth grade had gone on the stuff. Before the pills, he'd bounce in his chair all day long. I could have kissed the doctor who'd gotten him to sit still. My grades went up along with his.

"But Ritalin is for kids with attention disorders," I said.

Vangie said, "It's a stimulant. The kids on campus call it Vitamin R. She's high as a kite right now."

I felt sick to my stomach. No wonder she was looking better. And baking and quilting again.

I looked over the edge of the loft. I couldn't see Kym but that didn't mean she couldn't hear us. I lead them to the back of the classroom where our conversation wouldn't filter downstairs.

"Where did you get them?" I asked. "Did your doctor prescribe them?" Was this the same doctor who'd given her Ambien to help her sleep last week? I felt my brain cloud from the possibilities. What did combining these drugs mean? Could she get addicted? Or overdose?

"Show her the label," Vangie said.

Pearl put her hand behind her back like a two-year-old. "You can't have my Granny Goose. You can't have them."

I looked at Vangie. Granny Goose? Cute name for a not-so-cute pill.

I put my palm out and made a stern face.

She relented and gave me the bottle. "It's not a big deal. As people get older, they have less energy. The Goose just gives me a goose," she said, her thumb thrust in the air. "A good ole kick in the pants."

Vangie said, "Who told you that? Ross?"

Pearl stuck out her tongue. Vangie returned the gesture.

Pearl said, "She's jealous of the kid. Doesn't like the fact that he's in the spare room. *Her* room, she called it. Doesn't like that I make his breakfast, and pack him a lunch."

"And wipe his butt," Vangie said.

Pearl made a face.

"Come on, you two. Let's leave Ross out of this for the moment. Get back to the drugs."

I looked at the bottle. The name on the label was Carl Menkin.

"These are not yours," I said. I could only manage the really obvious. I tapped out a few. The pale yellow pills were round.

Pearl looked at me like I was a loon. "It's not a big deal, Dewey. I traded. That guy, Carl, he's not really hyper. ACHD, ABC, whatever. He doesn't need his Ritalin. But he did need the stuff I got at the clinic."

"You got some pretty powerful drugs that day. I thought that was for Ross's project. Was Carl involved?"

Pearl zipped her lip with an exaggerated motion.

Vangie threw up her hands. "She doesn't know Carl Menkin from a hole in the wall. How do you think she found this ADHD kid who needs the Oxy she got from the pill mill?"

"Ross." Of course. I introduced Ross to Pearl. My face flushed with shame.

Vangie said, "Ross is getting her Ritalin, and giving her pills to this other kid. Her Ambien, too, He uses it to come down."

What a mess. "Pearl, you can't be taking prescriptions without a doctor's supervision. Who knows what the long-term effects are? You could be doing yourself terrible harm."

Pearl laughed a harsh laugh. She leapt out of her chair. "You think I care if I live another twenty, thirty years? I can't stand the pain now. Now. I need things to change right now."

Vangie and I exchanged a glance. Pearl was in big trouble.

"Come, sit down. Let's talk this out."

Vangie and I settled on either side of her but Pearl wouldn't sit. I reached out for her. She twisted away. Her eyes flashed. I recoiled from the venom coming off her.

Pearl turned back and slammed her fists into the tabletop. Vangie and I both jumped. My heart pounded. "Now you want to talk? Where have you been, Dewey? Or you, Vangie? For months, all I wanted was someone to talk to. You're so busy. Both of you."

Vangie hung her head. Vangie kept her fingers in her lap. I heard a knuckle crack. "School," she croaked. Vangie's voice was tight with sadness.

I'd started my store remodel right before Hiro's death. I hadn't been available. "Pearl," I said. "We tried, but—"

Pearl sat heavily in the chair. She shrunk against the back, and her voice was gravely. She was disappearing. "I know. For you, there are not enough hours in the day. For me, there are too many. Twenty-four long, lonely hours."

I felt my throat swell as the tears came up. Vangie swiped at her cheeks with the back of her hand. I reached out for Pearl's hand but she pulled away.

"I only took the pill to feel better. That's all I wanted. To feel like myself again."

Pearl's eyes filled. My heart flipped wildly. Pearl had been dry-eyed through Hiro's funeral and, as far as I knew, for the last six months. Now she was crying.

"But I can't. I'm too old."

My heart softened. "You're not old. You're sad."

I used my thumb to wipe away a tear on her lined cheek. Her eyes were so black, I could see my own reflection, saw the pain lines on my forehead.

"You're supposed to be sad. The love of your life died."

"We met in the camp, Dewey. I was four. He was eight. I loved him even then."

Vangie and I exchanged a sweet smile. We'd heard this story so many times before. "I know, sweetie. That's why you're so miserable. You're grieving."

Pearl pouched out her lower lip. "I don't like to be sad. It sucks."

"We'll help you." I looked to Vangie.

She nodded and said, "I can stay with you at your house for a while longer. If you get rid of Ross."

Pearl nodded.

I smiled at Vangie. That would be a perfect solution. "You can hang out here at the shop. Every day if you want. Jenn and Ursula would love to see you more."

"It hurts."

I patted Pearl's back. "You'll quilt. You'll heal."

The real Pearl was in there. Buried under her unfelt pain. By pushing away the hurt, she'd lost herself. We had to bring her back.

I hugged Pearl. I was facing the front of the loft. In the quiet, I could hear that Ursula was talking quite loudly. "She's not here, I told you."

I pushed Pearl into Vangie's arms and took several long strides and peeked over the edge. A short man in a gray business suit and a cowboy hat was striding through the center aisle, coming from the direction of my office. Anton Zorn.

He turned and looked up. I ducked down. Vangie and Pearl looked at me and started toward me.

"Sshhh …" I said to Vangie and Pearl. "We've got to be super quiet. Zorn's in the house."

"What's up there?" he barked.

"Storage," Ursula said. "Listen, why don't I give Dewey a call on her cell? I'll tell her you're here. She probably went to the bank or to pick up lunch."

She started dialing before he answered. My phone, in my pocket, started to vibrate. The vibration that meant the ringer was about to go off. I pressed the off button, the mute button. The phone went quiet.

Ursula left me a perky message. "Detective Zorn is at the store, looking for you, Dewey. I believe he's trying to locate Vangie. I'll ask him to wait in the classroom until you return."

Her eyes looked skyward. Zorn, distracted by a car backfiring outside, rushed to the window. Behind his back, Ursula gave me a thumbs up.

She walked Zorn to the classroom. She knew how to deal with aggressive men. Her tone of voice was soothing. She kept one hand on his elbow and gently steered him.

As soon as they were out of sight, I grabbed Vangie. "I'll keep Zorn busy, out of sight in the classroom. You get out of here, as quick as you can. As quiet as you can."

Pearl said, "Take my car. I'll get home somehow. I'll stay with Dewey." She tossed her head and grinned. "I'm good at distracting."

"Give me those damn pills," I said.

Pearl handed them over. "Good bye, good mood," she said morosely. "Good bye, sense of accomplishment. Good bye, vim and vigor."

I squeezed her. "Come on. We've got real-life excitement. There's nothing like fooling a cop to get your heart rate up."

"Wait," Vangie said. "I can't keep running from this guy. Maybe I should…"

I put a warning finger up. "NO! You don't need to spend any more time with the police. Someone wanted those drugs that you found in your car. Let me find that stash. Then we can lead Zorn to Wyatt's killer."

Vangie chewed her cuticle and looked over the edge. I followed her gaze. There was no sign of Zorn, but there was no guarantee he would stay in the classroom either.

I gave her a tiny shove. "Come on, now. Go. And call Larry."

"Catch," Pearl said. She tossed the ring of keys. Too hard. The keys sailed over the railing and landed with a metallic clang on the floor below. A tiny beaded koi flashed.

Vangie gasped. I froze and grabbed her hand. We held our breath as we waited for Zorn to investigate the noise.

"Stay here," Pearl said. She raced down the steps. At the bottom, she looked up and blew Vangie a kiss. She picked up the keys and set them on top of a display of thread. "Detective Zorn is here?" she asked loudly as she sashayed out of sight.

I started down the steps pulling Vangie behind me. "Go out the front. We'll keep him busy."

"Dewey," Vangie began, her voice breaking. "Find those drugs. Please."

I hugged her hard. She ducked through the aisles, taking cover behind the bookrack and finally getting out the door. The little Mini went by the window just as I turned to see Zorn behind me.

Pearl was right behind him. "Why, Detective Zorn. Can't you take off that cowboy hat and sit a minute? Did you have some of the melon? It's so sweet for this time of year."

He ignored Pearl's charms. "Ms. Pellicano, I am looking for Ms. Estrada."

I tried batting my eyelashes. From the look on Pearl's face, I had no career as a charmer. "Have you spoken to her lawyer? I'm sure she's in touch with him."

His eyes narrowed. The shadow cast by his hat gave him a sinister cast. I felt my breath catch. "You're playing a dangerous game, hiding a murder suspect."

Pearl darted close to him, like a tiny pit bull. Her lips were curled. "Vangie is not the murdering kind."

He turned quickly and she reeled back. I stepped next to Pearl and put my arm around her. She was trembling.

Zorn spoke harshly. "That is not for you or anyone else to determine. I am the detective in charge. I will speak to Ms. Estrada without interference from either of you. The law is on my side, not yours."

Zorn was the worst kind of bully. One with real authority and power. I had to be careful what I said. He would have me up on obstruction charges. "I'm sure her lawyer could arrange for you two to meet." I smiled sweetly, despite the grinding pain in my belly.

"Things could get dicey at the department for your boyfriend, you know. Very easily."

I steadied myself. He had the capability to make Buster's life miserable too.

Zorn was an all-American cretin.

He had nothing on Vangie. She wasn't guilty of anything.

Except hiding a stash of drugs. I kept the stab of despair I felt off my face.

Zorn gathered himself. "I will issue a warrant for her arrest if Ms. Estrada does not present herself to me in one hour. One hour."

He turned on his stacked heel and left. I felt a trickle of sweat run between my shoulder blades. The wet sensation made me shiver. Pearl felt me quiver and squeezed me.

"Vangie did nothing wrong, Dewey. Don't worry."

"I know, Pearl, I know."

I had to go look for the drugs. They were evidence. Evidence that would clear Vangie.

"You stay here," I said to Pearl. I gestured to Ursula. "Can you keep Pearl busy?"

"Sure can," she said. "I need some help with the Strip Club fabric choices."

I didn't want Pearl around when I called Buster and let him know that Ross had been trading Pearl's prescriptions. He could get Ross out of Pearl's house. I didn't care what happened to him after that. We would get Pearl to a real doctor and get her some good meds.

I called Vangie. "Where are you? Did you go to Pearl's?"

"I did, but I'm gone. I left the car there and took my bike. I'm on my way to school."

"Good. Don't go back to Pearl's. I'm sending Buster over there to pick up Ross. I'll tell Buster to call you when it's safe."

I called Buster next. He had been napping but woke up quickly when I told him the scenario. He agreed to pick up Ross for questioning.

Tying Lois to Barb V would have to wait.

———

"I'll be back," I said to Jenn as I went out to my car after I'd talked to Buster. Ursula had taken Pearl and they were in the fabric stacks. "Call my cell if something happens and you need me."

I went back to the street where Wyatt had died. I parked in front of the hedges that had sheltered us from the wind that night. In the daylight, I could see the house, a corner cinder-block ranch, painted dark brown. I needed to get into the backyard.

Lois's purse was on the front seat, where I'd left it after taking it to Freddy's yesterday. I tucked it under my arm. If any nosy neighbors were about, I could claim to be returning it to its owner. Lois's street was nearby.

I went around to the front yard facing the cross street, alert to any activity. The neighborhood was quiet. Late-blooming coral roses climbed a white arbor in front of the walkway to the door.

I had the feeling that I'd been here before. The house looked a lot like the one where I'd taken oboe lessons when I was a kid. Maybe that was it. I'd only lasted a month but it must have left an impression on me.

San Jose was officially a big city, but in certain places, if felt like a small town.

I knocked on the front door. I wanted to make sure no one was home before I let myself into the backyard. I didn't need any interruptions. I couldn't forget that Vangie had been attacked here.

I looked up and down the street. No one was outside, so I stepped into Lois's backyard.

I made my way around a saggng clothesline. Clothespins jiggled by the wind were a sad sight. I imagined Lois washing her new fabric and hanging the colorful pieces. Lois wouldn't be using that line ever again.

A used-brick walkway with grass growing in the cracks led me past two raised beds made of decking lumber. Spinach and pretty purple kale grew among dead stalks. A lone tomato lay squashed in the dirt. In the back corner, a lemon tree was shedding fruit. The usual life and death cycle of a garden seemed portentous today.

At the end of the walkway was a bench, the heavy-duty plastic kind that did double duty as a storage bin.

I felt a chill, like someone was watching me. I looked up and checked the yard. A jay scolded me from a redwood, a flash of blue as he dived toward me. I ducked and he was gone.

I looked back the way I'd come, thinking about how Vangie had raced in from the street, with Wyatt dead in her car. She couldn't have gone far to hide the bag of drugs. I opened the storage bin, but aside from an open bag of fertilizer and a scattering of bulbs, it was empty.

I didn't see any other hiding place. The yard was wide open. There was no garden shed, no empty pots. Not even a convenient watering can.

The jay screeched again and I opened the lid wider. The sun came out from behind a cloud and suddenly I saw a clean spot on the bottom. As if something had sat there.

I closed the lid and sat down on the bin. Wyatt had the drugs with him in Vangie's car. She hid them here. When she came back for them, they were gone. Someone had hit her after she left. Someone who thought her backpack was full of drugs.

Who?

Maybe Vangie knew more than she was telling me. Something about Wyatt that she didn't realize was important. A friend, a favorite hangout. Something that might lead us to the drugs and his killer.

I'd go find her. I walked to the front of the house again. As I passed by the dining room window, I saw a sewing machine set up on the table. A pile of fabric sat next to a rotary cutting board. The fabric caught my eye. The colors were the same as the purse in my hand.

I backed up, nearly falling over a ceramic frog perched under a bush. What was the address? I glanced back at the street sign. Ninth Street.

My heart thudded. Lois lived on Ninth. The chimes tinkled, just like that night. The night that Wyatt had been murdered.

Vangie had said she'd been bringing Wyatt home. Wyatt lived with Lois? Was this the connection Zorn was hinting at? Wyatt and Lois knew each other?

There was only one way to find out. With both of them dead, the house would be empty. I needed in.

Kevin had given me a lock pick key ring as a joke last Christmas, but I'd been practicing. Lois's lock was an old one, without a deadbolt.

I stuck the torsion wrench into the lock, tapping the pins with the pick, starting from back to front. I heard the lock open with a satisfying click. I was in.

I stepped in and closed the door quickly. Yesterday's paper was still on the kitchen table. One coffee cup and plate were in the sink. A fading Trader Joe's bouquet of flowers were in a speckled vase in the kitchen window.

I bypassed Lois's violet bedroom and headed for the closed door at the end of the short hall.

I stopped, hand on the knob, and took a breath. What if I found something that lead to Vangie? Something I really didn't want to know.

She'd assured me she wasn't addicted. She wasn't dealing drugs and she hadn't taken any. The question,was, did I believe her? Could I trust her?

I let my breath out. Of course I could. She was Vangie.

I opened the door. My eyes had to adjust to the darkness. The plaid shade on the single window opposite the door was closed. I dared not open it and attract the attention of a neighbor. I flicked the light switch. Nothing happened. I left the door open, letting light from the hall show me the way to a lamp on the maple night-stand.

It illuminated the room well enough so I could see a matching set of furniture. Single bed, desk, and bookshelves. Nothing looked new. Lois could have decorated this guest room years ago. The blue corduroy bedspread had been tossed on the floor.

A pair of khakis were folded over the desk chair. A skinny striped tie was laid on top. It reminded me of Ross, when he'd come to apply to be Pearl's GrandSon.

The truth hit me. Lois had mentioned a grandson, helping her map out her route to the Crawl. Wyatt had been living with Lois. Not a grandson, a GrandSon.

Poor Lois. She must have found the stash of drugs. And got herself killed.

SEVENTEEN

ON THE DESK WAS a laptop. I lifted the cover. Wyatt's Twitter account was open. It hadn't been refreshed. A line at the top read 967 new tweets. The ones on his page had been sent before the protest, before he died. A mention of Vitamin R chilled me. The street name for Ritalin. Scrolling back, I saw requests for HH and Oxy.

Wyatt had been dealing drugs and somehow escaped the Task Force's sweep. No wonder he had been protesting so much.

The drug bust and Wyatt's death left the field wide open. A new dealer would surely take over.

I minimized that window and another popped up. An IM conversation. The date was last Friday.

The screen name chilled me. RosstheBoss.

Ross: Scored six bottles of Happy Place from Granny Rose.

Wasn't that the name of the woman Ross had been living with before Pearl? I jumped up from the chair. He'd gone straight from ripping off his last charge to Pearl.

Ross: 60 pills in each.

Wyatt: $25 a pop for the Abilify.

I did the math in my head. That was nine thousand dollars for Ross. Double that to Wyatt after he sold them on the street. Lucrative business.

Ross: A hundred Vavavoom from Dr. Aldana.

And he'd taken Pearl to the sports clinic and Dr. Aldana. My innards quaked at the thought.

Wyatt: $40 for the Vicodin.

They'd agreed to meet in the parking garage at midnight last Friday to make the exchange. Nearly fifteen thousand dollars worth of pills. With a street value of double that.

The pills that Wyatt had stashed in Vangie's car. And that went missing from Lois's yard.

I called Buster. "Do you have Ross yet?"

"No one's home. I'm waiting outside." He yawned loudly.

"Ross killed Wyatt, Buster," I said, my voice rising fast. I gasped, trying to force air into my lungs. I heard Buster breathe into the phone. He was leaning in. He knew me, I didn't get hysterical for nothing. "And Lois."

"Tell me."

I exhaled. "They were dealing. He stole pills from his last gig as a GrandSon and sold them to Wyatt. They'd set up a meet the night he died. He killed him."

"We missed this guy?" Buster was mentally head scratching.

"Tell Zorn so he can leave Vangie alone. He threatened to arrest her if she didn't come in for questioning," I looked at my watch. "Right about now."

Vangie was safe now. That felt good.

"Where are you?"

Uh-oh. I coughed, covering up my nervousness. "Can't hear you, Buster. Go get Ross."

"You get somewhere safe. Now."

"Don't worry, I'm going back to QP. I'll leave the heroics up to you. Go!"

I hung up. I had to get out of here. Now the danger wasn't from someone looking for the drugs. My bet was that Ross had Wyatt's drugs.

The danger was from a beat cop finding me inside Lois's house.

I wiped off Wyatt's laptop, feeling like an idiot. I couldn't leave trace evidence. Once I told them where Wyatt had lived, the police would be all over this place. I'd rather Zorn didn't know I'd broken in. Or Buster for that matter.

Once I was back in my car, I let out a whoop and texted Vangie. She was free from Zorn.

My work was done.

————

"We haven't had a customer in at least two hours," Jenn said when I got back to the store. She and Kym were playing canasta at the greeting table. "I sent Florence home." She smiled at me. "Maybe there'll be a last-minute rush?"

I shook my head. "Doubtful. You guys go home," I said.

Kym said, "You'll pay me till six, right?"

Even Kym's money-grubbing ways couldn't dampen my triumphant mood. I agreed and the two of them gathered up their things and went out the door, planning a quick trip to Nordstrom Rack before going home.

Ursula was at the cutting table. She had stacks of fabric strips in front of her.

"Hey, boss. Pearl and I are working on next month's Strip Club. To be honest, I've cut the next three months. I'm working on January now."

She waited for my approval. When it didn't come, she said, "You okay?"

"Where's Pearl?"

"Bathroom."

"Listen, can you take her out to dinner? I'll pay. She can't go home for a while."

Ursula raised her eyebrows.

"Ross, the kid living with Pearl, was involved with Wyatt. They were in the business of selling drugs with a unique twist. They'd figured out that old people could get pain pills without too much trouble. Wyatt could sell those at school, marking them up outrageously. Pure profit, plenty of it. Pearl was their victim, too. She was getting pain pills from their doctor and swapping them for Ritalin."

"Oh no! Poor Pearl," Ursula said with a shake of her head. She gathered up the strips and laid them in a plastic bin.

"Buster's at her house now, waiting for Ross to get home. He killed Lois and Wyatt. He wanted in on their action."

Ursula shook her head. "So much pain."

I picked up three of her project bins. She followed me, carrying one bin. We stashed them on the shelving unit just inside the classroom door. The classroom still had food and drinks laid out for the non-existent customers.

"Pearl might be a handful," I warned. "She's been taking Ritalin for the last couple of days."

"I know what to do," Ursula said.

I kissed her cheek, and she hugged me. Her arms felt warm and substantial, a reminder of what was good in the world. She'd survived. Pearl would, too.

She broke away, then asked, "Was Barbara the Damp in on the drug dealing, too?"

I looked at her questioningly. "I don't think so. Why?"

"The sweating. She's probably addicted to Vicodin."

I didn't have to ask how she knew. Ursula, poor sweet Ursula. She'd lived through more pain than most.

Pearl agreed to go to dinner with Ursula. I pulled two twenties out of the cash register and shooed them away. Ursula had convinced Pearl she wanted an authentic Japanese dinner and needed Pearl as her guide.

According to Crawl rules, I had to remain open for another hour so I left the front door open. We'd only cleared two hundred dollars in sales today. That was barely enough to pay for the help and the goodies we'd bought. Not a stellar day.

I hoped the rest of the stores were doing better.

The store was so quiet. And neat. With no customers, Jenn and Ursula had plenty of time to straighten up. I wished the place was a little messy.

My mom's punch bowl was still full, the pretty parsley that had been frozen in the ice cubes laying on top like seaweed. The quilt we used as a tablecloth had a stained ring. The cheese had gotten sweaty and the crackers were soft.

The table looked like a girl doing the walk of shame still in her party dress. Wilted and pathetic.

I pulled over the garbage can and swept everything into it.

The back door opened. I steeled myself to go out and greet a Crawler. Only the most desperate to finish were coming out today.

Those and the lookiloos. Freddy had tweeted that he had spent the morning chasing away people taking pictures outside his place.

Maybe I could put the greeting table outside, with a sign reading "Stamp Your Own Damn Passport."

I wished now I hadn't sent Ursula and Pearl away. At least then I'd have someone to complain to.

Before I could get myself to move, Sonya stepped into the classroom.

"Oh boy, am I glad it's you," I said. "I've had it up to here with the Quilters Crawl."

"Hey, girlfriend," Sonya said. Today her skirt had a hem embroidered with tiny mirrors. "I was hoping you could help a sister out."

She dumped out her tote bag and out came the Baggies containing the Monkey Wrench blocks. "I haven't the foggiest notion what to do with these." She held up a strip of purple and wiggled it at me.

I laughed. "They're to make quilt blocks. You make all twelve and you have enough for a small quilt top. Like this."

I pointed out the sample that Ursula had made.

"That came from that?" Sonya stared at the Baggies. "Impossible."

I gave her a smile. I remember when I was this clueless about how to make a quilt. I hadn't wanted to learn from my mother but Pearl and Ina had been there to teach me.

Helping Sonya make a block was the perfect distraction for the remaining hour. I could forget about Pearl and Vangie and Buster arresting Ross. Lose myself in teaching a novice to quilt.

I said, "Come on, we can do it. It's a simple block, really. Even I can show you how to make it. And that's saying something."

"Are you sure you have time?"

I laughed. "Ha. The Crawl's a total bomb. I sent everyone home early. Buster's busy doing what he does. Vangie's at school studying. Heck, yes I have time."

I pulled out a rotary cutting mat and blade. "We've got to cut these fabrics to these exact measurements," I said, pointing to the instructions that came with each block.

"Four and seven-eighths? That's a ridiculous number."

"Quilters use seven-eighths all the time. When the quarter inch seams are sewn ..." Sonya's eyes glazed over. "Never mind. The rulers are made for it."

"Math was never my strong suit," Sonya said. Her brows were knitted together as if we were designing a neutron bomb.

I giggled. "Seriously, it's not that bad."

Sonya grabbed a handful of her hair, lifting it off her shoulders and fanning herself underneath. The temperatures outside were typical October, mid-sixties. It was not hot in here. It was sweet that she was nervous.

I tried to put her at ease. "Really, it's no big deal. If we make a mistake, we can get more fabric. There's plenty where that came from."

She twisted her hair around her fist and producing several long pins from her pocket, anchored the twist. She pushed the sleeves of her navy-blue peasant blouse up so the elastic was above her elbows.

"Here we go," I said. "I'll cut the first couple, then I'll show you how to sew them together. Do you have a sewing machine at home?"

She shook her head.

"No worries. I'll mark the seam allowance and you can stitch them by hand."

"Thanks, Dewey. It'll be nice to have a memento of my Crawl experience. I may never do another one."

There may never be another Crawl. I didn't know the extent of the damage.

"Even if you do," I said. "This is your first, so it's special."

She nodded.

I cut a square from each fabric, then sliced those into triangles, holding them up for Sonya to see. It felt so good to work on a simple, solvable problem. Just cutting and sewing. Nothing life or death. I sighed happily.

"Slap that up on the design wall over there," I said pointing to the flannel board installed on the closet doors. "Put the two triangles together to make a square."

Sonya did what I said. I cut the rest of the rectangles and squares that made up the quilt square.

"Now look at the picture, and see if you can work out how these go."

After one or two missteps, she arranged them to look like the Monkey Wrench. Sonya clapped. "So that's how it works. It's like a puzzle."

I laughed at her enthusiasm. "Exactly. It all fits together once you know how to do it."

"I couldn't see how I was going to sew that sucker together," Sonya said. "I was picturing it all different."

"Easy once you know how, huh?"

I showed her how to draw a line for the seam allowance. "You'll sew on that line. Let me get a needle and thread."

I looked on the open shelves for a hand sewing kit but didn't find one.

"I know there's one up front," I said. "I'll be right back."

I glanced at the clock. Twenty minutes until the official closing time. Of course who was to know if I closed up a little early? The Quilters Crawl Police were off duty.

I shut out the lights and locked the front door. A flip of the switch turned the Open sign to Closed.

I came back down the hall and locked the back door. One more day of the Crawl tomorrow. Then I would have a year to rehabilitate myself.

Sonya wasn't in the classroom when I returned. Had I locked her out? Maybe she'd gone to her car for something. I looked out the window but didn't see her in the parking lot. I went into the hall.

I heard the fan come on in the bathroom. So that's where she was. The old fan had sounded like a jet engine. I enjoyed the purr of the new one for a moment before going back into the classroom.

I flipped through the Baggies that held the blocks she'd collected on the Crawl. Sonya had the block from Quilts Up in Santa Cruz, and Gwen's in Half Moon Bay. She had gotten around.

I recognized the fabric in one of the bags. It was the latest Jay McCarroll line. I'd bought in a special order, just for Freddy.

Sonya'd said she hadn't gone to Freddy's, yet here was his Monkey Wrench kit.

I looked in her tote for her passport. Stuffed in the bottom was what looked like a piece of patchwork. I reached in and pulled it out. It was stiffer than a quilt and much smaller. The item sprang open as I released it.

A purse. In that now familiar fabric. The second purse Lois had made.

Lois had had lots of fabric left over and she told Ursula and I that she'd make another. So when she left her purse behind on Thursday, she must have used this one on the Crawl on Friday.

Why did Sonya have Lois's purse?

Lois had been here the other day and met Sonya. The two had talked, even argued according to Barb V. What if what Barb V had seen *really* was an argument? What could Lois and Sonya have in common?

I flashed on Lois bragging to us about her grandson. Correction. Capital G. Capital S. Her GrandSon. Sonya had been the one to first bring the GrandSons to my attention.

What if Sonya knew all along it wasn't a graduate student's thesis? She could have posed as Ross's mother on the phone with Pearl. What if it wasn't Ross who was the brains behind the GrandSons and the drug dealing?

All this cozying up to me was a way to stay close to Vangie. She must have followed Vangie to Lois's, hit her and taken her backpack. I could only imagine her frustration when the drugs weren't in there.

She was here now because she thought I knew where the drugs were. But I'd thought the drugs were with Ross. So where were they?

I knew there wasn't enough room in there, but I glanced into her bag. Her passport lay on the bottom. Nestled next to a syringe.

EIGHTEEN

WYATT HAD BEEN KILLED by injection. Probably Lois, too.

My scalp crawled. I heard the toilet flush. Sonya would be out in thirty seconds. I stashed her bag on a shelf as I went by. I raced to the hall and grabbed the door handle from the outside. My brothers had kept me prisoner this way once a week when I was a kid.

Just in time. From inside, Sonya tried to turn the knob. She pulled and I pulled back. She tugged and I held on tight. I felt her go away and come back again.

She rattled the doorknob hard and I nearly lost my grip. The knob started to turn. I stiffened my arms and held on. My triceps were starting to complain. I reminded myself that I was a lot bigger than Sonya.

And she didn't have her murder weapon of choice.

"Dewey," Sonya called loudly. "The bathroom door is stuck."

I didn't want to answer, didn't want her to know I was right outside.

She hollered again, "Dewey!"

I leaned away as far as I could and still hold on. "Hang on, Sonya. That door's been sticking ever since I painted..." I let my voice fade away."

I heard her sigh and take a few steps away, back, I imagined, to my pretty mirror. I stomped my feet as though I was just arriving, and messed with the knob.

"I'll have you out in a minute."

Now what was I going to do? My phone was in my pocket for all the good that would do me. I needed two hands to keep her trapped. And how long could I hang on? I couldn't stand here all night. No one was coming.

Sonya stopped moving. I held my breath, hoping to keep my anxiety from floating under the door.

But she caught it anyway. "Dewey, what's going on?"

I didn't dare answer. I knew the fear I was feeling coursing through my veins like a toxin would show in my voice.

"Dewey, you can't keep me in here forever."

"I'm calling for help."

"No, you're not. I've got your phone."

I heard the strains of "Hammerhead Stew" coming from my phone. Crud. I realized the familiar weight was not there in my pocket. When had I dropped my phone? I hadn't even noticed. Maybe Sonya had been a pickpocket in another life.

My mind was racing. How could Sonya have killed Lois? She'd been teaching with Pearl when Lois died. Pearl's voice came back to me, complaining about Sonya being flaky and disappearing during the class. She'd been right. Sonya wasn't there the entire time. She'd gone to Freddy's and killed Lois. With a syringe full of drugs.

I kicked the bottom of the door in frustration. "You killed Lois?" I said, letting my outrage vent. "She was a sweet old lady."

"That sweet old thing was going to turn me in. Wyatt had given her a video of us for safekeeping. When she found it, she threatened to go to the police."

Poor Lois. I wished she'd have talked to me before going to Sonya.

Sonya banged on the door. "What are you going to do now, Dewey? You'll get tired way before I do."

I forced myself to sound confident. "Buster will come looking for me. He hates it when I don't answer my phone."

My phone rang again. Sonya answered, "Hey babe, call me later, willya? Store is busy."

Dang it. She did a decent imitation of me.

"Buster won't buy that," I said, but my gut roiled. I was afraid he might. Maybe she never answered, just pretended to. She was just trying to throw me off.

"By the way, he said Ross is in custody and he'll be working the rest of the night."

My heart sank. She really had talked to him.

Sonya launched herself, her tiny body jarring the length of the door. My shoulder wrenched and my hand slipped off the knob. I recovered before she did, twisting the knob back.

"Bathroom looks great, by the way. Love these new fixtures. I wonder what will happen to your new tile work if I let the water run." She turned on the taps.

My breath caught. The vanity that I'd had made from Mom's dresser would be ruined. Buster and I had spent hours refinishing that piece. Time I'd spent thinking about my mother, and the young wife she'd been when she'd first found that dresser in an antiques shop on San Carlos Street. We'd stripped away layers of paint that my mother herself had applied as the dresser went from the boys' room to mine and finally to the office at Quilter Paradiso. Blue, pink, yellow.

I gave myself a mental shake. I was getting distracted. The dresser was not my biggest worry now. There was a syringe with my name on it just behind me in the classroom.

Sonya turned the taps on harder. Water splashed onto the floor and started to leak out underneath the door. The hall was flooding.

"My shoes are getting ruined, Dewey," Sonya singsonged. "I paid three hundred dollars for these shoes. I'm not happy right now."

Her voice got louder and she rattled the knob for punctuation.

I wasn't going to answer. With the water running, she would have to struggle to hear what was going on out here. All she knew was that the door wouldn't open. I could be down the hall or outside for all she knew.

I looked for a way to secure the door.

If I had the right size of something, I could jam it under the doorknob. The souvenir wooden yardsticks might be the right length. From here, I could see one standing in the hall, next to the greeting table. Good ole Kym. She never cleaned up her spot.

I braced my feet and stretched my hand out. The yardstick was out of reach. I pulled back, and twisted at the waist, trying to give myself a little more length.

The water shut off. "Dewey, you out there?"

The door shook as she banged on it. I didn't answer. I liked her uncertain.

The light coming from the window in the back door faded. The sun was setting. The only light was the light in the classroom and a small sliver coming from the bathroom. Pretty soon I wouldn't be able to see my hand in front of my face.

I leaned as far as I could, skootching my foot along the hall, the soles of my sneakers slipping. I felt the yardstick under my fingertips. I exhaled and bent as far as I could. I needed to add yoga to my schedule.

I gave myself one final push. I had it. I swiped up the yardstick and wedged it under the knob, moving away as I did.

Sonya had the timing of a psychopath. She pushed on the door, snapping the yardstick into three pieces.

I ran, my feet sliding on the slippery floor. I went down just in front of the classroom door, my head hitting the jamb hard. I saw stars. I tried to shake it off, but the roiling made my head hurt more.

I had to get the syringe before she did. She was right behind me. I held onto the doorjamb for support and kicked. I felt a surge of energy as my foot connected with Sonya. She grunted in pain. She grabbed her shin.

I reached up and grabbed her tote bag off the shelf and tucked it under my arm. I had to avoid getting stuck. Whatever Sonya had loaded that thing with, it was lethal.

Sonya came into the classroom, steadying herself. The hem of her long skirt was wet and her hair had come half down out of her bun. She looked like a witch from a dark fairy tale.

Her wide eyes swept the room, finally coming to rest on the bag under my arm. I shifted, trying to hide the bag, the syringe. Her face twisted in anger. She knew that I knew.

I held up a steadying hand. "Let's make a deal. I'll give you the drugs. You get out of the country."

Sonya's hair was flying across her face. She brushed it back, holding it with one hand. She cocked her head at me. "Why would you do that?"

I twisted my face into what I hoped was a good imitation of disgust. "I didn't want that cop Zorn to get the bust. You don't know all the history between us. He's ruining my boyfriend's career. All he cares about is scoring points with the FBI and the DEA. I can't have Zorn getting the upper hand on Buster."

She swiped at the tote bag. "How about I just kill you now?"

I kept the bag out of her reach. "You'll never find the drugs. There were thousands of dollars worth of prescriptions in that bag. You can't really afford to let that go, can you? You need that money."

"Damned right I do. Do you know how much money a part-time college instructor gets paid?"

I did. "Didn't you want to go to Florence to paint? Go away, stop dealing drugs in San Jose."

Sonya grabbed a bin off the shelf. She spilled out the contents, dumping the fabric strips that Ursula and Pearl had cut. She piled the plastic bin in the doorway, grabbing another and doing the same. She was building a barricade.

"Don't you want in on my business? Everyone else wanted a piece of the action. My action. No one was as smart as me. No one saw the potential between the older women and the younger men.

That was all me. Do you think Wyatt would have been clever enough to figure out the GrandSons? No way. Oh, he could pull together several hundred stoned kids to gather in the park but he wasn't smart enough to run the whole show. He thought he was."

Sonya dumped another bin. This one was full of threads, and the spools scattered across the floor. I picked up my foot to let several roll past.

"And Lois? She thought she was brilliant, too, coming to me. When she saw Ross with Pearl, she went a little nuts. She told me I had to get Ross out of Pearl's house, then she would give me the drugs. Where are the drugs, Dewey? Lois told me she had my drugs."

"I don't know. I thought Ross had them." I backed farther into the classroom. Sonya was blocking the doorway. I needed to put space between us.

"I don't believe you. Lois showed me a scrip. She had them when she was here the other day. She must have given them to you to hold."

I squirmed my hand into the bag, and felt the barrel of the syringe. My head throbbed. Sonya's instrument of death. Would I be able to stab her with the needle?

My grip slipped, my fingers wet from falling on the floor. I wiped my palm on my pants. The syringe had clung to my hand and before I realized it, the syringe was skittering across the classroom floor.

I cried out and threw myself on the floor. My knee landed hard on a spool of thread. I cried out in pain, twisting up in a sitting position. As I asked my knee to ignore its pain and help me stand, the syringe traveled the length of the room and landed close to

Sonya's foot. She scooped it up, her eyes flashing in triumph. Her mouth twisted in a rictus smile sending chills down my back.

I scooted on the floor, backing into the far corner of the room, stopped by the inventory shelves.

She would kill me. She'd have no problem stabbing me with poison. I reached behind me, trying to pull myself up. My fingers touched cold metal. I glanced back. The iron that Pearl had ruined.

Sonya was nearly on me. I closed my fingers on the handle, feeling the iron's heft. I stood and swung with all my might.

The ruined iron landed on Sonya's temple with a satisfying thwack. The tiny woman went down in a heap.

I leaned on my knees, panting. Sonya groaned and I pulled the iron back to hit her again.

Her eyes fluttered and she stopped moving. A roaring in my ears subsided and I could hear someone pounding on the back door.

"Dewey!"

Buster. Even the sound of Buster's voice couldn't keep my knees from shaking.

I took the syringe from her hand and backed out of the room, watching her. I ran down the short hall and flung open the door. Buster rushed in. He held my upper arm and searched my face.

"I'm okay. Sonya's in the classroom," I said.

Buster led the way. Sonya seemed to be coming to. She moaned and tried to turn over. He put a foot on her back, keeping her down.

"Are you okay?"

I moved closer so he could put an arm around me. My shoulders heaved at his touch. I nodded.

Buster pulled Sonya around and handcuffed her. Then he picked me up and carried me to a chair. His big brown eyes looked into mine.

"I knew that wasn't you on the phone," he said. "I got here as fast as I could."

"Thanks, sweetie. Go turn off the water in the bathroom, please."

NINETEEN

BUSTER TOOK ME HOME. He'd left Sonya and Ross with Zorn. I took a steamy bath and wrapped up in Buster's terry robe. Buster had made tea for both of us. He was strumming his guitar when I came into the living room.

He patted the couch next to him. He kept his eyes on me, his brow knitted. He was worried about me.

I had never felt so tired. I put my feet on the coffee table next to where Buster had laid his guitar and sipped the tea. The hot drink did nothing to penetrate the cold spot in my belly.

I didn't want to talk about what had just happened but I couldn't stop the words from flowing.

"Buster, Sonya and her GrandSons were hooking women on prescription drugs. Like Pearl."

Buster was nodding. He knew. My eyes filled with tears. Buster put a comforting arm around me and drew me in close.

"Vangie and Pearl. This could have ended so differently."

"We—you—put the perpetrator behind bars," he said. "That's something."

I nodded into his chest. It was something. But was it enough? It was enough for Buster, because his job was to deal with the never-ending parade of bad guys. Human nature, he'd say, is to screw up. *My job is to make them pay their debt to society. Nothing personal.* That's how he stayed sane.

I wanted my life to be normal. No more dead bodies, no bad guys.

"I'm not doing this anymore."

Buster reared back. "What? Us?"

I patted his face and kissed his cheek. "No, stupid. Us is forever."

He leaned his head on top of mine, his chin digging into the top of my skull with an uncomfortable amount of pressure. "Forever," he said.

"I don't want to be the one who finds dead bodies, who solves murders. I'm finished."

This business had left me feeling tainted, as though Sonya had tarred me with her brush too. As if I'd taken too many over-the-counter drugs, leaving me logy and sluggish. Bath and tea and even Buster didn't help.

I couldn't shake off the feeling that putting Sonya in jail solved nothing. Lois was still dead. Pearl was still a sad widow. Vangie was still on overload with a dead friend. Ursula was in chronic pain and without health insurance. The problems that Sonya had unearthed—and exploited—were still there.

Buster was quiet.

"What if I went back to school?" I said. "Learn to be a drug counselor. Something useful."

"You could do that," Buster said quietly.

"I don't know how long it'll take," I said, warming to the idea. "Couple of years, maybe. We'd have to put off buying a new house."

"We can live here," Buster said. "I'm getting used to bumping my head in the shower. I think I've developed a callous."

I laughed and reached up to rub his head.

"Would you sell QP?" he asked.

The idea sent a chill down my back. QP was my connection to my mother, my connection to the world that I'd grown to love.

"I might need the money."

We were quiet and I rode Buster's chest as it expanded with his breathing.

"I have two things to say," he said finally. "One, you haven't had a choice when it came to the dead bodies and the bad guys. They entered your life and wouldn't let go. You did what had to be done. I know you didn't invite this mayhem into your life, and while I'll always worry about you, I'm proud of you, too. You've stepped up every time."

He stopped and I let his words sink in. It was true. There wasn't anything I could have done differently. People I loved needed me.

"Second, running QP is doing something useful," Buster said, kissing the top of my head with gusto. "You help people. Aren't you the one who's always telling me that quilting heals?"

I smiled. I had learned that over these last couple of years at QP. Quilters came in with broken hearts, broken marriages, broken

homes. They sewed and the pain eased. I'd seen women with difficult lives find solace and comfort in making quilts.

"At least sleep on it," Buster said.

———

We fell asleep fully clothed on the couch. This is what people mean
when they say love finds a way. Ordinarily when we watched TV,
we took turns spreading out. But that night, we lay entwined for
eight hours on the narrow couch.

The sun coming in the front window woke us. I opened my eyes
as Buster opened his. His lids fluttered shut and he yawned.

"Good morning," I said. The newness of the day washed over me.

We had a chance at a fresh start. The sun was shining. The
mourning doves were cooing. I heard my neighbor's dog bark ur-
gently. "Let's go," he seemed to be saying. "Time's a wasting."

Buster was by my side. I could do anything. My heart was telling me it was time to move on. Let QP run itself. Let the police do
their job. Fighting crime was their job, not mine. I had my own
destiny to fulfill.

"No more crime solving," I said. "I've slept on it and that's what
I've decided."

Buster nuzzled my neck. I got the feeling he wasn't listening.

My cell rang. I ignored it. Then Buster's cell trilled. I scooped it
off the coffee table and held it up.

"No, no phones. Not yet."

"I'm good," he said. He reached up and knocked the phone out of
my hand. It landed near the kitchen door. "Besides, I have a much
better idea on how to start the morning," he said, reaching under

272

my shirt. His fingers tickled and I screeched, involuntarily rolling away from him. I fell off the couch and Buster reached for me.

"Are you hurt?"

His concern was fake, so I threw a cushion at him. Buster ducked and laughed harder. He pounced, tickling me for real. I jumped up and ran a few steps. Buster tried to get up but his feet caught in the quilt I'd thrown over us last night. He went sprawling, his hands out in front of him in a protection mode. His pants slid down so his boxers were visible, making the whole scene even funnier. I danced and giggled, trying to avoid peeing myself.

The home phone rang. "I knew I should have gotten rid of that thing. Who needs a land line anyhow?" I let it ring and reached out, getting a fistful of boxers before Buster pulled away.

The machine kicked in after three rings. Freddy's voice came through the small speakers. Buster tugged his pants in order.

"Hey, you two crime fighters. What do two crime fighters do when they're not fighting crime? Wait, I bet I know."

Freddy made some weird kissing noise.

"Last day of the Crawl, Dewey. Twitter's blowing up. People are going to come out. You've got to fill me in. I'm dying over here. Was Lois a killer? That's what I heard. Did Vangie run over someone with her car? Come on, not knowing is killing me. You gotta let me in the loop."

Buster stayed on all fours and came after me, his large hand swiping the air in front of him. I did a jig, avoiding him. I grabbed a couch cushion and hid behind it.

"Please, Buster, make it stop. Go hang up that phone."

Freddy continued, unedited, "Call me as soon as you get done. Oh no, ewww. I just gave myself a visual. Ugh. The thought of you two making sweet, sweet love..."

"Your friend the buzz killer," Buster said. "It's like he knew that I was going to put the moves on you."

"When aren't you putting the moves on me?" I asked, laughing. "He'd have to know when you were asleep. I take that back, I feel you sometimes..."

"I'd have to be dead," Buster said.

He bellowed like an elephant. I fled into the bathroom and closed the door.

"Come out, little girl," he said in a villainy voice. "I will break this door down. I've been trained and can broach this obstacle in 3.3 seconds. I was first in my class at the academy in legal egress."

I was giggling too hard to respond. I didn't lock the door, instead jumped into the bathtub and pulled the shower curtain shut.

Buster opened the door a crack. "May I?"

I didn't answer. The chase was too much fun. I didn't want it to end.

Buster let himself in. The bathroom was tiny, and there was no place to hide but I tingled with anticipation anyhow. Buster was delaying his discovery of me and I loved every second.

He pulled the shower curtain back with a roar. I faked a scream and fell into his open arms. He scooped me up.

"Now I've got you," he said.

I kissed him. "You do. That you do."

That was all I needed. Buster in my arms. Together we could deal with whatever came our way.

QP was my legacy. The building had been in my family for a hundred years. My mother had built the business up. With the changes I'd made, the store fit my vision. I wasn't going to bail on it now.

As for the other stuff, I just hoped I could always be there when my friends needed me.

The Crawl didn't start for another two hours.

I pushed Buster toward the bedroom.

ABOUT THE AUTHOR OF *MONKEY WRENCH*

Terri Thayer is busy writing, quilting, and keeping an eye out for murderers at quilt shows. So as not to disappoint her fans, she is still trying to figure out a way to bring Buster to the guild's show-and-tell.

WWW.MIDNIGHTINKBOOKS.COM

From the gritty streets of New York City to sacred tombs in the Middle East, it's always midnight somewhere. Join us online at any hour for fresh new voices in mystery fiction.

At midnightinkbooks.com you'll also find our author blog, new and upcoming books, events, book club questions, excerpts, mystery resources, and more.

MIDNIGHT INK ORDERING INFORMATION

Order Online:
• Visit our website www.midnightinkbooks.com, select your books, and order them on our secure server.

Order by Phone:
• Call toll-free within the U.S. and Canada at
  1-888-NITE-INK (1-888-648-3465)
• We accept VISA, MasterCard, and American Express

Order by Mail:
Send the full price of your order (MN residents add 6.875% sales tax) in U.S. funds, plus postage & handling to:

> Midnight Ink
> 2143 Wooddale Drive
> Woodbury, MN 55125-2989

Postage & Handling:
Standard (U.S. & Canada). If your order is:
> $25.00 and under, add $4.00
> $25.01 and over, FREE STANDARD SHIPPING

AK, HI, PR: $16.00 for one book plus $2.00 for each additional book.

International Orders (airmail only):
> $16.00 for one book plus $3.00 for each additional book

Orders are processed within 12 business days. Please allow for normal shipping time.
Postage and handling rates subject to change.